YOUNG KNIGHTS

PENDRAGON

YOUNG KNIGHTS

PENDRAGON

Julia Golding

OXFORD
UNIVERSITY PRESS

OXFORD
UNIVERSITY PRESS

Great Clarendon Street, Oxford OX2 6DP
Oxford University Press is a department of the University of Oxford.
It furthers the University's objective of excellence in research, scholarship,
and education by publishing worldwide in

Oxford New York

Auckland Cape Town Dar es Salaam Hong Kong Karachi
Kuala Lumpur Madrid Melbourne Mexico City Nairobi
New Delhi Shanghai Taipei Toronto

With offices in

Argentina Austria Brazil Chile Czech Republic France Greece
Guatemala Hungary Italy Japan Poland Portugal Singapore
South Korea Switzerland Thailand Turkey Ukraine Vietnam

Oxford is a registered trade mark of Oxford University Press
in the UK and in certain other countries

British Library Cataloguing in Publication Data

Data available

ISBN: 978-0-19-273223-1
1 3 5 7 9 10 8 6 4 2

Printed in Great Britain
Paper used in the production of this book is a natural,
recyclable product made from wood grown in sustainable forests.
The manufacturing process conforms to the environmental
regulations of the country of origin.

To the Girton kids: Lucy, Edward, Toby, Thomas, Ben, Alice, Luke, Sam, Jacob, Toby, Noah, Silas, Caleb, Jude, Talitha, Molly, Grace, Johnny and Sammy. It is a privilege watching you all grow up together!

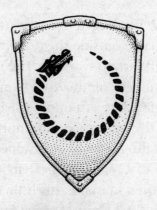

Chapter 1

THE stench of dragon was overwhelming. A burning ache at the back of Rick's throat, a stinging in his eyes—there was nothing else in Avalon that smelled quite like it.

Pausing before the entrance to the den, Rick Halfdane, the Fey King's newest dragon keeper, took a last breath of fresh air. The other keepers, a scarred and scratched collection of Dark Folk, stood in a semicircle behind him, watching, their amusement plain. All the dragon keepers were little better than outcasts in Avalon; it pleased them to have a human added to their number, a new underdog to bully. Money was changing hands as they took bets on his survival. His death wasn't in doubt—just how long it would take the dragon to kill him.

The sun had just edged over the horizon, flooding the rock ledge outside the dragon stables with blood-red light but no warmth. The long shadows cast by the towers of the royal castle sprawled across the cliff face, stamping King Oberon's authority on the landscape. The northerly breeze from the distant range of ice-capped mountains was cold and dry. White eagles circled above the turrets. Rick tried to make this little moment last: it might be his final glimpse of daylight.

'Go on then, changeling,' urged Gorth, the veteran keeper, uncurling his iron-tipped whip. A tough part-troll Fey, with a gnarled hide and tusks instead of teeth, Gorth had rated the human's chances as very low. 'Sun's up and the king's mount will be really hungry. Waiting will only make it worse.' He spat a hissing droplet of venom on the ground at Rick's feet, his forked tongue flickering. 'And to think I forgot to feed it yesterday; it'll be starving.'

The other keepers laughed. A couple changed their bets to shorter survival times.

He'd been set up. No point risking the only one he loved that he still had with him. He tapped the golden torc around his neck. 'Aethel, stay here.'

Obediently, his magical snake shimmered from ornament into life and slid to safety in a crack just over the rough lintel.

Deep inside the honeycomb of caves, the beast was already roaring as it sensed the arrival of food. Penned in by the rock, the dragon's claws scraped on the floor and walls, hollowing out a few more inches in the chambers it had already carved in its years of captivity. The noise made Rick's teeth ache, hitting the note that went right to the nerve.

Was there nothing about dragon keeping that wasn't the complete pits for a human? It was the all-out winner of the worst job in history, right down there with sewer cleaner.

Casting a last defiant look at his audience of ill-wishers, Rick entered the tunnel and reached for the protective breastplate that hung just inside. A little large for him, it had been made for the previous keeper who had been invalided out after serving this particular dragon for only a week. Next, Rick laced up his shin pads and gauntlets, and finally added a helmet to cover his hair. The gear would not be much help in the event of the dragon turning on a keeper, but it did give Rick the illusion of protection. He breathed through the shivery sensation that rolled inside him. He couldn't think too much or he would never find the courage to face the dragon.

'OK, if I get out alive, I'll get hold of a massive plate of chips somehow and eat every single one.' He had become fond of this human treat during his recent stay on Earth. Fey cooks hadn't yet discovered French fries so he had no idea how he was going to realize his dream. Still, it felt better to hope than despair. 'So, all I have to do is not become a dragon chip first.'

Uniform securely fastened, Rick grabbed a torch and proceeded to the meat dump. No one but the keeper was expected to come this close to the dragon; magical defences were useless as the creature just ripped straight through them. Brute force and bribery were the only things that worked. The Fey hunters dropped their catch down a specially constructed shoot in the rock. It was Rick's task to drag the carcass the last hundred yards; this was to remind the dragon that it relied on the keepers for every meal.

Thrusting his torch in to the dark recess at the bottom of the shoot, Rick cursed when he saw that the only offering was a half-eaten chicken. Rick hooked it off the floor and slung it over his shoulder. He should have expected this. The chance of surviving to eat his chips had just got a whole lot fainter.

'I hate this place,' Rick muttered, words inadequate to describe the deep loathing he felt for his life in Avalon. Painfully lonely, without anyone but Aethel to look out for him, Rick just wished he could be a normal teenager living in an ordinary family on Earth, ignorant that places such as this existed.

He turned the final corner to look down on the den in which the dragon, one of the warrior Stormridge breed, was stabled. The top of the pit was covered with thick fire-proof bars and long spikes pointing downwards so the dragon could not grip on to them and saw through the steel. That left the creature the floor and walls of its cell on which to vent its frustration. Whitish-grey rubble was heaped in one corner, torn up by claws. The air was thick with dust. As a chameleon species, dragons could change colour to suit their environment, but as all of them were kept in dungeons they had lost their rainbow skins. They had become dull, ugly and vengeful.

Rick peered in to every corner of the prison. Then he spotted his dragon clinging to the far wall, ragged wings flat against its back, tail tucked in to the new gouge it had made in its frenzy. It was enormous—the length of a tennis court, though a good deal narrower, with its pinions tucked tightly to its body. Skin pitted and uneven like a dried lava flow, claws sharp as scythes, this old dragon looked hideous and mean, and as though it would enjoy nothing better than to use its keeper's bones as toothpicks. It wasn't hard to see the parallels between Rick's and the dragon's status as Oberon's captives. The dragon hated life in Avalon as much as he did. Maybe more.

'Breakfast is served!' Rick called, throwing the chicken through the bars. It plummeted unimpressively to the ground a few feet from the dragon's tail. The other keepers had already told him he was wasting his time talking to their charges. It wasn't that the dragons didn't have the wit to understand—before Oberon took over, they had once ruled Avalon in their own right and were famed for their intelligence—it was that they just didn't care what any usurping Dark Folk had to say. 'Sorry it isn't much. The next thing I'm going to do is hunt down the hunters and make sure you get a decent meal. Double, to make up for today.'

The Stormridge did not move.

'We didn't get a chance to be introduced yesterday,' Rick continued, tone more cheerful than he felt. He was now supposed to lift the hatch in the bars, rope down, and enter the cave to muck out the creature's pen—the idea being that occupied with its meal it would not attack. Some hope. He eyed the pitchfork, wondering if he could use it to defend himself at a pinch.

If only he could do this by magic: use a couple of lifting spells to move the dung and zap the floor with a spring charm to wash the dirt away. But the problem was that dragons dampened magic.

Something about their own power meant no charms worked within a few feet of them.

Rick balanced his way across the bars to drop the rope into the pit. The pitchfork went next, landing prongs downwards, quivering slightly. He then opened the grill.

The dragon still made no movement.

'I'm coming down to clear up,' he continued, in what he hoped was a soothing tone. 'To make you more comfortable.'

A curl of smoke wound from the creature's nostrils. A sign of annoyance? Malice?

'OK, coming in.' Rick grasped the rope and quickly slid down. He could feel the unblinking stare of the dragon following his progress. He wanted to hunch his head closer to his shoulders to defend the back of his neck, but decided against showing weakness. He smoothly picked up the pitchfork and made his way over to the straw-covered area the dragon had selected for its bathroom, pretending that everything was perfectly normal and he didn't have a one-tonne dragon fixing him with a predatory gaze. *Don't shake*, he urged himself, noticing his legs were in danger of going into a little jittery dance all on their own. He approached the dung pile. During his induction he had learned that dragons were fastidious creatures and objected to living in a dirty stable. 'I'll just get rid of this for you.'

That did it. The Stormridge cannoned the short distance between them, its tail whipping the pitchfork from Rick's hands. Just in time, Rick dived behind the heap of rubble, narrowly missing being crispy fried by a blast of flame. Straw blackened and whirled up in sparks, a flock of tiny firebirds. He felt a scorching heat on his face. Hair smouldered. Then nothing.

Cautiously, Rick raised his head from behind his barrier. The dragon had reverted to wall painting mode, this time on the other side of its cell. The chicken, straw and dung had all gone up in smoke. All that was left was the smoking stump of his pitchfork.

Spooked, Rick didn't even bother to retrieve it. He made straight for his lifeline and hauled himself out of the pit, heartbeat thumping in his ears. Once safely above the bars he slumped against the wall. OK, OK, he was alive. The dragon hadn't killed him. It could have done, so very easily. Something he had said must have set it off—probably the idea that he did the cleaning up on its behalf. It was a prisoner, for troll's sake. He'd be annoyed if his jailer more or less told him to be grateful for mucking out his cell.

Rick peered down at the dragon again. Alien black eyes glared up at him.

Gingerly, Rick reached for a bucket and splashed water over the ashes. Grey liquid trickled out of the channel carved in the floor. The dragon made no objection so Rick quickly threw down two more pails of water. That left a smelly damp corner. Just as he was wondering what to do about that, the dragon breathed out a ripple of heat, drying up the remaining puddles.

'Clever!' Rick called before he remembered the dragon hated his guts. 'Um, I'll just get the straw.'

In silence, he scattered the straw through the bars. The dragon watched.

'Well, er, that's it for now. I'm going to go and complain about the food delivery but I think they did it on purpose—they want you to kill me.' Hobspit, he probably shouldn't put ideas in the creature's mind.

I know, human. That is the only reason you live.

The dragon's thought burst in to Rick's brain. Rick clutched his ringing temples. He'd heard that dragons used thought-speech, but no one had ever reported experiencing it. The sensation was like a claw raking across tender flesh.

'Troll breath—that hurts.'

Poor little lost human, snarled the dragon, not the slightest bit repentant, though its voice was less painful this time, as if it had adjusted its power. *I can bear hunger for one day only. Tomorrow I will eat you.*

Rick shuddered. 'I'll talk to the hunters.'

You do that, changeling. But, in any case, your time is up. The dragon's tongue flickered out to lick its mouth.

'I said I was sorry about the food. Really I am. Not my fault, but I'll try and sort it out.'

This is not about food. Dragons hear things. Either I eat you or Oberon kills you. At least I will make it quick.

'Oh wow, that's very public spirited of you,' Rick replied with more attitude than he intended. Stupid to sneer at a dragon when you were still in firing range. He hurriedly turned to go.

Perhaps you would do well to listen, changeling. Oberon has plans for your scrawny hide.

'What do you mean?' Rick came back and crouched over the bars but the dragon had closed its eyes and ignored him. He sighed and tugged off his helmet and gauntlets to sit for a moment with his back against the tunnel wall where he was out of direct fire but still within hearing. 'I guess you've been more than fair telling me that much.'

Sometimes it was very hard to stop from sinking into despair and find that part of him that could carry on fighting. Ever since he had learned a few days ago that the Fey had not swapped but stolen him from his parents, Rick had felt a great aching hole in his chest, a longing for another life. And every time he dared hope for something better, his own circumstances took a turn for the worse. He was under the thumb of a vicious cruel-hearted king, the tyrant Oberon; he had had his chance of escape only for a brief second before it was whisked away, like a meal placed in front of a starving man then fed to others.

He hugged his knee, the other leg sprawled across the passageway.

Human changelings like him, trapped in Avalon at Dark Lore training camp, were doomed to a life of slavery unless they saved themselves. The Fey Folk thought them only fit to be used and discarded like rubbish. For one brief moment, he and his friends had had hope—a plan to set up a new Round Table. When knights were invited by King Arthur to join his table they gained amazing magical powers that helped them to fight their Fey enemies on an equal footing—spell for spell. Rick had hoped to start a new generation of Round Table knights able to defeat Oberon, but he needed the original table founders, Arthur and Merlin, to do it. But before Rick could make his move, Morgan, the commander of the camp, had booted him out for spreading rebellion and sent him to be a dragon keeper. Now he could only return to the vital task of recruiting Arthur if he survived the dragon's dungeon and escaped from Oberon's well-guarded palace. For Rick, it was out of the frying pan and into the furnace blast of dragon flame.

Rick rubbed the empty place on his wrist where Aethel normally sat. He missed his mates: Roxy, still stuck at Dark Lore half a day's journey to the south; Tiago, their half-human half-Mage ally; and Linette, the human friend they had made on Earth. Now it looked like their plan to re-form the Table had failed as he was pretty much doomed to working with the dragons. The worst thing was that, after finding such good friends and working as a team, he was again alone. He wanted Roxy's cheek and undefeated spirit, Tiago's oddball way of looking at the world, Linette's wry humour and, well, normality—she was the only one with anything resembling a family life.

Get moving, human, or I will blast you now.

Rick sprang to his feet. Low though he might be, he wasn't quite ready to be dragon-kill. As he ran back down the tunnel to the entrance, he could have sworn he heard a wheeze of laughter echo in the den.

Chapter 2

SIX hours earlier.

On the top floor of Dark Lore House, Roxy eased out of her bunk in the dormitory she shared with twenty of the other girls. Moving soundlessly, she crossed the floor to the door, needing no lamp to see thanks to the faint moonlight spilling in through the high windows. After Dark Lore had melted under rebel attack last week, the Fey had reconstructed the house as quickly and simply as possible; instead of a beautiful castle, the changelings now lived in a four-storey office block. A girl turned over. Roxy paused, but the sleeper didn't wake. One of the toddlers whimpered slightly, caught in a bad dream. Roxy paused by the cot and laid her hand on the child's tummy, stroking to calm her down. The little noises stopped and the toddler curled up into a puppy-like ball.

OK. So far, so good.

Out in the corridor, things got more perilous. She had timed the troll-guard patrols and estimated that she had five minutes to get downstairs to Morgan's office.

I must be mad, she thought, as she crept along the passageway, keeping to the shadows as much as possible. Her goal for this night raid was to acquire—all right, *steal*—the commander's surveillance mirror. The scrying glass was an ancient object, spelled by Merlin himself; it had once been embedded in the middle of Arthur's Round Table like a smooth diamond hub, its reflection giving warning of the approach of enemies. It had long since become Morgan's possession, after she had defeated Arthur's knights when she split the round oak table with a formidable rending spell, breaking the knights' magical strength that was tied to it. The mirror had survived in one piece and she had taken it to Avalon as a trophy, along with the husk of the broken table. It was the crown jewel in Morgan's collection of magical artefacts; a unique object that no Fey knew how to replicate.

So what could a girl raised by pixies do but try to steal it?

The patrol was returning early. Ducking into a storage cupboard, Roxy crouched among the old Kemystery equipment. It smelt strongly of bog frogs—sulphurous and slimy. Heavy boots passed and the corridor fell silent again. Cracking the cupboard open, Roxy checked the way was clear then jogged lightly down the last staircase until she stood outside the door.

'Right, now work out what spells she has on this place,' Roxy muttered to herself. She wasn't out here for a midnight lark; if she didn't succeed in getting to the mirror the plan to escape and find Arthur wouldn't stand a chance. A distant enchanted ancestor to human CCTV, the mirror could track any place, any time in the past, if the user's magic was strong enough. The changelings would never be able to escape Morgan's vigilance so long as the mirror was in the commander's hands. No wonder she had always seemed one step ahead of them and caught Rick recruiting fighters for the resistance from among the changelings.

Roxy cast a revealing spell over the door, letting the magic catch like a golden net of mist on any charms that blocked her path. Three were shown up this way, including a fiendishly complex one on the lock that looked like a ball of wool after a kitten had got at it. Sticking her tongue between her teeth, Roxy set to work.

Ten minutes later, the door clicked open and Roxy grinned. Almost there now. Her pixie-bred side was humming with anticipation. Stepping into the room, she repeated the revelation spell. Hundreds of little charms were shown to be attached to objects in the room.

'Paranoid much?' she snorted. It fitted that Morgan had triple guarded then secured everything a fourth time as she had the temperament of a dragon sitting on its hoard. Roxy spotted the mirror lying on Morgan's desk. Checking for charmed trip wires or other hazards, Roxy tiptoed across the room.

Silence. No alarms. Nothing. Some instinct nudged her that that was wrong, but having come so far it would be stupid to stop now.

Just do it.

She stretched out her fingers and was on the point of lifting the glass from its satin-lined casket when the door blasted inwards and Morgan swept into the room.

Roxy froze in shock.

Fey and girl stood looking at each other in silence as Morgan waited for her reinforcements. The black-uniformed commander had a cruel beauty, like a cobra coiled to strike. Tall, pale-faced, with dead-straight dark hair that fell to her waist, Morgan glared at Roxy with cold fury. Feet stamped in the corridor as troll guards arrived with a pack of hungry wolf-like hobgoblins to corner her. The rank smell of the hobs matched in foulness their hairless bodies and hungry eyes; their barks split the air.

All Roxy could think was 'hobspit'.

Chapter 3

ICK'S work passed the noon inspection. Gorth was so surprised to see him alive that he allowed Rick to go for lunch, waving off his complaints about the inadequate meat supply.

'You get what you gets,' he said gruffly, wiping the back of his hand over his snout and flicking the snot to the ground as he glared down at the motionless dragon through the bars of the cage.

That was when Rick realized who had bribed the huntsmen to leave the Stormridge short. 'I'll speak to them myself then, shall I, sir?' Rick suggested. He thought he saw a crack appear in the dragon's eyelid, a cold eye fixing on Gorth.

'You do that, boy. See if it gets you anywhere.' Gorth muttered something about blasted reptiles never doing what they should and someone's wages going down the drain.

So that was how things stood. The Stormridge was not going to get fed as long as Rick was available for eating.

'I can only try, can't I? I mean, it's not as if you are all plotting against me or anything, is it?' Rick shrugged out of his protective gear.

'Now why would we do that?' Gorth gave a derisive grunt.

Because it amused them. Because humans were no more to the Dark Folk of Avalon than flies to a bored schoolboy, swatting them for no better reason than he could. The Fey had set up Dark Lore because they had needed human babies in exchange for the rebels Oberon sent into exile on Earth, otherwise the delicate physical balance between the two worlds would be put in danger. The king had decided he might as well make use of the changelings and given Morgan the task of turning the children into loyal warriors to serve him. They were only allowed to live so long as they were considered to have a purpose. Rick feared, given his new job, his own 'sell by' date was judged to have passed.

Gorth lumbered away to inspect the other dragon pens further along the cliff. Rick hung up his gear and retrieved Aethel from her place above the door. She curled around his arm, her tongue flickering over the sensitive skin on the inside of his wrist.

'I survived.'

Aethel's bright eyes seemed to suggest that that wasn't enough.

'The dragon didn't hurt me—it gave me advice, if you can believe it?' She didn't need to know about him being on the menu tomorrow. There were some things with which he did not want to burden his oldest and closest friend; she worried about him enough already.

The snake looked sceptical, curling backwards.

'Yeah, I know, but it doesn't have a reason to lie to me. It said that Oberon has plans for me— not good ones.' Rick rubbed his forehead wearily, trying to fathom the motives of the dragon; it was good policy never to trust anyone in Avalon. 'We can believe that, can't we? Would be true to form.' He descended the steep flight of steps that led to the bridge spanning the gorge separating the castle from the stables. 'I suppose the dragon might just be stirring things up, starting rumours, but what would be the point of that? I can't do much if it wants me to cause trouble for the king.'

Rick paused on the bridge, looking down at the silver waterfall that tumbled over the cliff, misting the delicate pink and white flowers that grew in the crevices. The water landed in a boiling pool, dark with shadows, then flowed on to curl around the castle, a natural moat. 'I'll have to check its story—and find out how to get it some proper food. Then I need to work out a way out of this place and go after Arthur. Yeah, that's what I need to do.'

The kitchens built into the northern wall of the castle were bustling at this hour. The upper servants were busy rushing to and fro from the royal apartments where the king and his counsellors were eating. Ducking between two grey-clad ogres from the kennels, Rick grabbed a plate of smoked fish and bread for himself. With skin like boiled leather, ogres stood twice the height of a man and had bulbous eyes, good for seeing in the dark. Jaws full of sharp teeth, as well as two stubby tusks, they were the elite warriors, able to bite the heads off their enemies. Most wore their hair short so it stuck out of their scalps like cornstalks after the combine harvester had passed over. Rick preferred to keep well out of their way. As he hurried to find a space at one of the long tables, a foot stuck out and tripped him. Rick, fish and bread went flying.

'Clumsy changeling, look where you are going!' tutted the owner of the foot, a coarse-looking Fey called Jacques, with steeply slanting eyebrows and a sharp nose. Rick rolled to his feet. His food was already being devoured by a hobgoblin pup, a skeletal beast that resembled a hairless wolf cub, which roamed the castle for scraps.

'I don't know why they let you eat with us,' continued Jacques. 'Filth like you should be kept separate.' He took a deep sniff. 'Can't you smell it—the human under the dragon reek? By the king's throne, it quite turns my stomach.' Two blue-scaled nix guards chuckled sympathetically, clicking their double row of shark teeth.

Ignoring the Fey, who wanted nothing more than to pick a fight, Rick returned to the serving table and grabbed some cheese and a hunk of bread, without bothering with a plate. Making a rough sandwich for himself, he walked out of the dining room.

Roxy stood locked in the stocks on the parade ground at Dark Lore Training Camp. Neck pinned, wrists trapped, she couldn't reach to brush a lock of red-gold hair out of her mouth and it was really bugging her. An added aggravation was that she was too short for this contraption and had been made to stand on a box to reach—the indignity giving a further twist to her foul temper.

She muttered a few choice words she had picked up in her brief stay in the human world, trying to spit her own hair free. There was no one around to help: as a result of her attempt to steal the mirror, the other changelings in the camp had been confined to barracks. It looked as if she would have to put up with the irritation of not being able to brush her hair away until sundown.

Movement on the horizon caught her eye. Roxy watched with growing amazement as a ribbon-decked pixie wagon appeared on the road, just cresting the hill beyond the fence. It was heading down the track to the perimeter gates of Dark Lore. Perched high on the baggage, directing the milk-white Fey horses in the traces, was Trix-E, her once-upon-a-time playmate; walking behind trailing armfuls of hedgerow flowers were Trix-E's parents, Frost-E and Miz-Begotten, the pixies that had raised Roxy from her early years.

She watched the pixies make short work of the gate, bribing the old troll on guard with one of their much sought-after charms. He stood back to let them through, tying a blue feather to his long, floppy earlobe. Roxy recognized the pink shimmer of the 'Be Irresistible' spell hovering around the earring and was momentarily distracted by imagining the effect it would have on female troll guards. She shuddered. Then she returned her attention to tracking the caravan as it approached.

Trix-E had changed very little since Roxy last saw her; she was still a tiny and unusually earnest pixie, with her gold hair tamed into plaits either side of her nut brown cheeks. She looked sweet and harmless but Roxy knew better than to trust appearances in Avalon; Trix-E may look child-like but she was the cleverest pixie Roxy had ever met. Even cramped in the stocks, Roxy's spirits lifted. The arrival of the pixies was the first good thing to happen all day and she began to think up some possible ways for them to help her escape. But what had brought her three vagabond friends here in the nick of time? The rules and routines of Dark Lore were the complete opposite to their way of life and she expected them to be repulsed from the camp like two north poles on magnets.

Miz-Begotten saw her first. With a little cry of pleasure, she dumped her flowers on her husband and danced over to the stocks. Her head at a level with Roxy's in this awkward position, she dropped a kiss on the end of her nose.

'Oh Rox-E, there you are! We were so hoping to be able to see you.' Her bronze hair fell in waves around her cream-coloured face, making her look fragile and doll-like—an illusion, as pixies were anything but delicate. 'We heard all about the dis-aster that melted Dark Lore and Trix-E insisted we pay you a visit to see how you are.'

'I'm fine—as you can see.' Roxy wondered if Miz-Begotten had even noticed the stocks. If she had, as a free-spirited pixie, she probably didn't understand what they were for. 'It's, um, lovely to see you again.'

Frost-E strode over looking like a blossoming bush, his copper-skinned face and shock of clover-purple hair peeping over the top. 'May your fingers be ever nimble,' he said, giving her the traditional pixie greeting.

'And the road clear before your feet,' Roxy replied, as was expected.

Frost-E tucked a blue lily behind Roxy's ear, clearing the annoying strand from her mouth. 'You look well, Rox-E.'

She resisted a snort. She did not look well: she looked trapped. Behind them she could see that Trix-E had dismounted from her seat and was making her way over to them.

'Rox-E!' called the little pixie girl. 'What in Avalon are you doing stuck in that?'

'Oh, you know me: I thought I'd just hang around here for the fun of it.'

Miz-Begotten wrinkled her nose in puzzlement, taking her words at face value. 'But it doesn't look very comfortable.'

Frost-E examined the wooden structure curiously. 'Is it fun, child? Should I have a go?'

Trix-E shouldered past her parents. She possessed more common sense than both of them put together—and all their extended family of hundreds, come to that. 'Of course you shouldn't, Pa; she was being ironic—a human trait.' She pulled out the hairpin securing a spray of magpie feathers to her head and set to work on the lock. In two seconds the stocks were open and she was helping Roxy step down from her box.

'Thanks, but you probably shouldn't have done that,' Roxy admitted, rubbing her neck and wrists. 'I was being punished.'

The concept of discipline was not one even the most level-headed vagabond pixie understood. Trix-E shrugged. 'Finders keepers. We found you unattended and have stolen you. You're ours again.'

Their lack of concern was catching. 'It's wonderful to see you all again! It's been so long!' She and Trix-E hugged enthusiastically, each vying to squeeze the breath out of the other, and then she kissed Miz-Begotten and Frost-E on the tip of the nose in the traditional pixie child to parent fashion. 'Are you really here to see how I am? What've you heard?'

Trix-E took her hand and led her over to the wagon. 'We heard rumours that King Malduc and his allies tried to stage a rebellion and that Oberon crushed it. We heard that Dark Lore had been badly damaged in the struggle.'

That about summed it up, thought Roxy, apart from the adventure she had been on with Rick and Tiago in the human world.

'You can see what happened. Doctor Purl-E is only just now beginning to reverse the melt.'

Trix-E reintroduced Roxy to Barleywater and Cauliflower, the same two horses who had pulled the wagon when Roxy travelled with them. The pair snuffed the girls' hair and stamped their huge hooves. The smell of their manes and the dust of the open road awoke so many memories in Roxy—ones she had deliberately suppressed in order to bear her tedious days in the camp; she would give anything to get on top of the baggage with Trix-E and head out for the Moonshine Mountains. It was tempting, but she couldn't just forget about Rick and the quest.

Trix-E glanced over her shoulder to check her parents were still busy with their task. Frost-E was balanced on top of the stocks suspending a parasol of lilac blossom from a tree branch; Miz-Begotten was doing a headstand. All was normal.

'Roxy, we did come to see you were safe, but I have to admit I have other motives.' Her little round face looked very sombre. 'On the road it is hard to ignore the signs. Oberon's grasp on power is getting weaker and this means he is clinging all the harder. One thing he is doing is finding a target for blame.'

Roxy smiled as she saw Miz-Begotten begin to spin on her head. 'Blame for what?'

'For the decline of magic. As the supply of green energy from the human world runs dry we are running out of magic.' She lowered her voice. 'The exchange that gives us magic and the humans their powers of invention was close to breakdown even before the rebels had a go at taking control of the Fey rings that generate the energy. There are rumours that we might have to ration magic soon—that or do something about the source.'

'You mean Earth?' Roxy's grin disappeared.

'Exactly. But that's not all. Oberon is looking for targets to blame closer to home, a place to direct his people's anger.'

'Like a . . . a scapegoat?'

Trix-E nodded.

'Not Rick?' gasped Roxy.

The pixie frowned. 'Who?'

'My friend, Rick. Oberon took him off to be a dragon keeper two days ago.'

Trix-E kissed the tip of each index finger—the pixie equivalent of touching wood, meaning 'may that fate not fall on us'. 'I wasn't talking about just one of you. I'm talking about all the human changelings.'

'All of us? But why? What have we done?'

Trix-E shrugged. 'Search me—then again, you'd

better not. Never know what you'll find.' She winked as she pulled out of her brightly embroidered shoulder bag a shell keyring that had until recently been in Roxy's pocket. She handed it back. 'The king's not interested in the facts but who he can use to divert attention away from his mistakes.'

Roxy tucked the keyring in her back pocket and rubbed her upper arms. Though the sun was out, her skin seemed to have chilled a few degrees. 'What can I do? I mean, I'm trapped here like all the others. What more can Oberon do to us?'

Trix-E leaned closer and whispered. 'Kill the changelings.'

'What!'

'Ssh!' warned Trix-E. 'Don't let the trolls know I've told you! Some of the strongest changelings might be sent to the emerald mines of the Blackore Peaks, but most of you will be taken away and . . .' She swallowed, crystal tears glinting in her eyes.

'And killed.' Roxy's skin felt ice cold with fear.

Trix-E nodded. 'He wants to shut down the camp—end the experiment of training changelings and use you as an example of what he does to his enemies. He plans to use you in the Fey Games.'

The Fey Games were held each year at the autumn equinox. Various magical beasts were pitted against each other in an arena for the amusement of the court. Roxy could guess how long humans would last against some of the monsters Oberon kept for his pleasure.

Trix-E sniffed and pulled a massive red-and-white spotted handkerchief out of the sleeve of her patchwork jacket, mopping the eyes of the draft horse nearest her who was crying silent tears. 'Barleywater is very sensitive,' Trix-E explained. 'She remembers you. Cauliflower won't show it, but he too has been awfully worried about you.'

Roxy put her arms around Barleywater's neck and hugged, relishing the simple animal warmth and horsey odour of earth and straw. 'So what should I do, Trix-E? Knowing you, you've got some ideas already or you wouldn't be here.'

'Prison break.' Trix-E waved her arms to the fence surrounding the camp. 'No other option. Security isn't very tight—not for a pixie anyway. We should be able to smuggle you out.'

'What? All of us?'

Trix-E looked awkwardly at the ground, seemingly fascinated by the curled tips of her shoes, half blue, half red. 'I was thinking of just you. Sometimes you can't save everyone.'

Not the right answer. 'But we have to take everyone.'

The next shift of trolls emerged from their guard-room to do their rounds. This wasn't the moment to elaborate on escape plans. Roxy gripped Trix-E's arm.

'Look, you don't know me—or only vaguely remember I travelled with pixies if anyone connects your family to me. Tell your parents to ignore me.'

'They won't like that.' Trix-E's expression said she was very pessimistic about Frost-E or Miz-Begotten keeping to a script for more than a minute, even if they understood what was at stake. The concept of changeling mass murder was not something a pixie mind could grasp—only an exceptional pixie like Trix-E could comprehend such cruelty. Take what Frost-E had just done to an instrument of torture. The stocks now looked like the winning entry in a village floral competition, sprouting blooms in a petal explosion. Job done, Frost-E had joined Miz-Begotten in spinning on his head.

'Please try. Give me a little time to think about this. But there's something you should know: Morgan's got this scrying mirror that keeps all of us under surveillance—we won't be able to get far even if we do get out.'

Trix-E frowned. 'Hmm, interesting. That will also make it harder to hide so many.'

'Try to understand: I must save my friends here. Think of it as stealing all of us from under her nose—that's much more impressive, and demands the skills of the very best pixie thieves.'

Trix-E chuckled, recognizing Roxy had found the right argument to convince her. 'All right, I'll scout out the territory and see if I can find a weak spot in the fence for all of you.'

'And the mirror?'

Trix-E winked. 'Like that will be a problem for us!'

'It's not funny. You don't know how powerful she is.'

Trix-E patted Roxy's arm. 'And she doesn't know how crafty we are.'

A troll guard spotted them and came marching through the glass doors of the foyer in their direction, truncheon swinging. Big, with tough blue-grey skin, tusks, and a venom-spit defence, he was typical of his species: good at carrying out orders, rubbish at independent thinking.

Roxy estimated they had five more seconds.

'Just don't get yourselves killed getting it.'

'Oi, you, little human girl! What are you doing out of the stocks?' shouted the guard. He blew three sharp peeps on a whistle round his neck, summoning backup. Quite why a ten-foot-tall troll needed back up for a girl half his size, Roxy did not know. She supposed she should be flattered.

'I . . . um . . .' Roxy grappled for an excuse that wouldn't get her friends in trouble.

'She was in the way.' Frost-E cartwheeled over, landing at the troll's boot tips. 'Do you like it?' He gestured to his flower arrangement.

The troll scratched his head, ruffling the wispy strands of the navy-blue mane that covered his scalp. 'Like it?'

'We're setting up shop there,' Frost-E continued. 'Charms for the charmless, potions to release your potential, ointments to clear annoyances: yours for a bargain price.' Frost-E ended his sales patter with a little tap dance.

The troll looked impressed. He scratched his hairy belly. 'Well, now you come to mention it, I do have a little private difficulty.' His cheek whiskers bristled—the troll sign of embarrassment.

'Come with me, my friend.' Frost-E cartwheeled back to the pixie market stall, formerly known as the stocks.

The troll took a step.

'Best if you cartwheel—it clears the mind!' Frost-E called.

With surprising grace, the troll followed, his truncheon whirling as he span.

Trix-E grabbed the harness to guide the wagon over to their new pitch. 'Trolls, pixies: we get along rather well considering how different we are. Speak later.'

Chapter 4

DRAGON keepers were supposed to limit themselves to the lower floors of the castle, but Rick decided the last thing he wanted was to eat his lunch in Fey company. He followed an obscure staircase up the outer wall. There were plenty of such passageways in the castle, as it spread across the hillside like a coral reef—full of pinnacles and hidden chambers more akin to a naturally growing organism than a planned building. The tallest tower at the centre of the castle, Oberon's private domain, was built like a conch shell—chambers spiralling upwards, narrowing to a thin spine. Finding a sunny window ledge, Rick sat in the niche, feet tucked up close, arms looped around his legs. For a moment he did nothing but enjoy the warmth; he hadn't expected to see the sun again today so he took time to relish the privilege. His mind turned to the Stormridge stuck down in the dungeon. That was plain wrong. Granted, dragons were lethal creatures, but they were also reptiles that needed to bathe in the sun, to fly, to be free. By being their keeper, Rick was, even if unwillingly, enforcing their captivity. He felt sick about that but what could he do?

A blue and silver butterfly flickered through the window to settle on his knee, flexing its wings, light catching its scales in rainbow flashes. Rick didn't move, knowing that even the slightest brush could damage it. The Stormridge had held himself so still, blended into the stonework—a useful skill. Rick needed to equip himself with this kind of magic if he was to survive in the castle. He searched his mind for a spell that would allow him to disguise himself in the same way. A Fey glamour should do it. He concentrated, dipped into the glowing well of magical power in his chest, and spun out a thread that turned his leather clothing to a marble white, veined with grey. Then he spread the pattern to his skin—it was weird to watch the creep as his skin changed colour, and so convincing he had to check to see he hadn't turned as cold as he now looked. No, skin warm as usual. The butterfly flew off in alarm, but Rick was pleased with the result: he now looked like a carving in a window niche.

He was about to drop the experiment when he heard bells tinkling throughout the castle and the soft patter of feet on the staircase. The court was being summoned to Oberon's throne room. Rick grabbed a torch from a silver bracket and pressed against the wall, holding it in front of his face to become a human statue. Out of the corner of his eye he could see a stream of Dark Folk passing, lesser members of the court who used this modest staircase, leaving the grand central spiral to their more important fellows. Just when he thought he had escaped notice, two familiar figures brought up the rear: Magmell and Shreddie, Rick's old minders from their stay in the human world.

'Second time in two days,' muttered Shreddie. The pixie had been given a promotion to court clerk, marked out by the parchment and quill she was carrying. 'What do you think is the matter, Magmell? Why does His Majesty want to address us again? Normally he doesn't care to keep us informed.'

Magmell glided behind her with his usual languid grace. A slender, dark-haired Fey of unreasonable good looks, he had always despised Rick and the other changelings.

'No idea, Pixie, but ours is not to reason why.' Magmell hitched up his new robe so it did not catch on his boot heels. The garish whirling pattern of scarlet and gold told Rick that Magmell had done even better than Shreddie and got a position as a special adviser.

A bead of sweat was threatening to run down Rick's forehead. He concentrated on keeping very still.

Shreddie sounded out of breath from her dash across the castle. 'As for our king, I think he's got a new strategy—everyone's saying it.'

'It's the human world he's going after.'

Shreddie stumbled on the stair. 'But we have the humans to thank for our jobs.'

Magmell helped her to her feet. 'I'm just thankful that we're not responsible for them any more. I couldn't stand them—particularly that arrogant boy with the snake. Come on, Shreddie. We can't be the last to arrive.'

The two disappeared from view. Rick breathed a sigh of relief and waited a few more seconds, checking the coast was really clear. It was strange to see his old minders but he was pleased that Shreddie at least had fallen on her feet; he didn't care what happened to the hard-hearted Fey, Magmell. Their conversation had been useful; he now knew that Oberon was about to announce something important and, if the dragon was right, it could well affect him. Could he risk following?

It would mean missing the start of his afternoon shift but, as the job was murder in the literal sense, maybe that was not a consideration.

His feet were moving before he was aware of having made a decision. He was going to spy on Oberon's court.

The door to Oberon's throne room was closed and guarded by formidable ogres. Rick knew better than to try entering that way and retreated to a nearby window. He had had an idea, copied from his friend Tiago. Tiago had become a fan of comic-book superheroes and had taken a tip from one called Spider-Man for a spell of his own devising. If you conjure a sticky substance on your palms and soles you can crawl along a vertical surface like an insect. Rick had been practising this since his return to Avalon and decided he was going to be a fly on the wall—an outside wall, as the skilled magic users in the room would be able to see through a glamour spell. Hopefully, no one would think anyone would be crazy enough to stick to a ledge five hundred feet over a chasm with a rocky moat at the bottom.

'Yeah, you'd have to be hobspitting insane to do that,' Rick muttered as he stripped off his boots, wishing Roxy was here to shake some sense in to him—or join him in the madness, which was more likely. He tucked his boots into his belt.

He tried the charm a couple of times to check he had got the details right, then slid to the edge so his feet dangled over the edge. Ah. His confidence took a nose dive as he suddenly discovered he did not have a good head for heights, not when the wind tugged at his trousers and cooled the bottoms of his feet. Was he really going to do this?

'Tiago does it all the time,' he told himself. 'Nothing to it.' No point putting Aethel at risk though. He tapped his snake necklace. 'Time to jump ship.'

Aethel glowed a heated warning. She refused to abandon him this time.

He didn't have time to argue. He stood on the window ledge gripping the inner edge with his left hand then swung his right out to slap his palm on the rock face. Contact. He tugged but it held, the sticking charm binding him to the smooth surface. Now for his feet. It was harder to get a good angle here. He realized he only needed the charm on his toes as the rest of his feet would not touch the wall. The right foot found a hold, then his left. His weight was now being supported by the charm; the next step was to let go with his left hand, but it was tough convincing his brain to do so.

'You've got to do it,' he told himself. His fingers released their death grip. Rick was on his own on the sheer wall. Looking sideways he could see the balcony to the throne room some twenty feet away. If he didn't speed up, he wouldn't get there until evening, missing the announcement entirely.

With great care, he released the charm from his right hand, moved it along, then his right foot. That left him spreadeagled on the wall. Not good. He worked out it was better to do opposites— right hand, left foot, left hand, right foot—and take smaller side-steps. After a good five minutes he reached the balcony. He did not dare rest on it—guards would no doubt have it under sur- veillance—but he could hang by the opening. He could see the backs of the closest courtiers all bending towards the throne. Oberon demanded his people lowered their eyes from his face when in his throne room, the explanation given that he was too beautiful to look on and would distract them. Rick suspected he just lapped up the visible signs of his domination.

'My people.' Oberon's voice was smooth and cold, like the waterfall that curled over the cliff by the ramparts. Rick had the impression that he and all the listeners were being misted in it like the pink and white flowers he had seen in the cracks. 'We have crushed the foe, Malduc, but it brought home to me how many challenges remain to threaten the decades of peace I have brought you. My consort and I have decided we must take decisive steps to secure our future. We cannot allow our magic to be held hostage again.'

A scattering of applause from folk planted in the audience grew to a firm ovation as the courtiers caught on to what was expected of them.

'But I have learnt that there are those who are already working to undermine this noble project.' Oberon's voice was coming closer. He must have stepped from his dais and be making his way to the balcony. 'Out there, our enemies are plotting. We must unite against this threat; crush it before they crush us!'

Applause rang out again.

'We must not let them spoil what we have built, what I have secured for you to enjoy.' Oberon glided on to the balcony, calculating that the frame of the open windows and his kingdom spread out behind him would make his point. Rick pressed himself flat against the wall, barely breathing— the king was so close to him now. Oberon wore a silver pinnacle crown on top of his ice-white hair. Long fluttering robes wafted around him like swan wings.

'To save all this, we must take the battle to Earth. The humans have meddled with our supply of energy for too long and fouled the pure wells of magic with their *industrialization*, their *consumption*.' Oberon spoke the words like curses. 'That will stop. We will get rid of those humans that pose a threat and reduce the rest to the level of other creatures of wood and plain, living at harmony with nature. Humans are ruining the source of the green power we rely on for our very existence. Earth, therefore, must be ours.' He paused, clasping his hands to his chest in a gesture of modesty. 'You see, my dear subjects, I am a merciful ruler. I do not slaughter and kill needlessly. Only a billion or so of the vermin need die.'

The applause was slow to start this time as the audience absorbed the full impact of his words. Even for the Dark Folk, the policy of mass murder was a tough sell—despite being assured it was necessary.

'So prepare yourselves for war. We must secure our future, and only humanity stands in our way.'

Ready this time, the audience cheered.

Oberon stepped back into the throne room. 'I have brought one of the human ringleaders to the castle. He will be put on trial before you so that you will see my solution to the human problem is just. I would not want anyone to say later that they had not been given a fair hearing. The trial will take place before supper, and his execution directly after.'

Fair hearing? Oberon was making a mockery of the law he claimed to uphold. And who for pixie's sake was the ringleader? Rick couldn't think of anyone who fitted that description. All the changelings were too downtrodden or brain-washed to think of rebelling.

Unless Oberon meant him.

Occupied by surviving dragon keeping, Rick had not had time to wonder why he had been sent to the palace rather than killed outright as a rebel. Now he knew: Oberon had always intended for him to be paraded in a show trial. By succeeding in his mission on Earth against huge odds, and then disabusing the changelings about their true position in the kingdom, he had made himself a threat.

And now he was going to die anyway because his shock made his spider-spell fail.

Chapter 5

STICKY grip turned to rapid slide. Rick's nails scratched for a hold as he shot down the smooth face of the castle like a tear down a cheek. The roof of the building below rushed towards him. His pool of magic had sunk out of reach in his panic. White doves flew off in alarm as he rattled past their perches. Silver mirrored tiles flashed below—an unforgiving surface to crash into. This was it.

Then his death slide stopped. He swung one-handed, only a few feet above the roof that would have ended his fall.

What had happened? He looked up and saw that Aethel had sprung up his arm and wedged herself in a crack in the rock so that he hung like a side of beef from a butcher's hook. Painful for both of them—but it had saved his life.

Relieved that his fall had stopped, Rick found his ability to spin magic had returned. He stuck his hands and feet to the wall and took the pressure off Aethel. She slid out, a new notch to the base of her neck where it had caught on the stone.

'Thanks, Aethel. I owe you. Hobspit, look what I did to you!' He touched the dent with a finger-tip. Aethel's eyes blinked once, as if to say it was worth it. She wound round his arm lovingly. Rick began to edge down to the roof that had almost been his death, looking for an open window to re-enter the castle. 'Did you hear what Oberon said? He's planning to put me on trial and then execute me. After that he's invading Earth and killing a billion people! We need Arthur and that Round Table, like, yesterday. We've got to stop Oberon.'

Further along the ridge of the mirrored roof was a large chimney with an opening wide enough for Rick to climb down. If no fire was lit below, he should be able to get down unseen and unhurt.

'No way am I staying around here to give Oberon his show this evening. We're going to Dark Lore to grab Roxy, and then fetching Arthur so we can get started on gathering knights to the Round Table.' Put like that, it was a scarily ambitious 'to-do' list. 'Any ideas how we can escape the palace?'

Aethel stared at him with her emerald eyes.

Rick balanced along the ridge and hugged the chimney pot. He took it as a good sign that there was no smoke curling out of it. 'Could I ask the dragon?'

Aethel flinched.

'Yeah, you're right. That would be suicidal. The Stormridge is starving. He'd eat me before I got out my request.'

Aethel made a waving shape in the air, trying to convey her idea to Rick.

'What does that mean? You know, Legless, sometimes I wish you could talk. Tell me in a moment—let's get off this roof first.' He dropped both legs into the chimney and began edging down. He wondered if he was insane to choose this route. He had no idea which room he would end up in. With his luck, it would be in the dungeons.

The first shaft joining the stack was too narrow for him to enter so he had to inch his way down another few feet. The second was just wide enough but it was horribly like being toothpaste squeezed out of a tube into an unknown set of jaws. Unable to see where he was going, blinded with soot and barely able to breathe, he fell onto a beautiful hearth rug woven in the design of a frosted leaf skeleton. His blackened hands and knees left four distinct prints on the white and grey design.

'Stop where you are!' The cold point of a sword reinforced the demand. All Rick could see were the small bare toes of the speaker and the bottom of a fine white robe decorated with seashells and mermaids. 'What are you doing in my chamber?'

'Forgive me, your ladyship.' She had to be a lady for none but high ranking courtiers would dress so finely and have such pure, precise tones. 'I fell out of a window and then, um, got lost on the roof trying to get back in.'

From her impatient tut, she was not impressed by this explanation. 'What are you?'

'A dragon keeper, ma'am.' He really wished she would let him look up. His neck was killing him in this position. Strangely, he was not scared of her. She didn't sound much of a threat.

'I didn't ask what you do but what you are—what species? You are not one of the Mage, are you? Let me see your eyes.'

Finally. He sat back on his haunches, knowing that his hazel eyes would excuse him of Mage blood. All of that species had silver irises. Rick raised his gaze to hers and realized that he was, after all, in big trouble—no comfort that it was a different sort of trouble from being a rebel Mage. Almond-shaped periwinkle eyes stared back at him. He had seen a pair just like those not so long ago—in the face of the king. This young Fey was clearly one of his kin. She was quite tall and slight, with long brown hair the colour of hot chocolate. The hand holding the silver sword was smooth and pale. This Fey had never done a day's manual labour in her life, or he was a hobgoblin.

'What are you? No Mage, I can see that. I've been warned against them by my father.' The sword began to dip slightly. 'Should I call my guard?'

He wondered why she even bothered to ask his opinion. 'It is your decision, my lady.'

'But if I do, they will kill you.' She bit her lower lip thoughtfully. 'Perhaps you are a secret messenger from my mother?'

'Who is she, my lady?' Rick hoped he could claim he was a messenger and excuse his presence in the forbidden part of the castle once he knew who this girl was.

'If you don't know that, then you can't be. But you don't look dangerous, just very dirty.' Making her choice, she sheathed the sword in the scabbard that hung at her side. It suited the warrior-maiden, like a very expensive piece of jewellery. 'Is it true, that you fell?'

'Yes, my lady.'

'What was a dragon keeper doing up high enough to fall out of a window on to our roof?'

She was no fool. 'I was exploring. I know I should've kept below but it's only my first full day in the castle and I wanted to see what was upstairs. I apologize if I've offended you.'

She flicked her wrist, beckoning him to rise. 'It's an unwise wish, Dragon Keeper. If you had entered any other room from that chimney you would've been killed on sight.' She handed him a linen towel and a basin. 'Wash before you take another step. You have already ruined my carpet.'

Aethel squeezed Rick's wrist. Carpet. That was what the snake had been trying to say all along. Rick had learned how to enchant a carpet to fly a few days earlier. He was standing on his escape vehicle. Unfortunately, so was the young lady, and she showed no signs of backing away. He swiped the towel across his face, thinking hard.

'My stars, you aren't Fey!' the girl exclaimed when he removed the soot from his face. She took a step closer and waved a hand across his chest. 'But you are magical like us. What are you?'

She was going to guess sooner or later; it was better that he show good faith by telling her. 'A human changeling, your ladyship.'

Her reaction was unexpected. Her mouth curved into a delighted smile. 'Really? How fascinating! I've never been allowed to meet one of you before. My father says you are ill-trained, vicious and stupid.'

Rick supposed he was probably confirming that impression after tumbling into her room without an invitation. 'And who is your father?' He thought he could guess.

'The king, of course.' She wrinkled her nose in an expression of wry humour. 'I'm the daughter of his first wife, Queen Titania. I was hoping you had a message from her.'

'I am sorry to disappoint you, your highness.' And he did feel sorry, she had looked so hopeful for a moment.

'My father has banished her and forbidden any contact so I should not expect to hear, I suppose.' She poked Rick in the chest. 'But you haven't disappointed me. You are the most exciting thing to happen to me in many weeks. I've been grounded, you see; I'm not allowed out for two months.'

Despite himself, he had to ask. 'Grounded? What for?'

'I just went riding in the Spore Forest with the hunters and their pack of hobgoblins without permission.' She picked up his hand to inspect it, contrasting it with her own long fingers. 'It was very amusing. I got to unleash the hobs. But you should have seen Father when we got back—he was purple with rage.'

Rick could understand why. She was lucky the hobs had not turned on her.

'I'm not supposed to leave the palace without my guard, but they act like a bunch of old nanny goats, not letting me have a moment's fun. I think my father believes I will sneak off and try to join my mother. The thought did cross my mind, of course, because she is so much more fun than him, but . . .' She gave a shrug and dropped his hand.

He bowed. 'I believe I have the honour of addressing the Princess Cobweb?'

She giggled at his formal tone. 'That's correct, changeling. Have you heard of me then?'

Not much, but even the inmates of Dark Lore had heard snippets of court gossip about Queen Titania's unruly children. Cobweb's name had featured frequently for her daring escapades. 'Yes, your highness.'

She seemed pleased to hear it. 'And who are you?'

'Rick, Elfric Halfdane, your highness.'

She snorted. 'What a silly name, Rick Elfric Halfdane!'

Perhaps he didn't like her after all. 'Just Rick or Elfric—not both. It's a human name, your highness, from Anglo-Saxon England.'

Cobweb was losing interest, her gaze drifting to the mess he had made of the floor. 'Oh, I've not heard of that place.' She knelt down to brush the silk clean.

He began to say that it wasn't a place now, but a place in time, but she had turned to other matters.

'You'd better move, Rick Halfdane. You are making the stain worse and this is my favourite rug.' She pushed him off the mat, treating him somewhat like an errant pet, a dog that had inadvertently tracked mud into her bedroom. He tried to resist. 'Oh, budge, human, or I will call my guard,' she said curtly, reminding him that she was a princess used to being obeyed.

He stepped off, not wanting her to guess his plans for her favourite carpet. Besides, now he remembered the hover charm, surely a chest or chair, anything large enough to bear his weight, would do?

A bell tolled in the courtyard below, soon picked up by all the others in the castle. Far below, guards ran across the marble pavement, their rapid footsteps echoing off the high palace walls.

'An alarm for an escape,' murmured the princess, jumping to her feet. 'I wonder who has fled?'

Dread settled like a stone in Rick's stomach; goosebumps stippled his forearms.

Cobweb came to the window beside him, her hair flicking restlessly in the breeze, long strands catching on his clothes. She bunched it carelessly and tied it back with a silver clasp, then leaned forward to look out. 'Can you see anyone? Oh, troll's breath, it is so boring being a princess sometimes: I miss all the fun!'

Rick didn't consider the hunt for an escaped prisoner the definition of 'fun'. He wondered when the princess would realize that the alarm was for her uninvited guest. 'No, your highness, I can't see anyone. Perhaps I had better go. I'm late for my duties.' He bowed, hoping the princess would let him leave without a fuss.

'Oh, you can't do that,' she said blithely. 'I've a guard on my door day and night, and if you try to leave they'll kill you without asking questions first. I'll get Archer—see what he says we should do with you.'

Before he could protest, the princess glided over to the floor length wall mirror opposite the chimney breast and pulled it open. It swung on a side hinge, revealing another room the mirror image of hers through the gap.

'What is it now?' came an irritated voice from within. 'No, I will not try to persuade Father to lift your punishment, so there is no point asking.'

'Grump!' huffed the princess. 'If you're going to be like that, I won't share my excellent secret with you.' She turned her back and flounced out of the room.

'What kind of secret?' The occupant of the room through the mirror trailed after her and stepped across the threshold.

'That kind of secret!' said Cobweb triumphantly, pointing at Rick, who was pondering if a charmed cushion would be enough to hold him up.

Rick found himself facing a boy who had to be Cobweb's twin. They were of identical height with features of the same cast, yet he was her reverse in complexion, his skin the velvet chocolate colour of her hair and his spiky crop the creamy white of her skin.

'Get down, Cobweb!' shouted the boy. He tugged a bow from his back and fitted an arrow to the string before Rick had time to realize what he was doing. A silver dart flew towards him, bedding itself in the pillow at chest height, impact foiled by Rick's padded keeper's jerkin.

'Archer!' squeaked Cobweb, dashing to put herself in the way of the second dart before he could release it. 'What are you doing?'

'It's the escaped prisoner—the human!' Archer conjured up a magical shield to protect his sister's back, as if he expected Rick to launch himself to sink his teeth in her neck.

She slapped his arm. 'Don't be foolish. He's a dragon keeper. He fell out of a window and needs help getting back to the lower regions.'

'Ye-es,' drawled Archer, as if she were very dim, 'the human IS a dragon keeper. Our father wanted his spirit broken before he puts him on trial tonight. Humans are vicious, dangerous creatures, Father says. How many humans do you think he'd let run around the castle unchained?'

Rick had heard enough. He quickly cast the charm over the cushion, thinking he'd better take his chances outside rather than in.

'Stop right there, human!' ordered Archer, as Rick climbed onto the window ledge. A silvery lasso charm curled round his ankle and snagged him off balance. The cushion sailed off without him, only to be pierced by a dozen arrows from the vigilant guards on the castle battlements. Feathers flew as the pillow tumbled to a saggy end on the ground fifty feet below.

'Well, that takes the prize for idiocy!' Cobweb couldn't seem to decide with whom she was angrier: her brother for attacking her guest or Rick for trying to leave. 'What has got into you both?' She blasted the shield charm with a bolt of her own magic then hurried to free Rick's ankle from the biting lasso.

'But he's human!' bellowed Archer.

'So what?' she shouted back, with matching force.

Rick shuffled so his back was against the wall, feeling a little safer that way, though he knew his fate was hanging by a thread—a spider's thread.

'Archer, apologize!' ordered Cobweb.

'Not in a million years.' He folded his arms.

'I said you would help. Don't make me break my word!'

'And why should I help him? Our father's guard is searching for him even now—he says the human is a threat to the kingdom.'

'Pah! Our father? He thinks everyone is a threat—our mother, our old nurse because she tried to smuggle in a message, *me* because I went for a ride without permission! It is quicker to count the folk he doesn't think pose a risk to him!'

'You mustn't talk like that!'

'Why not? Mother tried to please him and look what that got her—divorce and exile!'

'You never liked the rules!'

'You always liked them too much!'

White sparks were spitting from the ends of their fingers. They looked on the point of flying at each other's throats. Then, to Rick's amazement, Archer blew a raspberry in his sister's face. It seemed to be some familiar ritual between the twins, signalling the end of an argument.

'Oh, all right, you win this one, Cob. Sorry, human.' He flicked the apology in Rick's direction as a rich man might throw a scrap to his dog.

'You going to be reasonable now?' she asked warily.

Archer shrugged. 'I suppose so. He doesn't look much of a threat. Father has been a bit extreme lately.'

'Since he married Miserable Mab.'

'Yes, ever since then.'

The twins nodded, coming to some silent accord. They turned to face Rick together.

'We'll help you out of here,' began Cobweb.

'On one condition,' continued Archer. 'That you tell no one we aided you.'

'And you carry a message to our mother.'

Archer raised a brow. 'That's two conditions, Cob.'

They turned back to Rick. 'Do you accept?' asked Archer.

Rick couldn't waste time running messages. 'Where is your mother to be found, your highness?'

'The Sylvan Palace in Deepdene Forest, not far inland from the Island of the Dragon. Father sends all his enemies in exile up there as it's miles from anywhere—they can be no threat to him.'

All his enemies? 'Isn't that the island where Arthur Pendragon is held?'

'Yes, but no one's seen him for years. I expect he's long dead. Our mother is the most recent exile in those parts.'

But Arthur, equally, could still be alive and well, ready to help strike back against his jailer. 'Then I'll take the letter—and thanks, your highnesses.'

Cobweb batted her brother in the chest. 'Aw, see, he's quite sweet really.'

'Say that again and I *will* shoot him,' said Archer.

Chapter 6

ROXY sat among the other changelings at supper in the grey painted canteen. The room smelt of cabbage. The children were crowded at a long table with no cloth and only paper plates. The glow-worm lights flickered from bright to dim, indicating that the magic supply hadn't yet been fully restored. Tonight, the food had hit a new low: nothing hot, only apples and cheese with stale bread. The children on her table were complaining in whispers but Roxy was keeping a low profile, not even daring to add her grumbles. She had noticed something far worse than the food. The troll guard inside seemed in a suspiciously good mood, gazing on the human children with something like affection.

If the trolls were happy, it meant bad news for the humans. Time had run out. Roxy had to organize a breakout before Morgan executed the changelings.

She bit into her apple, finding it rotten at the core. 'Yuck.'

'Everything all right?' asked Tabitha, the changeling who was sitting beside her. A Quaker child, taken from Maryland in the early days of European settlement of America when she was a few years old, Tabitha still chose to dress in the plain clothes her parents had favoured, a white bonnet framing a pale anxious face. She might look as delicate as a dandelion seed but she was one of Roxy's chief conspirators.

'No. Tabs, we have to get out,' Roxy murmured, masking that she was talking behind a bread roll. Commander Morgan La Faye was seated at the top table and had Roxy under particularly close watch. 'But there are just so many of us: I'm not sure we can do it.' The Fey had stolen about a hundred babies and young children over the years, all from different places and time periods, and raised them in the strict confines of Dark Lore.

Tabitha whispered a prayer for help. 'We're not ready, Roxy. We've only had a few days to come to terms with your discovery that we were stolen not rescued by the Fey. We haven't got a plan.'

'We don't have a choice. We have to get everyone together tonight and make a run for it.'

Tabitha took a shuddering breath then nudged Edgar, the stocky medieval peasant boy with a shorn head, prominent ears, and sleepy hazel eyes. These two had formed an alliance from the early days of imprisonment. He looked after her like a sheepdog a frail lamb, while she stopped the others teasing him for what they mistook as his slow brain. He was only slow in the sense that the tortoise was in the fable—and Roxy had seen enough examples of his behaviour to know that slow and steady often wins the race.

'Ed, emergency meeting,' whispered Tabitha. 'Please spread the word.'

Edgar shuffled to his feet and made his way along the tables of children. To the trolls it would look like he was being his usual awkward self, but Roxy could see he was tapping key individuals on the back. He then approached Morgan at the top table overseeing the canteen. The commander took little notice of the peasant boy as she dismissed Edgar as a half-wit. He stopped a few feet from her and bowed with a bumbling lack of grace.

'Come on. I don't want him doing this alone.' Tabitha tugged Roxy from her seat.

'Tabs, what are you and Ed up to?' Roxy hurried after her.

'You'll see.'

'Commander, sir,' Edgar said in his strident voice. Morgan demanded they address her as 'sir', believing 'ma'am' sounded weak. 'I learned in Human History this afternoon that today in my village would have been a holiday.'

Morgan raised a brow as if to ask 'so what?'.

Edgar bravely continued: 'Do I have your permission to . . . to . . . gather the other changelings to mark the day as we should?'

She tapped her sharp fingernails on the table, leaving little dents in the white linen cloth. 'What kind of holiday?'

The changelings were not normally allowed to celebrate any special days, so poor Edgar was briefly at a loss.

'Saint Pringle's Day,' interjected Roxy, recalling her favoured brand of crisps on Earth.

'St Pringle? I've never heard of him.' Morgan was losing interest.

'*She* is the patron saint of changelings,' Roxy replied. 'And Edgar is a very religious boy.'

Edgar did his best to look pious.

'Changelings don't have patron saints,' snapped Morgan.

'They did in my village,' Edgar replied stoutly.

'We don't want to insult St Pringle, do we?' suggested Roxy, knowing that the Fey Folk were fearful of anything that might bring them bad luck, including religion. They gave the idea of a creator God a distant respect, like subjects of an emperor who rarely paid their land a visit.

'Hold your tongue, girl.' Morgan fixed Roxy with a withering look. 'I don't want to give you any favours—not after what you did.'

'No, sir. It's not for me, but for Edgar.' Roxy tried to look humble but did not think she succeeded very well.

Morgan studied the boy's face. 'And what does this celebration entail, Edgar?'

'Oh, um . . .' He glanced at Tabitha for aid.

'We meet for an hour of singing, praying and fasting,' the little Quaker interjected quickly.

'Sounds tedious.' Morgan gave her a vicious smile.

Tabitha blushed, her hands fretting at her sides, not liking to tell an untruth even in a good cause. 'It is very uplifting—for a human.'

'And is this the last request you will make of me, peasant?' Morgan seemed amused by the idea.

'Yes, commander,' promised Edgar.

'You may gather here then, after supper—and those who want to share this celebration with you. I can't imagine many will be enticed to join you.'

Edgar scratched his head, looking puzzled. Only Roxy and Tabitha were able to see the cunning behind the pretence at innocent confusion. He gave a sigh. 'Oh dear: did I forget to explain, Commander, that we have to gather under the stars?'

Morgan scored a little furrow in the cloth, considering. 'It is convenient for you to be occupied for a few hours after supper as I have work for the guards to do. You have until ten o'clock to mark your little superstitions, then you must all come back here. I have an announcement to make.'

'You are very kind.' Edgar bowed and ambled back to his seat, with Tabitha and Roxy following behind. Once seated, Tabitha squeezed his hand in congratulation for a job well done. Roxy whispered a 'thank you'. They had been granted a rare permission to gather out of Fey control; the rest had to be improvised from there. With the pixies to help, she was fairly confident they could get past the fence. What followed next was the difficult part.

Who in Avalon would risk Oberon's wrath and take in a hundred humans?

No one.

Morgan stood, signalling the end of the meal. The changelings got to their feet even if they were still eating.

'Be back here at ten o'clock precisely,' she ordered. 'Until then you may celebrate St Pringle's

Day with the peasant, Edgar, if that is in accordance with your beliefs. This is the last favour I will grant you all.' She swept from the room, signalling the trolls to follow her.

When the door closed, the spell of respectful silence was broken.

'Last favour? She means *only* favour,' grumbled Simon, a changeling of Edgar's age. 'And you go and waste it on what? A hobspitting dull service! I would've asked for a day off classes tomorrow—or something vaguely fun. You really are thick, Ed.'

Tabitha glared at the freckled-faced boy, son of a woodcutter from Sherwood Forest who had been stolen only a few human years after Edgar. 'Please be quiet. Ed is not stupid. He hasn't wasted his request—as you'll soon find out if you use your brain and follow us.'

'It's fine, Tabs,' mumbled Edgar, 'he'll see in a moment.'

With a final sniff, Tabitha did a very good job of sweeping regally out of the canteen, leading the way to the parade ground. The changelings that Edgar had already alerted followed at once; six of them carried the babies who were too young to understand what was going on. The others, not wanting to miss anything, shambled out behind them. This service for the made-up St Pringle was not something they could afford to miss.

Roxy came along last in the line. She was only just realizing whom Tabitha was expecting to convince the changelings of the seriousness of what was happening and lead the escape. It was up to her.

'Quick, guards, down there!' Prince Archer dashed into the corridor outside his room and pointed into a dark stairwell leading to the cellars. 'I saw the human flee that way.'

Coming to attention, the two ogres on guard outside the princess's chamber hesitated.

'Sorry, sir,' said the one with a captain's badge on his tunic, 'but we were told our lives would be forfeited if we left her highness unattended.'

'So you will let a dangerous creature run amok in the castle? What kind of protection do you call that? Quickly now, he's getting away!'

'I'll go, your highness,' volunteered the captain. 'Private Norse can stay on guard.'

Archer struck his forehead as if astonished by the suggestion. 'What? Face the human on your own? I can't let that happen. I caught a glimpse of him: blood dripping from his teeth, madness in his eyes, a smell to fell an ox—he made me shudder, I can tell you. It'll take more than one ogre to put him down. Look, I'll stand guard and you both hunt him. That way no order is ignored.'

Relieved to have been given an honourable solution, the ogres saluted the prince. 'Yes, sir.'

Archer thrust a flaming torch into the hands of the nearest ogre. 'Go on, hurry—he's had time to get away. You'd better run at the double!'

Unsheathing their swords and grabbing another torch from the wall bracket, the ogres set off on their wild goose chase down the stairs. As soon as they were out of sight round the turn, Archer softly closed and bolted the door to the stairwell.

'All clear!'

Cobweb peered out of her room. 'They believed you?'

'Evidently, sister, or I would not have said "all clear".'

She stuck her tongue out at him. 'Come on, human, time to go.'

Warily, Rick edged out from behind the curtain where he had been hiding in case the ogres checked the princess's chamber. Cobweb threw a light grey cloak over his shoulders and fastened it under his chin with a spider brooch. She pulled the hood over his head so that his face was lost in the depths. 'There, keep that on like that and we can tell everyone you are my new bodyguard.'

The twins had already explained to him that they planned to get him out by hiding him in plain sight. They were going to stride through the castle and take him to the royal stables—for horses not dragons—and send him on his way as if he were entirely within his rights to do so. Any furtive behaviour was far more likely to alert the ogres that they were up to something. Rick agreed in principle, but the idea of boldly walking through the busiest parts of the castle was pretty terrifying.

'What am I then?' he asked Cobweb.

'Hmm, you aren't tall enough for a Fey and not blue enough for a nix.'

'Just keep hidden and hope no one asks.' Archer passed Rick a bundle to hide under his cloak. It contained food supplies taken from the princess's dinner tray and the letter for the twin's mother. 'If they do, Cobweb, say he's a Pixie-Fey half-breed. There are a few around the castle. Now stop fussing and let's get going: those guards won't be fooled for long by that trick I played on them.'

'Wouldn't it be better if just Archer took me to the stables?' Rick suggested. 'I mean, isn't the princess supposed to be grounded?' As soon as the words had left his mouth, he knew they were a mistake.

'Grounded!' snarled Cobweb, starting out for the stables immediately. 'Oh yes, I stay behind and miss all the fun—as if that's going to happen!'

Archer jogged to catch up. 'He has a point, Cob.'

Her reply was a rude Fey sign made by linking thumbs and fluttering her fingers. Rick sighed and hurried to catch up. He couldn't help the dragging sensation in the pit of his stomach that told him this was a terrible idea.

Having slid down the banister of the central staircase, Cobweb strode out into the courtyard, not even registering the bows her appearance prompted from the castle staff. They all bowed again as soon as Archer came into sight, like a second gust of wind through a field of corn. Rick hoped they were all too busy even to notice the undersized bodyguard struggling to keep up. He saw six soldiers surrounding the poor cushion, in deep discussion over how it had come to be there.

'You shot my sylph-made pillow. Why?' demanded the princess, coming to a halt beside the inquest.

'*Your* pillow, your highness?' The Fey in charge of the courtyard guard paled and scooped it up from the ground with a grimace. 'We saw that it had been enchanted. It seemed suspicious, what with the escaped human on the loose, so we took preventative action.'

'No, you took stupid action and ruined it. Was there a human inside it, hmm? No, I thought not.' She folded her arms and picked off each warrior with her glare.

'But how did it come to hover so unnaturally . . . ?' ventured the Fey guard.

'I threw it out of the window—I cast the spell, of course!' She shouted this as if it should have been blindingly obvious.

'But in the middle of an emergency . . . ?' The guard snapped his mouth shut, realizing there was no flattering way of ending that sentence.

Archer stepped forward and wrested the cushion from him. A sad drift of feathers spilled from numerous holes. 'Temper, temper, sister. You should never have thrown it at me if you did not want it shot. The guards were only doing their duty.'

The idea that she had lobbed the spelled cushion at her brother was clearly considered highly plausible for the remaining questions in the guard's eyes disappeared. The Fey guard bowed again. 'Please accept my apologies, your highness.'

'Oh, all right,' she sighed. 'But next time something flies out of my window be more careful! I really liked that cushion.' She managed a funny sounding sniff that Rick did not find in the least convincing. He guessed the twins were enjoying their chance to confuse their usual guards.

'Oh, Cobweb, you're so sentimental. I know: why don't we go and see your horse? Take your mind off the loss of your favourite pillow. Leave these good soldiers to pursue the missing human.' Archer turned to the guard. 'I assume the stables have been checked?'

The Fey nodded, eager to impress them with his efficiency after the lapse over the princess's belongings. 'Yes, sir. First place we looked, seeing how he is likely to be on the run and needing transport. All the griffins are under lockdown and the horses are all in their loose boxes.'

'Carry on then. We have our own escort so we will leave you to your duties.' With majestic coolness, Archer seized his sister's arm and pulled her past the soldiers. Rick strode behind as calmly as he could, wishing he had more of the twins' composure about this deception. Then again, it was not they who were slated for execution if they were caught.

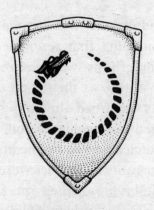

Chapter 7

THEY crossed two more courtyards in the bewildering tangle of buildings that made up the royal apartments. If Rick had not been so worried about exposure he would have had more time to note the beautiful architecture, but all he could manage were brief glimpses, laid down in the mind to be remembered later. Towers branching like coral trees on a reef of silver and blue, smooth plains of mosaic tiles and marble pavements, fantastical growths of twisting vines fanfaring their way through masses of apricot trumpet flowers: Oberon was a tyrant but his home was an incredible tribute to what Fey skill and magic could do when combined.

Even the stables were a work of art. While the poor old dragons were confined out in the caves, the horses and griffins were treated as privileged guests in a building that resembled a comfortable inn. The griffins were housed separately in the upper storeys as their loud screeches and nesting habits disturbed the horses. Each loose box was crafted from golden wood, the red brick floor scrubbed clean, even the bedding straw was silvery and fragrant. The horses were magnificent, and clearly deserving of their special conditions: fine grey Arabians, golden Halflings for pixie riders, black Barbaries with gleaming manes. They whickered in greeting to the prince and princess. One grey kicked his door, excited at the prospect of getting out. Cobweb went to him and scratched his nose.

'Sorry, Gerent, but not today. We're still grounded.'

Rick guessed he was not about to be offered the princess's own mount, or the matching jet black Arabian in the stall next to it who was being fed an apple by Archer. Cobweb strolled along the boxes looking for a suitable candidate. She picked a friendly looking Barbary with a rose tinge to his chestnut coat and a straw-coloured mane.

'Yes, you'll do, my beauty,' murmured Cobweb. She opened the loose box door and led the horse out by the halter.

'Cobweb!' her brother groaned.

'What?' Her face was wreathed with impish glee.

'Queen Mab's favourite? Is that wise?' Archer folded his arms.

'No, of course not, but Peony is the fastest and I think the human might require a touch of speed to get away from pursuers.'

While Cobweb might consider it funny to provoke her stepmother, Rick thought he really didn't need any more counts against him. 'Won't the horse be recognized?'

'Oh, cast a glamour, you muttonhead!' Cobweb was already heaving the Barbary's tack off the peg—a beautiful hand-tooled set of red and gold leatherwork, embossed with a dragon. Rather fitting, really, considering Rick's short-lived profession in the castle. Archer had obviously decided not to argue with his sister for he was now helping her saddle the eager Barbary.

Rick had long since given up any illusions that he was in charge of this escape. With a deep sigh, he tied his bundle to the pommel.

'You can ride, can't you?' asked Archer.

'Of course.' In theory. He was glad for the hood to hide his blush of shame. As an Anglo-Saxon prince he should have been born in the saddle, but his incarceration at Dark Lore had not included the luxury of riding lessons. He had studied many books on the subject and once or twice conjured himself a pony out of pieces of furniture, but he guessed that a spelled illusion would be a very different matter from a real horse.

'Hmm.' Archer was more astute than Rick had realized, hearing the lie in his voice. 'Peony is exceptionally well trained. Our stepmother is a terrible rider and relies on her horses to do all the thinking for her. If you don't get in his way, he should see you safe.'

'OK.'

Archer frowned. 'What is this "OK"?'

'It is human for "all right", or "I agree".'

Archer tapped his chin thoughtfully, matching that to what he knew of human culture. 'You mean like "Amen"?'

Rick decided laughing at a prince was not something he should dare to do today. 'Um, sort of. But not really.' He adjusted the stirrups to what he guessed was the right length. 'OK is used all the time now, whereas amen is saved for prayers in my country.' And he would certainly need a few prayers to get out of this castle alive.

Archer shrugged. 'I last visited the human world in 1603, just a few Fey years ago, and they never said this "OK" to each other. Humans are strange creatures.' He added a bag of oats to the saddle. 'A couple of centuries pass and they do not understand what their ancestors say. They can't spell the air like we do to make all languages comprehensible.'

'Years pass a hundred times faster than here. You get out of date very quickly if you don't keep an eye on what humans are doing.'

'Never been that interested in humans,' admitted Archer. 'Can't see the point as they are all going to die or be reduced to the level of the apes again if my father has his way.' He patted Rick on the back in his first friendly gesture. 'You stay hidden in Avalon; you'll be "OK" if you do. Need a hand getting up?'

'I'm fine, thanks. But you must realize I can't stay hidden and let your father do that.'

'You can try to stop him, but it won't help. He is the most powerful of the Fey, so what chance do humans have? Even the dragons had to bow to him eventually.'

Cobweb walked Peony in a circle to check all was well with his tack.

'What's that about Father?' she asked, blue eyes alert.

Archer patted Peony's neck. 'I'll tell you later. It's time our messenger left. Head north. Deepdene Woods is about a week's ride away.'

Rick nodded. He would go there, but first he had to get Roxy from Dark Lore. They were a team and he couldn't leave her behind.

'If my father's guards capture you, destroy the letter,' added Cobweb.

'Yes, your highness.'

'Good luck, Rick Halfdane.' The princess led horse and rider to the stable door. The road to the castle gate stretched before them. Clipped hedges of thorny plants lined the way.

'Show my token,' said Archer, handing Rick one of his silver arrows. 'That should get you through the gatekeepers.'

Rick gripped it tightly in his fist. It wasn't much of passport but it was better than nothing. 'Thank you. For everything.'

'Don't let us down.' Archer ushered him forward.

'Don't get caught!' added Cobweb.

'OK.' Rick grinned at the prince. Archer smiled back while Cobweb looked puzzled. 'Your brother will explain what that means.' He kicked his horse into a gentle trot, surprised to discover that he could do the basics of riding after all.

'Cobweb, Archer! What are you doing with my horse!' The screech was enough to shatter windows. Out of the corner of his eye, Rick caught sight of an orange-blonde Fey in an eye-scorching pink gown running towards the stable. Behind her trailed a large entourage of soldiers and ladies-in-waiting. A pinch-nosed face, ruby red eyes, Amazonian figure, and black emerald crown:

Queen Mab had come to pay her favourite horse a visit.

'Go!' shouted Cobweb. 'We'll deal with this!'

Rick urged Peony into a canter and prayed he would reach the gate before news of the horse theft reached the guard.

Tabitha and Edgar chose the football field for their meeting. Close to the boundary fence and out of sight of most windows of Dark Lore House, it was the most private place in the grounds. A couple of troll guards followed the changelings—they could not hope to be completely out of surveillance— but, fortunately, the trolls were soon distracted by the pixie stall. When Roxy began singing a hastily improvised hymn to St Pringle, set to the tune of 'God save our gracious Queen', they soon lost any interest in the human ceremony and drifted away to buy spells from Miz-Begotten, Trix-E and Frost-E.

'Gather round, friends, for the sermon,' announced Tabitha loudly. The guards took no notice as the changelings closed ranks and sat in a tight-packed circle with Roxy in the middle. A couple of the little ones wailed but a sleep charm soon settled them. She rubbed her hands on her jeans, wondering what she should say. Nothing for it but to get straight to the point.

'Look, everyone, remember what Rick and I told you about Oberon stealing us? Well, it's just got a whole lot worse. My informants have told me he's going to get rid of us. Tonight.'

'He's making us dragon keepers like he did Rick?' gasped a little North African lad, a relative newcomer to Dark Lore.

'No, Ahmed. Worse. We are to be killed off in ones and twos at the Fey Games. Some might be used as slave labour in the emerald mines, but only the strongest, and they'll still end up in the arena.'

'How long have we got?' asked Ahmed.

'No time at all. I think our meeting at ten o'clock is when Morgan intends to tell us our fate.'

Silence met that announcement. The prospect was so horrific few could get their minds round it. They all knew the Fey regarded them as lesser beings, like a herd of sheep; but the news they were all being sent to the slaughter just because Oberon had tired of housing them in his kingdom was a complete shock.

'So what do we do?' asked Simon. 'You have a plan, don't you, Roxy?'

Roxy dug her fingers into her palm, so tense she felt she might snap. Their lives now depended on her. 'Not much of one. We have to run.'

There was a mutter of agreement.

'But go where?' Simon pressed.

'I can only think of one place where we might stand a chance: Earth.'

It was the only place where they could hide. As only Fey bloods had the necessary magic to make the doorways between the worlds, Roxy would have to convince the pixies to conjure one. Nerves strung tight with anxiety, she waited until the excited buzz of conversation subsided. The thought of taking the changelings, including the babies, to the human world, all so ill-prepared for the twenty-first century, was daunting. They wouldn't have any idea how to hide when Morgan sent her hunters after them. Not to mention what the humans would make of this bunch of misfits with varying degrees of magical power.

'Shh, everyone!' warned Tabitha. The troll guards had turned their attention to them. One swung his truncheon, looking as if he was contemplating coming to break up their meeting.

Edgar jumped to his feet. 'All praise to St Pringle! Let me hear you say it!'

Alert to the danger, the changelings all echoed his words, adopting meek and unthreatening stances, heads bowed, eyes closed. Edgar led them in another chorus of the hymn to St Pringle. The trolls went back to their bargaining.

'Thanks, Ed,' said Roxy. 'I'm not sure if this will work but basically my plan is to get through the fence then conjure a doorway to Earth. There we split up to confuse Morgan's hunters and arrange to meet up later, somewhere safe from detection. We need to mix in with the normal population so we'll make the doorway to a big city—I suggest London; some of you might have heard of it. Divide into groups of five or six, try not to attract attention to yourself and make your way to . . .' She paused, wondering where a huge group of clueless humans were least likely to be noticed. 'To Paddington Station.' The trains from Oxford came into that terminus and she was hoping she could get a message to Tiago and Linette to come to her aid if they were still in England. Luckily, she still had in her pocket her spelled shell from her mission to Earth; it connected to Tiago's. Roxy knew she would need their help finding them somewhere to stay.

'What's this Paddington Station?' asked Ahmed.

'Did you not listen to your Human History briefing?' sneered Simon. 'Humans invented a form of transport called the steam engine. It pulls little carriages, moving humans from one place to another along a track. Stations are where you get on board, like the Fey's Dew Track.'

Sometimes Simon could be really annoying, decided Roxy. 'Get with the times, Simon. That's so last year. Steam trains are out. They are electric or diesel now.'

Simon bristled like a hedgehog. He didn't like being corrected one little bit. 'But you still get on board at a station. I was right about that, wasn't I?'

'Yes.' She had to allow him that. 'OK, sort yourselves out into groups.'

This produced much muttering and arguing, but finally the job was done. Most had chosen wisely, putting an older student in charge of younger ones. Roxy was not surprised to find no one had wanted Simon. He was trying not to look upset but she could tell he was worried he was going to be left on his own. She was always a sucker when it came to outsiders.

'Simon, you can come with me and Ahmed,' she volunteered. 'Tabs, Ed, you too. Jane and Knut—can you look after the nursery children? Choose a team to help you. Everyone: your priority is to make sure the little ones are protected.' Had she thought of everything? She didn't know. 'Paddington shouldn't be hard to find. Act like the people around you and ask any local for directions; they should be able to tell you how to get there. We'll rendezvous twenty-four hours after we arrive.'

'But how are we going to get there in the first place?' asked Ahmed tentatively, fearing Simon was going to mock his ignorance again. 'I thought you had to be Fey to make the doors between our two worlds.'

'You're right. But, fortunately, help has arrived just in time. Give me a moment.' Roxy stood, shaking the pins and needles from her cramped legs, and jogged over to Trix-E.

'Hey, pixie girl, I want to buy one of your charms,' she said loudly.

'What kind of charm would a human need?' Trix-E nudged the nearest troll. 'Still, business is business, I suppose.'

'I'll tell you,' said Roxy, 'but it is going to stay between the two of us.' The troll edged closer to eavesdrop. 'Girl talk.' The troll's blue mane bristled and he went back to examining the spell Frost-E had been demonstrating. The charm appeared to increase hair to extraordinary lengths. The pixie was now lost under a bush of purple curls.

Taking advantage of this admittedly riveting sight, Roxy pulled Trix-E behind the flower-strewn stocks and quickly repeated the plan.

'Yes, that could work,' said Trix-E. 'Leave the rest to us.'

'The mirror?'

Trix-E smirked. 'You must be losing your pixie touch, Roxy, if that old concealed trap in the box lid caught you out.'

'You got past it?'

'And the other safeguards. I'm delighted to report that the mirror has moved on to a new owner.' She opened her bag of charms to reveal the bevelled edge of the scrying glass.

'Grand. But what about getting through the fence? We'll need one amazing diversion if we're to get away.'

'Don't worry. We already had one planned to get you out. When would you like to leave?'

'Has to be before ten.' Roxy looked up. The stars were already popping out of the darkening skies, forming their familiar patterns—the Club, the Seashell, the Sword. The shadows were lengthening; the edge of the forest now stretched almost to the fence. Only the flicker of fireflies lightened the space under the tree canopy. 'We'll run there. If you can cast a doorway in the forest for us, we might be able to get through before Morgan realizes what's happened.' She took Trix-E's hand. 'And you must come too. They'll soon guess we had help from Fey bloods and I wouldn't want you to be punished in our place.'

Trix-E's earnest face creased in a frown. 'But we can't leave Avalon!'

But they had to or they would face gruesome punishment. How could she make them understand?

'Please, Trix-E! I can't leave you to suffer for us—I can only keep you safe on Earth.'

The pixie snorted. 'Safe! On Earth? Isn't that a contradiction?'

'It doesn't have to be for ever; just till we sort out a safe haven for all of us.'

And then Roxy intended to come straight back to save Rick and complete the quest for Arthur. At least when they transferred to Earth she would have more time to think of a way of saving Rick. Life passed a hundred times faster, so an hour there was but a few seconds in Avalon.

Trix-E sighed. 'I suppose you are right, though that wasn't part of our plan. I'll turn Barleywater and Cauliflower loose and tell them to make their way to our cousins. Ma, Pa and I can hide out on Earth for a while until the hunt dies down here.'

Roxy had the nagging feeling that there had to be a million more details that she should be thinking about. 'I don't know how the Fey magic works on making doors. Can you take us anywhere?'

Trix-E shook her head. 'No. There are a limited number of connections. I think of it like the fronds of a sea anemone reaching out from one place to another. You can choose one of them but there is a rough geographic limitation, a circle within which you can reach.'

'I know that we can get to central England from here. Can we reach London?'

'What is that?'

'A big city. I thought it would provide us with maximum cover as there are so many humans there. And our oddness will be less noticeable.'

'I'll take a peek and see if I can find the place. But what is a city?'

Roxy had forgotten that there was nothing in Avalon that resembled a modern conurbation. Nearly everything here looked like it had grown naturally in place, whereas on Earth humans dropped their buildings on to the land like litter. 'Look at Dark Lore House at the moment. You'll recognize London because it will be lots and lots of buildings like that, a railway that goes under the ground in special tubes, a very big clock by the river, a man's statue on top of a column, and crowds of people.'

'Intriguing. That should be enough for me to find it for you.'

'Stick with me when you get through, won't you? I don't like to think what will happen to the three of you if you get lost.'

Trix-E laughed. 'Surely the humans have more to fear from us than us from them? But don't worry: I don't intend to let you out of my sight either. So when shall I set off the distraction?'

'Give me five minutes.'

Trix-E slipped a red stone into Roxy's hand.
'What's this?'

'Your charm, of course. We can't stand here in deep conversation and part without a sale.' She turned and announced loudly. 'Mind you follow my instructions, human.'

The inquisitive troll looked up from the display on the stall.

'Thank you, pixie.'

'Those spots on your face should disappear immediately.'

'They are called freckles.'

'No matter. Those unsightly blemishes will go if you wear the stone on a chain around your neck.'

'Thank you.' Roxy gave her friend a mocking smile, fully intending to get her own back for the 'unsightly blemish' crack when they were safe.

'You're welcome.'

Roxy jogged back to the changelings. They had divided themselves into their escape parties in her absence.

'Everything settled?' asked Tabitha anxiously.

'Yes. I think we have time for one more song to St Pringle, then we go through the fence. Who wants to make the hole?'

Simon and Edgar both raised their hands. Good choices, because they were the strongest of the changelings.

'We need something to cut the wire. I've got just the tool.' Roxy pulled Rick's sword out from under her jacket. She had been carrying it with her since he had been taken, hoping to get the chance to return it to him. Having shrunk it with a spell, she now returned it to its proper size. As a magical instrument it should make easy work of the fence if any charms had been put upon it.

'What's the signal to go?' asked Tabitha.

'I'm not sure, but I think we'll recognize it when we see it.' Roxy looked round the circle of anxious faces, feeling entirely unequal to the task of commanding them in this escape operation. She wasn't used to being regarded as a leader—that had been more Rick's thing than hers—so had no idea how to inspire them. What would she like to be given if she were in their shoes? Easy: hope.

'Don't be afraid. We'll be fine. Earth is our home, remember? Once we get there, our lives will be so much more than they can be here.'

'But we have no one left there,' said Ahmed, voicing the fear they all shared.

Roxy shook her head. 'That's not true. We'll have each other. Humans are nothing like you were taught. I made a really good friend there, despite how different we are, and I can't believe that was a fluke. We can rely on ourselves to start with.' She smiled as she took in the crowd sitting around her. 'Besides, there are enough of us to start our own village if we want.'

Tabitha offered Ahmed her hand, then gave his slim fingers a friendly squeeze. 'She's right. We've got so used to being alone and persecuted here, we've forgotten that we can be so much more if we stick together.'

'Exactly. Are we ready then?'

'Yes, we're ready, Chief Roxy,' replied Tabitha. A little laugh went round the circle, some of the tension disappearing.

Five minutes were up. Roxy scanned the grounds to see the signs of the diversion she had been promised. Trix-E had already released the Fey horses from their tethers and was whispering to them, no doubt giving them their instructions. Frost-E and Miz-Begotten were talking to the guard on the gate as if they had all the time in the world.

A bellow from the trolls gathered around the stall:

'Get your paws off me, you filthy human!'

'What do you mean: human? I'm not the changeling here!' protested another.

Roxy jumped to her feet. The trolls were one by one changing into . . .

'What are you doing over there?' asked Edgar, confused.

Where there had been a dozen blue-maned guards, now there were a cluster of red-haired

Roxys. The only one who still looked himself was the troll who was not wearing a charm. Brilliant. The spells had all been booby-trapped to cast a glamour over the wearer. There wasn't time to admire the fiendish simplicity of the idea.

'Quick, this is our signal.' She thrust the hilt of the sword into Edgar's hands, seeing out of the corner of her eye that the three pixies were already backing away from the quarrelling troll-Roxys and slipping through the gate. 'Cut the fence.'

The trolls were now trying to wrestle each other to the ground, shouting and grunting. It was weird watching herself fight herself: the punches were way more powerful than she could have managed.

Tabitha tugged her shirt. 'Come on, Roxy. We're leaving.'

Roxy turned in time to see the first little group of changelings carrying the babies dart through the gap. 'Quick, we need to throw up some kind of shield to stop the guards seeing what's going on until it's too late.'

'Hag's haze?' suggested Tabitha.

'Perfect.'

The two girls drew on their magic and twisted it into tendrils of mist. Manipulating magical power was like working with a lighter-than-air clay that could be shaped into many forms; Roxy concentrated on making her enchanted fog seem as natural as possible. Now, when the trolls looked towards the football field, they should see nothing but indistinct shapes moving about in a white mist.

But the haze came too late. Morgan had arrived.

Chapter 8

ALERTED by Queen Mab's shrieks and magic distress-flares, Oberon's sentries rushed to close the castle gates. Triggered by magic, the clipped hedges snaked and snarled, thorns growing to scythe points, creating an impenetrable barrier. Even Peony, hooves sparking on the cobbles, could not run fast enough to reach them before the gap narrowed. Any second now Rick was either going to have to pull up and surrender or there would be a horrible collision of horse, boy and thorns.

A tantalizing glimpse of darkening sky gleamed over the top of the needle-sharp battlements. Freedom was so close.

As Rick ducked an arrow that whizzed overhead, he had a wild—possibly a stupid—idea. He muttered the hover charm he had already successfully used on objects, but this time applied it to his mount. The horse tossed his mane and slowed, distressed as he felt the weightless sensation grip his body. His skin twitched in alarm, as though flicking off a hundred flies. 'It's OK, Peony. Keep calm. Keep moving.'

The horse's hooves were no longer touching the ground. Peony reared, almost unseating Rick. A shower of arrows mixed with a few bolts of magic passed under his legs.

Perhaps this was not such a brainwave after all. Peony was now spinning in a circle, going nowhere but up. Fortunately the archers did not want to injure the queen's favourite mount so were not shooting at Peony's exposed underside. 'Ssh. Hush now.' Rick clung on to Peony's neck. 'Think of flying like swimming a river. You're swimming the air.'

The Barbary neighed in protest.

'Please, Peony. It's this or they'll kill me. I was told you were bright enough to make up for a dim rider like me—you can do this!'

His plea must have got through because the horse tried again to master the unfamiliar motion. Peony stretched out his neck and began to canter. Rick feared for a moment that they were standing still, like one of those magic lantern horses which stayed in place while seeming to gallop, but then he realized they were gaining speed and going forward. Problem was that, though they had climbed out of reach of the thorns, they were on a collision course with the towers flanking the main gate. The bowmen were readying their missiles, waiting for a clear shot.

'Higher!' urged Rick.

Spiralling to gain height, Peony whinnied, no longer sounding terrified but rather impressed by his new skill. He charged towards the topmost point of the tower.

'We're going to crash!' warned Rick, knuckles white on the reins.

With an elegant spring, Peony jumped the roof like a champion in a steeplechase. Rick was the clumsy one, almost bouncing off, but he kept his seat by a combination of clutching Peony's neck and juggling his balance.

With a neigh that sounded to Rick like the equivalent of a horse laugh at his expense, Peony galloped off cross country, taking a second leap over a silver-green loop of the Dew Track. Arrows flew after them like a flock of hummingbirds armed with lethal beaks. One struck the bag of oats on the back of Rick's saddle, but the rest passed over without injuring either boy or horse.

'Fantastic! Well done!' Rick patted Peony's neck in enthusiastic praise as they flew out of the archers' range. He checked his own supply of magic for sustaining the hover charm and discovered that there was still a fair amount remaining—at least three-quarters of his fuel left in the tank, to borrow an Earth phrase. As Peony did not object to this mode of travel, Rick decided to remain airborne.

'We're going to Dark Lore,' he told the horse, not really expecting him to understand. He had underestimated Peony, however. The Barbary smoothly shifted direction like a glider banking on an air current, turning his nose northeast in the direction of the internment camp. Ahead lay the silver-topped Moonshine Mountains, darkened in the growing shadow of night, to their right was the glimmer of the ocean over Thirfo Thuinn, the Land under the Waves, and the beach where Oberon's forces had defeated the Wild Ride only a few days ago. The gleaming network of the Dew Track provided a path like a vein in a frosted leaf. He knew the pursuit would follow; the highly trained troops who used sycacopter wings would be mobilizing. But at the speed Peony was flying there was a decent chance that the hunters would not catch up with them. Peony could be at Dark Lore well before midnight. Rick couldn't wait to see Roxy's face when he flew over the walls to pick her up.

'What is happening here?' Commander Morgan strode out of Dark Lore House, her personal ogre guards flanking her. She blasted apart a pair of wrestling Roxys. 'Idiots! Can't you see you're under an enchantment? Which is the real human?' She shot spells right and left, leaving a trail of felled trolls in her wake. 'She's going to be the first to die at the Fey Games!'

Morgan's quick wits seized on the display of pixie charms and her eyes sparked with fury. 'Take off your spells, those of you who have bought something from the pedlars.' The trolls were not quick enough for her liking. 'TAKE THEM OFF!' The stall exploded in a flash of her power, the little spells setting off a chain reaction of pops and fizzes like fireworks. Reluctantly the guards began removing their feathers, bracelets and beads. The Roxys vanished to be replaced by confused-looking trolls.

Roxy slipped through the gap in the fence and ran into the forest. The changelings only had seconds to make good their escape. They had to get to Earth immediately.

Trix-E and her parents were waiting for her. A gateway between the worlds shimmered in the air like a heat haze, the size of a tunnel in the London Underground, blue lightning licking and crackling at the edges. The other changelings had already gone through.

'I think you are going to be really pleased with

me.' Trix-E held out her hand to Roxy. 'I found your busy place, Lon-Din.'

'London,' murmured Roxy, but she was distracted by the baying of the hobgoblins. 'I hope Barleywater and Cauliflower will be safe.'

'They'll be fine. They said goodbye. Come on.' Pushing her parents before her, Trix-E gestured to Roxy to proceed. 'I'll close the gate behind me.'

Roxy passed over the threshold, forest floor giving way to pavement. The noise level suddenly went up; music boomed, people shouted, cars hooted and growled. Dazed, she looked around her and found herself in the middle of a crowd of dancing girls dressed in sequinned bikinis and plumes. Vibrant floats wound their way slowly through the streets, decked out in lights, flowers, and streamers, people jigging around on their decks. 'What the . . . ?'

'Welcome, everybody, to this year's Notting Hill Carnival! Let's get the party started!' boomed the loud speaker.

Frost-E did a little shimmy on the spot, falling into step with the string of dancers twirling around him.

Miz-Begotten grinned at Roxy. 'And I thought Earth was boring. I think we're going to like this place!' she shouted over the music, plucking a feather from a girl's bustle and sticking it in her hair. 'Let's party!'

Deciding extreme caution would be a good idea for the final approach to the camp, Rick landed in a clearing of the Dark Lore forest and covered the last half mile on foot. There was just enough moonlight to see his way. Tangles of barbed brambles loaded with blood-red berries snagged at his cloak. Fireflies flicked on and off in the bushes, a ghostly pulse warning of danger. Fallen trees sprawled across his path, trunks spawning luminous fingers of fungi that released puffs of green spores when he brushed against them. When the spores reached his skin, they triggered a burning sensation and left an angry red rash behind. Even Aethel seemed disturbed by the wood, curling down to wind round his wrist, ready to defend him. The air smelled of swampy ground and rotting leaves.

'Lovely,' muttered Rick, yanking his ankle free of a particularly persistent bramble bush.

Peony nudged him in the small of the back, urging him on.

They reached the edge of the forest where a short stretch of rough ground separated the boundary fence from the trees. Brushing aside a spray of leaves, he caught a clear glimpse of Dark Lore. The place was so brightly lit, spotlighted in hovering glow-balls, it appeared almost as if it were on fire. Trolls and ogres milled about in the exercise yard in front of the main doors, marshalling five packs of hobgoblins who were straining on long leashes. Crouched on all fours, these wolfish creatures were among the most relentlessly bloodthirsty in Avalon. Their excited howling carried on the wind. Aethel hissed a warning. Peony took a step back, tugging on the reins. The hobgoblins wouldn't hesitate to bring down and eat a horse, and the Barbary was scared.

Rick held firm. He had not come this far to back off now. 'I can't see any changelings.' Were they locked up? Signs indicated that Morgan had ordered a massive hunt, which suggested someone had gone on the run.

Then Rick noticed the gaping hole in the fence.

'Aethel—Peony—they got out!' The cut in the silver wire mesh was exactly human child sized—too small for a troll, ogre, or even a Fey. The rough grass had been flattened by the passage of many feet heading for the forest. Roxy's attempts to spread rebellion must have succeeded. Though happy for them, Rick couldn't help a twinge of disappointment that Roxy had not waited for him or, for that matter, come to rescue him. Perhaps she didn't feel the same way about them being a team.

Or maybe, more likely, she'd had no choice.

Peony nudged him in the back again, this time with impatience.

'Yes, I know: we've got to fly.'

Relieved the human had got the message, Peony waited for Rick to be seated, then immediately set off into the open for take-off.

'Peony! What are you doing? We'll be seen!'

From the increase of barking from the hobs they had already been spotted. The Barbary was unrepentant: he was taking charge of the escape. Rick cast the spell for take-off.

Bolts of magic shot past. It was the castle all over again, but this time the ones casting the spells had no inhibitions about hitting the stallion. Peony banked sharply left and dived behind the roof of Dark Lore for protection, hooves rattling the tiles as he cut it fine; he then headed due east towards the sea. Not a bad idea because any earth-bound pursuit would have to give up once it reached the coast. They had to fly high and fast if they wanted to outstrip any followers.

Rick checked his magic. 'I can keep this up for another hour, maybe two. How far can you get us?'

Peony snorted as if to say that was plenty. His confidence in his own abilities was being boosted by his new-found skill.

'I hope you're right.' Rick glanced behind, half-expecting Morgan to be on his tail. Aethel curled up his body to his neck, settling at his nape to watch his back. Morgan was fully capable of a hover charm, though she preferred to fly on dragons or use sycacopter wings as they did not deplete her magic so quickly. Fortunately, the sky was clear.

A shower blew in from the ocean, reaching them as suddenly as if someone had turned on a tap. The cold drizzle slapped Rick's face and quickly chilled him to the bone, but he had no time to worry about his own comfort. They could make use of this turn in the weather. 'Can you take us into cloud, Peony?'

Flicking his bedraggled mane in answer, the horse gained height, plunging them both in the obscuring grey mist. Without being told, he also shifted north; anyone who was following their last known position would soon lose them.

'Phew!' Rick patted Peony's neck. 'I think we're safe now.' He rubbed Aethel, taking comfort from the familiar metal circling his collar. She had gone quiet, which meant she was content with their progress.

It was only a temporary kind of safety. Rick was very aware that he was on the run on a horse stolen from the current Queen of Avalon, in a kingdom where almost any of the Dark Folk would feel free to kill him on sight. Not good, however you looked at it. He would prefer to have some company to share his danger but even the Dark Lore inmates were gone.

'Where are the others?' he wondered aloud.

There were a hundred changelings and signs suggested they had only recently fled into the forest. Surely he would have heard them even if he had not spotted them? If they had had Fey help, they could have made a door to Earth.

And if that was so, that meant Rick was the only human changeling left in Avalon. He truly was on his own.

Peony was forced to land after two hours of hard flying. Both horse and rider were frozen, and Rick's supply of magic running low. Even Aethel was shivering with cold.

Peony located a tiny ring in a forest clearing, visible in the dark thanks to the ghostly shine of the whitecap mushrooms. The ground was damp, but Rick was too tired to care. He clutched the cloak tight to his body and lay down, curled around the ring as close as he could get without crushing any of the fungi. Peony stood over him, silently electing himself as first watch so that the human could replenish his magical power from the connections to Earth that seeped through such rings. His big body sheltered Rick from some of the rain, making it slightly less miserable to be sleeping out in the open. Aethel coiled against Rick's chest, offering what comfort she could.

Despite his exhaustion, Rick found it hard to relax enough to go to sleep, his mind whirled with all the things that had happened to him that day. The Stormridge—exploring the castle—the twins—the escape. His stomach grumbled, realizing that he hadn't eaten for hours. He reached in the bundle he was using as a pillow and pulled out a crushed pastry Cobweb had given him. He took a bite. The sweet savour of nutmeg and apple filled his mouth, silencing his hunger pangs. As he chewed, he listened to Peony tearing up the grass in his strong teeth, a strangely soothing sound of normal life carrying on despite the extraordinary situation in which they found themselves. Rick was grateful that the horse had made no protest at being stolen. In fact, Peony seemed to be enjoying the adventure more than his rider now it was underway.

Rick must have fallen asleep, for the next he knew was a blast of hot grass-scented breath in his face. He rolled over, coming awake in an instant. It was still dark, though if he had to guess, it felt like the hours before dawn rather than the middle of the night. Aethel was humming with tension.

'What?' he whispered.

Aethel held still. Now Rick could hear it too: a strange creaking noise overhead, like the sound made by a flight of swans, but much louder. And he was lying out in the open by the mushroom ring! What better way of marking 'come and get me'?

Two dark shapes blocked out the stars above. Whatever they were, they had begun their descent, spiralling down to land. Trying not to make any sound, Rick rose to his feet, picked up his bundle and led Peony out of the clearing and into the shelter of the trees. Had they been seen or had the shadows hidden them?

There came two thumps, then a glow-worm lantern flared. Rick was dazzled, his night vision ruined by the sudden eruption of light.

'Elfric Halfdane?' called a high voice. 'We know you're here: show yourself!'

Peony whinnied, alarmed not by the speaker but the two creatures the riders had brought with them. Aethel slid quickly under the cover of Rick's sleeve. Cobweb and Archer were standing in the clearing; behind them crouched two small dragons, not much bigger than Peony, tethered to the ground by iron chains. They snapped fretfully at their riders but were unable to see them as they were blinkered.

What were the twins doing here? Had they changed their mind, and come to recapture him?

Cobweb was growing impatient. 'Where is he,

Archer? You said he was here.'

Archer stepped further away from his dragon, removing himself from the influence of the magic-dampening field that surrounded them. He pointed directly at Rick's hiding place. 'Over there.'

'Come on, human, we haven't got all day.' Cobweb folded her arms and tapped her foot.

Rick emerged from the bushes, brushing off the leaves that had got caught on his hair. 'I'm here. How did you find me?'

Archer held out his hand. 'My arrow. I'll have it back now.'

Rick took the silver dart from under his belt where he had stuffed it earlier and passed it over. 'How did it lead you to me?'

'I have a summoning charm on all of them so I don't have to bother collecting them after I've fired. I just followed the magical link and it brought us to you.'

'Neat,' said Rick, thinking how annoying that was. He had been so easy to corner. 'What now?'

Cobweb scowled at the damp ground, looking for a place to sit. 'What do you mean?'

Rick preferred to hear the bad news immediately. 'Have you come to take me back?'

'Stars, no! We're on the run like you. Our wicked stepmother Mab took exception to us lending you Peony and turned very nasty.' She rubbed her arms. Now Rick was closer, he could see she had a number of scratches and bruises. It appeared they had had to fight to escape.

Archer moved closer to his sister and put his arm around her shoulders. 'Our father was not listening to us. He'd just heard all the changelings had escaped Dark Lore.'

Rick felt a fierce swoop of pride in his friends. So his guess was correct.

'Our actions were the last in a series of disappointments. I really think he might've killed us in his rage.' Archer rubbed a scorch mark from his sister's sleeve.

Rick hated to think he'd got them into trouble. 'I shouldn't have got you involved.'

Cobweb snapped her fingers. 'Bog frogspawn! Father has had it in for us since he exiled Mother. We are not convenient, not now Mab has taken over. We were going to get chased out sooner or later.'

'What are you going to do now?'

'Go find Mother with you, of course.'

He looked to Archer, whom he considered the more sober-thinking of the two. 'But aren't they going to be after you? I don't want to be rude but I could do without the extra pressure. I mean, I know they want to catch me, but two children of Oberon's blood must be an even higher priority.'

Archer nodded. 'Naturally. That's why you need

us and we need you. As much as we like you, human, we didn't come after you just to keep you company in your hopeless flight from Avalon's best huntsmen.'

Well, at least that fitted with what he knew about Fey motivation. 'So why did you come for me? You can carry your own message to your mother now.'

'We want to travel to Deepdene Forest through Earth. But I realized after talking to you that I haven't been there for several of your Earth centuries, so we need a guide.'

'You,' said Cobweb cheerfully.

Chapter 9

'YOU expect me to be your guide?' Rick rubbed his eyes, feeling a headache forming.

'Of course.' Seeing Cobweb was shivering in the cold and damp, Archer pointed at the fallen tree Rick had hidden behind. Branches snapped off, danced to the clearing and neatly formed a pile. With a sweep of his fingers, Archer set it alight.

'Are you going to tell me how this plan will work?' Rick asked, holding his palms towards the flames.

Archer poked the embers with a stick, sparks whirling up to the grey sky. 'How much do you know about Fey doors?'

'Not much,' admitted Rick, 'except that you

have to have Fey blood to have the right kind of magic to conjure them.'

'There is more to it than that. Thanks to the connections we made by building the power rings, Avalon maps roughly onto Earth, the two worlds in alignment. They act as a kind of anchor stopping the random fluctuations that would otherwise exist.'

'I see. So Earth's like a boat moored to Avalon?'

'You could put it like that.' Archer didn't sound as impressed at Rick's image as he was. 'What it means is that if you want to go north in Avalon, you can do so on Earth and then make the jump across.'

'I think I can see how that would work.'

'If we cross here, we can travel in your world, avoiding my father's hunters and gaining time. We can then arrive at Mother's tomorrow, rather than after a week of travelling here.'

In fact, that didn't sound a bad plan. Rick would even get a chance to contact his friends and meet up with Roxy.

'Do the Dark Folk do this a lot?' asked Rick.

Cobweb laughed. 'Why do you think there are all those stories of Fey processions through your countryside—not because we want to be there, I can tell you! We use Earth as a shortcut.'

Archer chucked the stick on to the flames. 'But it's no longer easy to go there undetected. The old ways of respect for the Dark Folk have vanished, so unauthorized travel to your realm is strictly forbidden.'

'Not that we worry about rules,' added Cobweb, her eyes glinting in the firelight like two burning coals.

'You don't.' Archer frowned at his twin. 'I happen to think they are very sensible. Not to mention the risk of upsetting the balance.'

Rick had forgotten about this until Archer reminded them all of the inescapable mythmatics underlying travel between the two worlds. That was why the changelings had been brought over in the first place—so they could balance out the Fey sent into exile. It then hit him that Roxy had just taken a hundred changelings to Earth without returning their Fey counterparts, creating an over-load on one side. He had been warned on his first visit that Earth could only put up with so much before it started shaking itself apart. He had to get to Roxy before that started to happen.

'When can we go?' Rick picked up his bundle.

'So you agree to help us?' Archer was surprised to have got Rick's cooperation so easily. Then again, he didn't know that Rick was eager to go north to liberate Arthur.

'Yes. Not that I don't have some questions. I don't mean to be rude or anything, but what's with the dragons? You can't seriously be planning to take them to Earth.'

Cobweb puffed a lock of hair out of her eyes. 'What's wrong with our dragons?'

'For one, thanks to the magic dampening field around them, you can't use a glamour to disguise them. Humans might just be a tad suspicious if you turn up there with two creatures from legend.'

Archer prodded his twin. 'Told you so. I said taking the dragons was a bad idea.'

'Yes, but you didn't have a better one. Mab had us cornered.'

Rick held up his hand to stop them descending into another of their squabbles. 'You'll have to let them go. They might find their way back to the stables.'

Cobweb sniffed. 'Unlikely. They hate us Fey bloods. They'll flee—after eating us if they get a chance.'

'We can't leave them here tethered to die of starvation.'

She folded her arms. 'Very well. *You* let them go.'

'I will if I have to.'

Cobweb shrugged, as if to say that was his funeral.

'And another thing: when we get to Earth, you're going to have to do as I say.'

Both twins spluttered with laughter this time.

'Oh yes?' Archer wiped a tear from his eye.

'Yes, or I won't go with you.'

'And you'll do what exactly? Stay here until the hunters catch you?'

Put like that, Rick's case wasn't very strong. 'But if you won't do what I say, then why ask for a guide?'

Cobweb put her hands on her hips. 'You may *suggest* to us what we should do, but we keep the final say. We are of royal blood.'

And so am I, thought Rick. He snapped a twig into three pieces and threw the bits at the hottest part of the fire. 'OK, but I'm warning you: if you do something really stupid, I'll leave you to sort it out.'

'I am never stupid!' protested Archer.

Rick raised an eyebrow and looked at Cobweb.

'You worry too much,' muttered the princess. 'What does it matter if humans are surprised by how we behave?'

Rick was truly tired of having to embark on a half-baked plan with scant chance of avoiding trouble, but he had little choice. 'You create the door then. Make sure you choose somewhere away from humans. I'll release the dragons.'

The two Fey retreated to give him room. Rick rubbed his temple, remembering the dragon-speech he had held with the Stormridge.

'I'm going to let you go. Please don't attack.'

III

There was no response. The two dragons were quieter now, lying with heads on their forelegs.

'I need your promise.'

Why should we promise you anything, human? The one on the right lifted his head, sniffing in Rick's direction. His voice was much quieter than the Stormridge, whispering through Rick's mind like the hiss of escaping gas.

'Because I'm trying to help you.'

We need no help.

'Are you sure about that? The prince and princess are all for leaving you tethered to the ground like this. You'll either starve or be recaptured. Is that better than giving me your word?'

A dragon does not make promises.

Rick scratched the back of his head, frustrated by the creature's stubbornness. Yet he knew he could not abandon them staked out in a lonely forest clearing with little chance of anyone coming to their aid. 'A dragon helped me yesterday morning, so I suppose I'm going to trust we can be allies rather than each other's enemies.'

Not enemies. You are prey.

'Fine. Be like that.' Rick moved forward, watching for the least threatening flicker from them. Nothing. First he removed the blinkers and halter. Two pairs of stone black eyes glared at him. He had the distinct impression only the stronger desire to allow the tethers to be undone stopped them trying to bite or blast him. He examined the harness. Each saddle was secured under their belly. If he slipped the buckle loose, they should be able to squirm free of the harness, leaving the tethers and saddle behind. With any luck, it would take them precious seconds to do so, giving him time to flee.

'Is that door ready?' he called. Looking over his shoulder, he saw Archer standing in the entrance, a rainbow light flickering around him. Cobweb had already gone through with Peony. Rick unfastened the first buckle and moved to the second dragon. 'On the count of three, get ready to close it behind me. One,' he pulled the strap, squeezing the scaly stomach a little tighter, 'Two,' he released the buckle and dropped the strap, 'Three!' He sprinted the distance and dived through the door. A tongue of flame followed, but was snuffed out as the passageway between the worlds was broken. His shoulder hit the ground hard, sending a jolt of pain through his body. Heat licked at his ankles. Archer beat out the smouldering bottoms of Rick's trousers before the blaze could spread.

'Ungrateful lizards,' muttered Archer.

Very relieved to have survived, Rick was able to shrug it off. 'Can't blame them—what have they to thank any of us for?' He brushed his hands on his thighs, feeling the sting where they had hit the tarmac. He had to hurry the twins along: they couldn't stay this side of the door without further upsetting the balance. 'Where are we?'

'No idea,' admitted Archer. 'I thought it looked suitable—plenty of cover among these wagons for our arrival.'

Rick got up. They were surrounded by cars. The roar of a plane taking off nearby gave him the clue he needed. He shook his head wearily. 'I think, Archer, you have brought us to Heathrow long-stay car park.'

The prince smiled. 'I assume that is rather brilliant of me? No humans in sight.'

'Not exactly. This car park must be one of the most closely watched places in England. And, if I am not mistaken, the police are arriving right now.'

Roxy felt like pulling her hair out in frustration. She had totally lost control of the changelings as soon as they arrived in the middle of the Notting Hill Carnival. Had she really been so stupid as to tell them to blend in by copying what those around them were doing? She caught a glimpse of a couple of children joining in with a team of acrobats, plunging their routine into chaos. Another was walking solemnly behind two police officers, mimicking their every move, which caused much laughter from the crowd. Six had leapt up on a passing float with the delusion that they would be an asset to the steel drum band. As for the pixies, this was their idea of heaven. Frost-E and Miz-Begotten had forgotten the serious purpose for their presence here and were dancing away with enthusiasm never before seen in the carnival. Trix-E was desperately trying to retrieve them but it was like chasing down wallabies: they hopped out of the way every time she reached one of them.

A jolly Afro-Caribbean lady with turquoise glittering eyelashes nudged Roxy. 'Who are your friends? They've got some seriously good dance moves.' She broke off into a raucous peel of laughter as Frost-E was delighting the crowd with his spinning-on-his-head routine.

'I know: they are quite something, aren't they?' Roxy was torn between wanting to chuckle and groan. She should have guessed something like this would happen. At least no one was questioning whether or not they were human; the carnival was so full of oddities they were strangely unremarkable. Still, she had better come up with some kind of explanation for them. 'They're actors. You know, from the cast of the new fantasy film they're making at Leavesden studios.'

The lady applauded the double somersault Miz-Begotten had just performed off the shoulders of a startled bystander. 'I hope they get a whole lot of screen time. I'd pay to see them.'

Trix-E had managed to hook her mother by the elbow and was talking furiously to her. Miz-Begotten was bobbing on the spot, looking as if the scolding was entirely floating over her head.

The seashell in Roxy's jeans' pocket tingled like pins and needles in her thigh. Smiling her excuses to the lady, Roxy slipped to one side and put the shell to her ear. 'Tiago? Is that you? How did you know I was here?'

'It's not Tiago, Roxy.'

'Rick!' she shrieked. 'Oh, I've been so worried about you! How did you get here—you are here, aren't you? England, I mean?'

'Yes, I am but . . .' he paused, catching a snatch of the music blaring behind her, 'where are you?'

'A carnival—don't ask. Big mistake. The pixies have gone AWOL and I've lost the rest of the changelings. I got everyone out.'

'But what about the balance?'

Roxy thumped her forehead. 'You're right. Oh, troll breath and dragon dung! But I had to act so fast—all I could think about was saving our lives. What shall we do about it?'

'No idea. Tiago was the one who understood this kind of thing. Have you tried contacting him yet?'

'Yes, I was just going to try again when you called me. I've only been here a few hours; he might just be out and left his shell behind.'

There was a brief pause. 'But you should have been here for days by now.'

'No, I guess we've been here about six hours or so.'

Rick took a sharp intake of breath. 'Then that means time in Avalon and on Earth is running more or less at the same pace. How can that have happened?'

They both were silent for a moment, running through the explanations. 'Who made your door? Did they do something?' asked Roxy.

Rick cleared his throat. 'Er, that was the other thing I needed to tell you. I didn't escape on my own. I'm here with Oberon's son and daughter, Prince Archer and Princess Cobweb.' He put his hand over the shell, muffling the noise for a moment while he spoke to Archer; then he returned to Roxy. 'Archer says that he did nothing special when he made the door—the same spell as normal.'

'Do you think I did it then—I upset time when I brought a hundred changelings over?' Her voice rose uncomfortably at the end of the sentence.

'It's a possibility. Oh, hang on a moment, Cobweb wants a word.'

A new voice took over on the shell. 'Is that the human girl, the one Elfric Halfdane calls "Roxy"?'

'Yes, your . . . um . . . Cobweb.'

'Rick tells us you have disrupted the timeline.'

'It might not be my fault.' But she had a terrible feeling that it was. What would come next? The complete disintegration of time?

Cobweb tutted. 'I hope you understand what you have done. We need the Earth's ability to travel faster. You have inconvenienced us.'

Roxy bit her tongue to stop herself making a rude response. Cobweb seemed not the slightest bit bothered that Roxy might have imperilled the whole world by upsetting the balance.

'We will sort out the mess you have made. Don't do anything else—and stay this side of the doors between our worlds,' ordered Cobweb.

Who did this girl think she was? Supreme ruler of the universe? Still, if she could help . . .

'You can do that?'

'Yes, once we have freed ourselves from this thing Rick calls "custard".'

Rick took back the shell. 'She means custody.'

'What!'

'Yeah, we . . . er . . . sort of turned up suddenly in the middle of Heathrow. I think we could've got away with it if it weren't for Peony—he's Queen Mab's horse . . .'

'Rick!'

'Um, yeah, that's a bit complicated. I'll tell you about it later. They won't release us until I give them the name of a responsible adult to vouch for us. I have to admit Cobweb and Archer are a bit startling to look at.'

Roxy couldn't help smiling, even though it sounded a horrible situation: two Fey under arrest—priceless! 'Tell them you are on your way to the carnival. Dark Folk blend in here no problem.'

'Good idea. Archer's going to charm a visitor to the police station to pretend to know us. We're just waiting for the right person to come in. We should be out soon.'

'Grand. It's really good to hear from you, Rick.' She wished she was close enough to give him a hug.

'Yeah, you too, Roxy. Mad this, isn't it?'

'You can say that again. I'll keep trying to contact Tiago and Linette. Can you come and join me?'

'I can't, as I've promised to take the twins north. I think it would be best if you found a way to meet up with us. Their destination in Avalon is really near King Arthur's island, and we need him more than ever. Oberon is on the war path and he'll come after us. We'll be slaughtered if we can't set up our own Round Table as soon as possible—that quest has to take priority.'

'You're right. I'll come to you.'

'Got to go: someone's just come in to report a stolen wallet. Speak later.'

'Yes, later.'

Roxy slipped the shell back into her pocket. Rick was safe—apart from the annoying detail of being in a police station. She was a little worried he wouldn't know how to negotiate his way out of human trouble, as he was always the most clueless about modern behaviour—having a firm prejudice for things Anglo-Saxon. But hopefully he'd manage for a little while without her to set him straight. Now for her other friends. She whispered the charm to call Tiago, letting it tingle, knowing that if he still had his shell, he would be feeling that prickle of an active communication charm.

There was no reply.

Perhaps he had given up on carrying the magical shell, not thinking there was anyone to call him? She would have to find a phone and try the conventional means of contacting him on Linette's mobile. First, though, she needed to drag the pixies away from the party, which was like taking a couple of misers away from their bags of gold. Trix-E would not be able to do it alone.

Roxy pushed up her sleeves. 'OK. Operation End of Party here we come.'

Chapter 10

IN a dank multi-storey car park behind a shopping centre, Rick and the twins said goodbye to the man who had claimed, under Archer's persuasion spell, to be their father. After releasing them from custody, Mr Goddard, a grey-haired businessman with multiple gold bracelets and a taste for loud suits, had given them a lift up the motorway to Reading, so befuddled he had not even batted an eyelid at the horse tethered to his roof rack. Peony galloped alongside thanks to Rick's hover charm. To outsiders, Peony looked like a flapping tarpaulin on a badly secured load.

'Thanks, Father,' Archer said formally, shaking Mr Goddard's hand. 'We'll not be needing you any longer.'

Their victim scratched his head. 'Are you going to be OK from here, son? I dunno, it feels wrong to just abandon you here.'

'Of course we will, Father.'

Cobweb flicked her fingers in a releasing spell for the harness and Peony floated down to land. He trotted over and nudged Rick in greeting.

'Enjoyed your flight, did you?' Rick murmured.

The businessman's bracelets rattled. 'Blimey, where are we going to keep that horse? We only have a semi in Croydon. Come to think of it, where did he come from?'

Cobweb slapped his arm playfully. 'Oh, Father, how could you forget? You gave him to me for my sixteenth birthday!'

'I did? So I'm a good dad, am I? Generous and thoughtful?'

'Yes. You're the best.'

Mr Goddard glowed with pleasure, then his smile dimmed. 'What's your name again?'

'Cobweb.'

'I called a daughter of mine "Cobweb"?'

'Don't be silly—of course you didn't.'

He heaved a sigh of relief.

'That was Mother's choice.'

'Who?'

'Your wife. The one you had twins with, Dad.'

'What? Don't tell me I'm married too? What

will my girlfriend say?' Mr Goddard's phone rang—a tinkly little tune. 'Crikey, that's her now. What can I do—she'll never forgive me! How can I be married all these years and not remember it? I should never have gone on Steve's stag weekend to Las Vegas!'

Rick tugged Archer's sleeve. 'Drop the charm, won't you, before we ruin this man's entire life. He's already lost his wallet; I don't want him to lose his mind too.'

Archer snapped his fingers. Mr Goddard's expression went vague for a second and then he jolted out of his nightmare.

'What? Where am I?'

'You were mugged,' Rick said quickly. 'Lost your wallet. You've reported it and are now heading home, with only a little detour to Reading.' The phone rang again. 'That's your girlfriend checking up on you.'

Leaving Mr Goddard to put his life back together in its normal shape, Rick led the way up the high street, guiding their party through the small flocks of elderly shoppers with trolleys, and parents pushing buggies stuffed with infants and bags. Humans carried so much clutter in this century. Peony attracted the most attention; unlike in Anglo-Saxon England, travel with a horse was not seen as the usual thing in this time period.

'Where are we going?' asked Archer.

'To the train station.' Rick felt rather proud that he had mastered how to travel about during his short stay on Oberon's mission, not that he had, as yet, used the railway himself. 'The quickest way north is to catch a train from there and get a connection to take us onward. I'm guessing Manchester will be far enough.'

He might has well have been speaking a foreign language to them. 'What do you mean? Train? Connix-shun? What are these things?' Archer scowled, not liking to be in the dark. The translation spell that allowed him to understand Rick's English had gaps where Fey knowledge gave up.

'It is a bit like the Dew Track, but without the magic. You'll see when we get there. Trust me.'

They turned into Reading station and entered the ticket hall, Peony's hooves echoing on the tiles. Rick was puzzled that everyone stopped what they were doing to look at them. He hadn't thought the twins were *that* remarkable. There was no time to worry: the display showed the next train was due in ten minutes and, better still, it went all the way to Manchester without them having to change.

Having been given no warning of this trip to the human world, Rick felt woefully under-prepared. As he had arrived without money, he would have to rely on a little glamour. If he was lucky, he could persuade the ticket seller that the leaflets he had grabbed from the newsstand were in fact twenty-pound notes.

He approached the window. The bespectacled woman at the counter was reading her computer screen and didn't look up.

'I'd like three single tickets to Manchester, please.' Rick glanced over to the twins who were looking down their noses at a cleaner who was protesting to them about Peony's recent contribution to his floor. 'You had best make that first class.'

The woman flicked a surprised look in his direction. 'Are you sure, love? More expensive seats. We don't get many youngsters asking for them.'

'Absolutely sure. And can you please tell me where we can put our horse?'

She surprised him by chuckling. 'Good one.'

'Horses aren't allowed on trains?' Come to think of it, he'd never seen any on the streets, so how did they move them long distances?

The woman must have caught his surprised tone. She raised a brow. 'You were joking, weren't you?'

Fortunately, Peony had wandered out of sight now, having gone to graze on a fruit and veg stall by the entrance. 'Of course—yes, absolutely. Just out of interest: what large items are allowed on trains?'

'Well, you can take a bike on most services as long as there is space, but you have to put it in the guard's van at the rear.' She tapped her keyboard and named an exorbitant price for the tickets.

Rick pushed over the wad of transformed leaflets, feeling guilty about the fraud. She handed him three little cardboard rectangles.

'There you go, love. Take care with that horse of yours now!'

Rick returned her cheery wave and hurried out of the station to Archer, Cobweb and Peony. A small gathering surrounded them as the stall owner protested at the horse's attempts to devour his stock. Peony stood oblivious and quite content, munching on a carrot. Archer and Cobweb looked on, mildly amused, as if watching some inferior performance played out for their entertainment.

'Sorry, sorry!' muttered Rick, thrusting yet more conjured notes in the stall holder's hand. 'Quick, we've got to move!' He tugged Peony down an alley out of sight of the station entrance. The twins followed reluctantly: the place smelled foul and was littered with food wrappers and cigarette butts.

'What's going on?' asked Cobweb. 'Aren't we getting a train after all?'

Rick had no desire to admit his ignorance of human ways so pretended this had all been part of his plan. 'Yes, but we have to cast a charm over Peony. And ourselves as well, I think. We stand out too much.' He muttered a spell, transforming

Peony's appearance into a racing bike, taking his cue from the one a cyclist was sitting on at the traffic lights across the road. He then cast a glamour over his clothes to match the biker—tight black shorts and yellow top, helmet and goggles. The twins copied his outfit. 'There, now we blend.'

They returned to the station, cutting quite a swathe through the crowd in their matching cycling strip, with Rick mounted on Peony's back. The worst moment came at the barrier when Rick feared there would not be enough space to get Peony-the-bike past. Although the horse looked like a bicycle, he still took up the same amount of space as normal. They were going to miss their train if Rick didn't think of a way round this.

He had forgotten the intelligence of his mount; the horse solved the problem for him by jumping the gate.

'Oi! None of them fancy stunts in the station!' shouted a uniformed attendant, running across the concourse towards them.

Rick swung off Peony's back. 'Sorry!' he shouted, hurrying the other way to the guard's van. 'Get on board!' he told Archer and Cobweb, ushering them ahead of him through the open door. Would Peony fit? The horse snorted and entered the carriage as if he were a natural born commuter. A whistle blew, the doors clicked shut, and the train began to move out of the station.

'We did it.' He patted Peony's neck. 'Well done.'

Archer frowned at the austere surroundings of the luggage van. The racks were packed with boxes and suitcases. Two bikes leaned against one wall. The horse took up a huge amount of room, his head brushing the ceiling. 'I'm not travelling in here. I'm a prince.'

'But we can't leave Peony and there won't be room for him, not even in the first class carriage,' argued Rick.

'Oh, he'll be quite comfortable,' said the prince loftily. Indeed, Peony did look happy as he had found a little wagon full of crisps, biscuits, and drinks, and had begun to nibble a packet of shortbread.

'I'll put a block on the door so no one comes in,' volunteered the princess.

'How?'

'If they try, they'll forget and go do something else instead. It's a very useful charm and explains how I get away with most of the things I do at the castle.' Cobweb grinned at him, her blue eyes sparkling. 'I thought it up myself.'

First Class was fortunately just the other side of the door from the luggage van. Rick chose seats so they could keep an eye on whether Cobweb's charm was deterring people from entering.

'So, hadn't you better do something about the balance?' he asked the twins, worried that they'd already left it dangerously long.

'Don't nag,' grumbled Cobweb. 'We'll get to that when we decide, not when you say so.'

Rick bit his tongue hard, knowing she would delay further just to annoy him.

'Not bad,' said Archer, running his palms over the broad leather seat back. 'Where are the servants?' He clapped his hands, causing the woman opposite to drop her copy of the *Financial Times*. The conductor appeared at the far end of the carriage. 'You, my man, I'll have a glass of fresh dew—sparkling—and honeyed petals of the paradise flower.'

The conductor hastened up the carriage, not to serve their every whim as Archer anticipated, but to check that First Class had not been invaded by a gang of yobs. 'Can I see your tickets, please?'

Rick handed over the three cardboard rectangles he had purchased. 'Sorry about my friend; he was just joking about the dew.'

The conductor glared at the tickets, trying to find something wrong with them. 'You get a complimentary drink and sandwich, nothing more, so don't push your luck, sonny. The attendant will be with you shortly, once she gets her refreshment trolley out of storage.'

Ah.

'Great. Thanks. We won't be bothering you again,' said Rick politely.

Giving them a final hard stare, the conductor moved off. The other passengers in First Class were in revolt by the time the train reached Birmingham. The hapless refreshment lady kept taking their orders, going to fetch her trolley, then promptly turning and walking off, forgetting what she was supposed to be doing.

'We are going to get her fired,' groaned Rick as he watched her do this for the tenth time. He was working his way up to a panic: neither twin seemed the least bothered about the balance or the effect they were having on the other passengers; they were too busy enjoying themselves.

'I'm hungry,' complained Archer.

'Yes, well, that is our fault. I think Peony has eaten everyone's lunch.'

'Where did you say this was going?'

'Manchester. It's a big city in the north.'

'That's no good. We'll need a deserted spot to make our doorway to mother's palace. I don't want another taste of custard.'

Cobweb meanwhile was leafing through the magazine she had found on the table. 'How about there?' She jabbed her finger at a picture of a steam train crossing a Scottish glen.

'That's not on our route,' Rick explained patiently. 'Trains have timetables they have to keep to.' He looked out of the window: the city of Birmingham had given way to pretty stone-walled fields and sheep. He checked the watch on the wrist of the lady across the carriage. The hand did not seem to have moved much in the last hour.

'I don't give a mermaid's scale for timetables; that field suits our needs. I'll just tell our driver.'

She started to get up. Rick pulled her back into her seat. 'You can't just waltz up to the driver and tell him to drive the train to Scotland! We are going to Manchester.'

'Well, if the humans don't want to come, they can get out.'

Rick looked out of the window again, seeking some peace in the green landscape. What he saw was the opposite of soothing. The same field and flock of sheep were there; the train was not making any progress. 'Archer, Cobweb—look!'

Archer frowned. 'Should it be doing that?'

Rick glanced round the carriage: they were the only ones still talking; everyone else had stopped, one man with a bottle of water half way to his mouth. Time had hit the pause button.

'No! Time goes forwards here—just like in your world. It must be the imbalance. You told Roxy you could fix it, remember?'

Cobweb pouted. 'If I fix it, will you agree to go to Scotland?'

'And get me a sandwich if Peony has left any?' added Archer.

'Yes, yes, anything!'

The twins grinned at each other.

'Go get the food then, Rick; we'll just pop outside for a moment,' said Cobweb.

'But the train's moving—sort of.' Rick rubbed his eyes. It was all very confusing. He supposed that the three of them, as inhabitants of another world, had brought with them some immunity to Earth's time collapse, but the sensation was beyond strange. It wasn't that everything had stopped, just that it was caught at the last moment, so the train felt as if it were moving, the people still living and breathing, but no advancement was being made.

Cobweb opened the door into the guard's van with a releasing spell. 'Just pull that handle if things start up again,' she said, pointing to a lever with 'Emergency Stop' written on it. 'Hello, Peony. Enjoying yourself?'

Rick eyed the lever with its dire warnings of a hefty penalty. He closed the door into First Class behind them. If he had to pull it, he would prefer no one to see him do it.

'I like cheese,' said Archer, opening the rear door and jumping down on to the track. 'And I wouldn't mind trying a packet of those circular golden things that Peony seemed to like.'

'Crisps,' said Rick.

'I want chocolate. Fey smugglers bring that into Avalon so I've tried that before and I know I like it!' called Cobweb, leaping down behind her brother.

'What are you going to do?' asked Rick, hanging out the open door.

'How many changelings came through, did you say?'

'About a hundred.'

'What do you think, Archer?' Cobweb surveyed the field.

'I believe there are enough.' With a complex weave of words and hand gestures, the prince created a doorway to his world; it shimmered over the pasture like a rainbow. A little of Avalon's time seeped through the entrance, stirring the sheep to life. They resumed feeding, uninterested in the magical force field creating beautiful splinter patterns in the sky.

Archer gave a whistle and the sheep lifted their heads. 'Denizens of Earth, we offer you a new life in Avalon. The grass there is greener, you will not be slaughtered for your meat, and you can run free. Do I have any volunteers?'

The nearest ewe gazed at him vacantly. The rest of the flock wandered off.

'They aren't as intelligent as creatures in your world,' called Rick. 'If this is your plan to restore the balance, just take their agreement as read. They'll only end up at the butcher's if they stay here.'

Cobweb tried approaching one of the sheep but it darted away. 'How do we get them to go through?'

'If one goes, the rest will follow.'

'Ah, I have it!' Archer conjured up the image of a ram running through the gateway. The ewe watched it suspiciously then turned back to the grass. Perhaps sheep were more intelligent than Rick gave them credit for.

'Or they use dogs,' he offered helpfully.

Cobweb was quite annoyed now, as the sheep spurned her attempts to give them a new life. 'You do it then, human,' she said, stamping back to the train, 'and I'll get our food.'

Rick gave her a hand back up into the carriage then jumped down. The twins' idea was quite brilliant in its simplicity. They needed a dog, though, or they would be chasing the flock from one end of the field to the other all day.

Rick shook Aethel off his wrist. 'Hey, sleepy

head, time to do a bit of work. Do you mind if I transform you?'

The snake looked up at him with resignation. Casting a quick spell, Rick made Aethel appear like a collie. The result was extremely odd because the dog still moved like a snake, sliding along the grass, keeping low. The sheep, however, paid attention this time. With a bleat of protest, the ewe led the flock away from the strange dog, jogging neatly through the gateway Archer had created.

'Count the sheep!' shouted Rick. 'We don't want to send too many.'

'How tiresome.' Archer yawned, making Rick laugh. 'What's so funny?'

'Nothing. Carry on.' He would have to explain the joke, but later; he and Aethel had a pocket of rebel sheep to round up.

'Ninety-nine, a hundred!' called Archer.

There were seven sheep left this side of the gate. Rick and Aethel held them back. 'Do you think that's enough? How does the balance work? Separate objects or total mass?'

'No idea,' admitted Archer. 'I never listened to my Feysyks tutor.'

'Let's send these through too. Roxy took some pixies with her, and my guess at the number of changelings was very rough. Then there's us to add.' Rick released the sheep and they ran quickly through the gate.

'I would imagine that, in the grand scheme of things, the worlds can cope with a slight imbalance.'

They watched the dirty tails of the latest changeling sheep bob out of sight through the shimmering curtain of magic.

'When I close the gateway, the exchange is complete,' said Archer. 'That's when we'll know if we've got it right.'

'OK. Let's get back on the train.'

'But I have to do it from here, where I cast the spell.'

'I'll get on then. And you—just don't hang around. I'd prefer not to pull the emergency stop. We've created enough trouble as it is.'

Archer looked surprised. 'We? I thought we had been immensely helpful to you humans.'

Only after creating the problems in the first place. 'Yes, of course you have. Let's get on with it.' Rick dropped the charm on Aethel and scooped her up from the grass.

Cobweb leaned out and pulled him up from the track level. He saw that she had pushed the ravaged trolley into the First Class carriage. Not much was left on the top layer.

'Did you succeed?' she asked, snapping open a chocolate bar.

'We won't know until Archer closes the door, he says. Get ready to help him up.'

Archer raised his hands above his head and swept them down.

Immediately life returned to the people in First Class; the train picked up where it had left off—at seventy miles an hour. Archer was running after them but his field was already far behind.

'He'll never catch up!' Cobweb reached for the emergency stop.

Rick batted her hand down. 'Sorry. I've a better idea.' Around the bend of the track, he could see a signal on green, like a traffic light. 'Can you cast a glamour from a distance?'

'Of course.'

'Turn that light red.'

'Why?'

'Just do it!'

With a huff of annoyance, Cobweb muttered a little charm. The signal light went red. The driver applied the brakes and the train slowed. Taking a shortcut across the neighbouring field, Archer deftly vaulted a fence and reached the train. He swung himself up without assistance.

'That was fun!' He smiled at his sister, brushing his hair out of his eyes with grimy hands. Rick wondered wryly if the prince had ever got them dirty before.

She handed him a cheese sandwich in an unopened package. 'I saved this for you. Now, let's go tell the driver we're going to Scotland.'

'But . . .' Rick remembered his promise, extracted under pressure. He closed his mouth.

'Exactly.' Cobweb patted him on his shoulder. 'Don't worry. I'm sure the humans will all like where we are going—it looks so beautiful.'

How to explain to a couple of Fey the concept of appointments, business meetings, and shopping trips?

'I'll leave the persuading to you.' Rick gestured towards the front of the train. 'He'll be up the other end. Just drop the glamour on the light, will you?'

Cobweb pulled the rear door closed and let the signal go back to its normal colour. 'He'll understand once he knows he has a prince and princess on board. I'm sure he will consider it an honour to serve us.'

Chapter 11

ROXY stashed the pixies temporarily in a cafe while she went in search of the other changelings in her group. She found Tabitha, Edgar and Ahmed huddled in a bus shelter, bewildered by the party going on around them. Gathering them up and taking them to Trix-E to be fed and looked after, she turned her attention to locating Simon. Annoying though he was, she didn't like to think of any of the changelings alone at the carnival. Yet it was almost impossible to make a proper search as the crowd kept shifting and blocking her view. In the end she climbed a cherry tree in a front garden and straddled a branch. What had he been wearing? Dark Lore didn't have a uniform, changing style of clothes at the whim of Morgan. Since the Great

Meltdown, even that routine had stopped. With no one enforcing a dress code, the inmates had drifted to wearing whatever they could get their hands on, most returning to the clothes of their era, as it was where they felt they belonged. Simon had been wearing an approximation of late-medieval peasant clothes: loose trousers and tunic from homespun material. He would look like a hippy in this crowd.

There! Roxy spotted him backed up against some bins behind a fast food outlet. Unfortunately, some other kids had found him first. Two were holding his arms while a third searched his clothes for valuables. Roxy leapt from her perch and headed towards the trouble.

'Hey, man, where's your phone?' grumbled the mugger, a skinny teenager with bad skin and uneven teeth.

Simon's answer was a head-butt.

The boy cradled his face, swearing inventively. Roxy didn't understand half the words he used. 'You broke my nose! I'm gonna kill you!'

Simon was doing a good job of defending himself, almost shaking off the other two attackers, but he was never going to get free without a helping hand.

'Hey, you, get away from him!' Roxy pushed the mugger sideways and then proceeded to kick one of his accomplices in the shin.

The mugger grabbed her in a half-nelson. 'Your girlfriend, is she? Perhaps she's got something worth taking?'

'Leave her alone!' Simon heaved one arm free only to be elbowed in the stomach. He doubled up, gasping.

'I may be small,' panted Roxy, gathering her magic, 'but I pack a powerful punch!' She slammed all three with a blast of elfshot. Like red snooker balls struck by the white, they flew apart; one landed on a pile of crates, bringing them crashing down, another collided with a drainpipe and ended up sitting in a puddle, and the mugger fell into the open top of a wheelie bin, legs flailing in the air in a most satisfactory fashion.

Roxy dusted off her hands. 'OK now, Simon?'

He nodded, somewhat shamefaced that he had had to be rescued by a pint-sized girl.

'Why didn't you use your magic?' Roxy asked.

He mumbled something.

'What?'

'I'm not very good at magic,' he admitted, limping out of the alley. 'I can't control the power and I didn't want to kill anyone.'

He rose in Roxy's estimation. Many changelings wouldn't have spared a thought to that; they would have just used their magic and worried about the consequences later.

'Did they hurt you?' She suspected only his pride had been battered.

'No. I didn't understand what they wanted. I was just trying to blend in like you told us—you know, make friends and that—when they approached me.'

She patted his arm consolingly. 'Perhaps we'd better not try to make friends with strangers. Let's stick together.'

'Yes, I'd be happier with that. Earth isn't what I expected.'

'I know. Different to study something than experience it, isn't it?'

'Definitely. So, where are the others?'

'Over in that cafe. Or so I hope.' She grinned. 'But knowing the pixies . . .'

Simon managed a flicker of a smile. 'Yeah, we'd better hurry before something else happens.'

The pile of empty plates on the table in front of the pixies indicated that they had run up a very large bill in the short time Roxy had left them to their own devices. She took the seat next to Trix-E.

'These are great!' the pixie enthused, holding up her cake. 'This is my ninth. What are they?'

'Muffins.'

Trix-E giggled. 'What a funny name!'

Roxy smiled. She supposed it was now she came to think about it. 'I'm not sure how we are going to pay for all of them.' She only had twenty pounds on her, left over from her stay in Oxford. 'How many have you eaten between you?'

'Oh, about thirty, I think.' Trix-E gave a little burp. 'But don't worry: we've got lots and lots of money.'

Roxy's smile turned into a frown. 'Oh yes? And where did that come from?'

'You won't believe how easy it is to steal in the human world—purses and wallets in every back pocket and bag. Most were stuffed with these useless little bits of plastic and paper with some human queen's head on it—we threw those away—but quite a few held coins.' Trix-E upended a sock full of coppers onto the table. 'We're bound to have enough.'

Roxy buried her head in her hands. Where to start? 'Trix-E, you do realize that stealing is generally thought to be wrong, don't you?'

The little pixie folded her arms across her chest. 'Says who?'

'Says anyone who owns anything.'

The pixie grinned. 'But, as you know, we pixies don't: we just temporarily act as custodians to things that come our way. The essence of trade is to keep things circulating, so that is our role—to wrest goods out of hands that would clutch and cling, and throw them back into the market so someone else can use them.'

There really was not time to debate the pixie world view that all theft is property (temporarily). Having lived with them so long, Roxy half agreed with them.

But first things first: she had to get them out of here and find a place for the changelings— that was if Rick's new friends could restore the balance as they had promised. That done, she and Rick had to get to Arthur and found a Round Table for protection—all before Oberon caught up with them.

Ahmed tugged at her sleeve. 'Hey, Roxy, something very strange is happening. Look, that teapot—the waitress is pouring but the tea isn't reaching the cup.'

With growing horror, Roxy looked around the cafe. Everything had stopped—a customer mid-sip, a cat on the windowsill licking its hind leg, the steam billowing from the coffee machine. The changelings were the only ones still moving.

Roxy leapt from her chair. 'She promised she would sort it out!'

'Who?' asked Trix-E, waving her hand in front of the cat to see if she could startle it back to life.

'Princess Cobweb.'

'What!' snorted Trix-E. 'You expected help from her? She's notorious for causing trouble, not solving it.'

'Yeah, I see that now. What can we do? We'll have to go back, won't we?' Roxy hugged herself, dismayed by the prospect. 'Round up the others, make a door, and restore the balance.'

'Great plan—I don't think.' Trix-E put her hands on her hips. 'Go back straight into the arms of Morgan and her hunters? Even though we have her scrying glass, she'd still find you if there were a hundred changelings stumbling about in Avalon. You'd be slaughtered before you knew what'd hit you.'

'What if you made the door to somewhere we could hide out?'

'And where would that be? You hid with us when you were younger, remember, and someone betrayed you. How can we hope to conceal a hundred humans, few of whom are actually pixie-sized?'

Roxy paced up and down. 'I need to think!'

'You, my dear Rox-E, need to rest. You've not slept since we got here, which means you've missed a night. It will all be clearer tomorrow.'

'If there is a tomorrow.' Roxy piled up the coins on the table and added her twenty-pound note. 'Come on, let's at least get out of here before they realize we want to pay with two-pence pieces.'

The changelings grabbed their takeaway cups. Frost-E and Miz-Begotten took the last muffins from the counter display.

'Where are we going, Roxy?' asked Edgar.

She felt almost ill that he still trusted that she would have a plan to look after them.

'Somewhere safer than this, Ed.'

The sight that greeted them on the streets of Notting Hill was weird in the extreme. The frozen moment had caught many revellers mid-leap, dance or—in the case of one set of acrobats—somersault. A child sat in a pushchair watching with dismay as its ice cream tumbled to the floor, mouth opening in a wail, tears about to fall. A girl and boy, arms around each other, paused with lips puckered, on the verge of kissing. A champagne cork hovered an inch above the neck of the bottle, foam just fizzing out, as a waiter served a birthday party on a restaurant terrace.

'I don't know what to do,' admitted Roxy, gazing around at the tableau of still life. 'I've gone and messed up the world big time.'

And then, just as suddenly as everything had stopped, it all started again. Scoop of ice cream hit the pavement, child bawled, lips met and cork hit the restaurant canopy to the sound of loud cheers.

'What the . . . ?'

Trix-E patted her on the back. 'There. All sorted. You know, according to gossip, humans are brutish creatures of incredible ugliness, lacking any sense of humour or fun.' Trix-E swept her hand to the crowds around her. 'I accept the ugliness bit,' she winked at Roxy, 'but no fun? You must be joking.'

Roxy's team found a quiet place to spend the night in a wooded area of Hyde Park in the centre of London. Edgar and Simon built a campfire while Roxy and the pixies set up a magical barrier to deter the park keepers from discovering their encampment. Through necessity, the pixie travellers were skilled in the small spells of concealment and tricking the eyes.

Once the fire was lit, Tabitha and Ahmed toasted a packet of marshmallows Frost-E had obtained in the cafe. Roxy opted instead for the sandwich Miz-Begotten had smuggled off some unfortunate customer's plate. She shared it with Simon, who hadn't eaten either.

'Do you think Morgan will chase us to this world?' Tabitha asked, passing round marshmallows on sticks.

'I hope not. Oberon wanted to get rid of us and we did the job for him, in a way.' Roxy bit into the bread roll. 'It would be vindictive in the extreme to chase us here.'

'Vindictive is just what I would call Morgan,' commented Trix-E. 'If she can get at you, she will.'

'We need to prepare for battle then.' Simon cracked his knuckles.

'Do you have to do that? It sets my teeth on edge,' grumbled Roxy. 'But we can't fight as we are. We might have our own powers but we don't have the training to put up a defence against Morgan's troops, let alone Oberon's armies if he decides to come after us.'

'The way I see it,' said Trix-E, 'you changelings need someone to look after you.' She smiled fondly at her own parents who were building a tower out of sticks and marshmallows. They had managed six feet already. 'None of you are old enough to take on the job of training the others—raising you all. I know I would be lost without my Ma and Pa.'

Roxy had always thought Trix-E did the job of taming her own parents but perhaps there was more to it than that? The empty place in Roxy's heart that would have been filled with love for her own family ached horribly at the thought of what she missed.

'We do have a plan—Rick and I, that is.'

'What plan?' asked Tabitha.

'We learned during our last mission here that the only way to defend ourselves against Oberon is to use Round Table magic—do what Arthur and Merlin did.'

'Oh, I always loved the stories about them! How did that work?' asked Ahmed.

'The Table acted like a kind of power source into which the knights plugged themselves to gain magic. We are fetching Arthur and Merlin so they can help us to do the same today.'

'Ah. You mean you will get them to look after you,' said Trix-E, nodding sagely.

'I wonder what they will feel, being asked to foster a hundred of us,' murmured Tabitha.

Roxy could imagine how that interview would go. King Arthur could be forgiven for thinking that his destiny was not to play nursemaid.

Trix-E cocked an eyebrow. 'How are you going to find them?'

'Rick and I are going after Arthur. He's in prison in the far north of Oberon's kingdom. Rick is on his way there in this world and can cross over. I have to go and join him; he shouldn't face Arthur alone. We're not quite sure what he'll make of us after all these years. Still, surely he will agree that Oberon needs challenging?'

Trix-E ate the last marshmallow before it dripped off the stick she'd been holding over the fire. 'We pixies don't take much interest in politics but I'd say that you're not alone. Not all Dark Folk will be against you if you stand up to Oberon. Some might even join you.'

'We can't all go with you—while you're fetching Arthur, the rest of us need a safe place,' said Tabitha. 'We can't camp out in a park for long.'

'We need to go to a strong place where we can

draw on lots of magical power for the Round Table when we're ready to set it up.' Roxy sketched a circle on the grass. 'Perhaps base ourselves near one of the rings.'

'But won't the Fey watch them?' asked Ahmed.

'Not if it is out of service,' said Trix-E, smiling.

'Do you know one?' asked Roxy.

'Oh yes: Stonehenge. It was a bit of a failure—something wrong with the primitive calibration—but I think it works well enough for your purposes. With a few well-placed glamours, we can set up camp there without attracting too much attention and secretly restart the exchange.'

Ahmed, who had been listening quietly, slipped his hand in Roxy's. 'But you can't go: you're our leader.'

She ruffled his hair. 'You don't need me; you've got the others to look after you—Trix-E and her parents, Tabs and Ed . . .'

Simon cleared his throat.

'Even Simon.' She winked at Ahmed who rolled his eyes.

'Are you sure it'll be all right?'

No, she wasn't the slightest bit sure. 'Absolutely. How could Arthur turn down this opportunity? He'll jump at the chance for a fight against the ones who imprisoned him.'

With those brave sounding words, she packed a few essentials for the journey, including Rick's sword. Trix-E sidled alongside her and slipped her hand into the bundle.

'Trix-E, I really do need everything in there,' said Roxy.

'I'm not taking, but adding.'

Roxy peeked inside. The scrying glass, still wrapped in a blood-red satin cloth, now nestled among her belongings. 'You're giving that to me?'

'Of course. Things must be kept in circulation—not stay with one owner: that's the pixie way.' She ran a finger over the smooth edge. 'Besides, it'll be of more use to you than me. I've enjoyed having it for a time, but I don't think I have the right kind of magic to use it—there's something human mixed into the spell. You might have better luck turning Merlin's object to your will.'

'Thanks. If I do find out how to use it, it'll be a real help in locating Arthur.'

'Have a go now. I'm curious to see how it works.'

Taking it out and unwrapping it, Roxy laid the mirror on her knees. It was heavy, about the size of an ostrich egg sliced in half, smooth and cold. She could feel the ripples of power under the surface, the swirl of untapped magic waiting to hatch.

'It's really, really strong.'

Trix-E bent over her shoulder, their two faces reflected back up at them—pixie and human. 'Don't burn your fingers now.'

'Any idea how this works?'

'No.'

'Thanks.' Roxy laughed and the spurt of her breath misted the surface of the glass. She wiped it away, clearing a space as if it were a clouded window. Instead of their reflection, the surface now whirled with flickering images. Rick was sitting in a seat with the world flashing by. He looked stressed, his hair sticking up every which way as he thrust his fingers through it in exasperation.

'Who is that?' The end of Trix-E's blond plait fell forward to brush the surface, the scarlet feather ornaments resting on the glass. Rick vanished.

'Rick. He was on a train so it must be now.' Roxy tucked the plait back under her friend's patchwork hat—another gain from the carnival.

'Well done, Roxy! You got the mirror to work.'

Roxy wrinkled her nose at her reflection in the glass, her pale face distorted so it looked like Saturn with its asteroid belt. 'Well, I was thinking of him when I laughed. Perhaps that is part of the spell.'

'Try again. See something else.'

Roxy held the image of Tiago and Linette in her mind and breathed on the glass again. Her reflection flicked off to be replaced by . . .

'Nothing. It didn't work. I thought I did exactly the same as before.'

'Spelled objects of this kind aren't easy to deci-pher. You must've missed a step.'

'When I've time, I'll have to practise. At least that shows me where I need to be.'

'On a train heading north, playing catch-up.'

'Exactly. Look after everyone, Trix-E.'

'Look after yourself, my friend.'

Chapter 12

THE Southampton to Manchester express arrived at its destination. The hitch for the passengers was that this was the middle of a moor in Scotland.

'What the blazes is going on?' asked the conductor, scratching his head as the mutterings of discontent grew around him. He rubbed the condensation from the window, hoping that the misty dark green mountains would transform into Manchester's streets.

Rick slid down in his seat, trying to look inconspicuous. The twins had disappeared up the front of the train some hours ago and not returned. He had noticed they had succeeded in getting their way when he saw the sun sinking over the Lake

District on the left-hand side of the train. He was surprised no one else had twigged to the fact that the train had gone seriously off track. Perhaps the twins had cast one of their forget-about-it charms on all the windows.

Cobweb breezed back into the carriage, looking very pleased with herself. 'Isn't it beautiful?' She gestured to the star-netted sky over the dark expanse of wilderness. A crescent moon peeped over the crest of a hill. A distant road with passing cars looked like a string of diamonds and rubies. 'See, I told you it would be perfect: we are far enough north now and not a polly-man in sight to stop us.'

'Policeman,' Rick corrected her automatically. 'Can we get off now?'

She nodded. 'Naturally.'

'Ladies and Gentlemen.' It was Archer's voice on the speaker system. 'Welcome to bonnie Scotland. Your driver, Jock Campbell, and I wish you all a very pleasant stay. He says there is a very good pub about a mile east of here if you need refreshment. He says he does. We hope you have all enjoyed this excursion from the humdrum of your lives. Goodbye and goodnight.'

'What!' the conductor thundered. 'Jock, you stupid idiot—you must be drunk!' He pushed his way through the crowds of irate passengers, heading for a reckoning with his colleague.

Cobweb settled back in her seat with a contented sigh.

'What did you do to the driver?' whispered Rick.

'Oh, nothing. It was easier than you would think. He just believes he's dreaming. He really wanted to come home so we let his wish come true.'

'This is outrageous!' screeched the businesswoman, stabbing at the buttons of her Blackberry. 'I'm contacting my lawyer!'

'An extra complimentary packet of crisps, madam?' asked the trolley attendant feebly.

'I wouldn't touch the food on that if I were starving! It looks as though it has been fed to pigs!'

'A horse actually.' Cobweb smiled at her. 'Don't you like our little surprise?'

Rick tugged her away from the lady before she got crowned with a briefcase. 'Let's get out while we can.'

They entered the guard's van, shutting the door behind them before anyone followed. The enclosed space smelled like a stable due a good mucking out. When Cobweb opened the rear door, Peony was delighted to jump down onto the soft heather and gallop a little to stretch his legs. At least the mess was a problem Rick did not have to leave for some unfortunate person to sort out. He whispered a rapid cleansing charm, sluicing the manure out and on to the tracks. He then followed the horse and Cobweb. Archer must have climbed out of the driver's cab as he was standing with his sister, grinning from ear to ear.

'Been enjoying yourself?' Rick asked gruffly.

'Enormously.'

'What about the poor driver?'

'Oh, he's only a human.'

That was the last straw. All the frustration of the past few hours boiled over. 'You Fey are just so arrogant! Only a human? He probably has family who rely on him—what are they going to say when he gets kicked out of his job and sent for psychiatric treatment for driving his hobspitting train TO SCOTLAND?'

Cobweb wagged her finger at him. 'Now, now. No need to get angry, Rick Halfdane. The railway servant was only doing what he was told.'

'Yes, but how is he going to prove that to his employers, you pair of Fey maniacs?'

Archer raised his eyebrow at his sister. 'The human has a bit of a temper.'

'Speaking to us in a very disrespectful manner too,' said Cobweb.

'My temper is not the issue here—it's that poor man's job!'

'Oh well, if it makes you feel any better.' Cobweb pointed her finger at the driver's cab. 'I can't bear travelling with a grumpy companion.'

'What have you done now?' Rick covered his face with his hands.

'I tied him up with the Fey fetter charm. Now he'll remember being knocked out and taken hostage. Some mysterious person . . .'

'Also known as me,' interjected Archer proudly.

'Took over the train and drove it as his what-you-ma-call-it.'

'Getaway vehicle,' Archer supplied. 'I read a newspaper about that in the driver's cab. Very exciting.'

Rick threw his hands in the air. 'I give up.'

Cobweb pouted. 'Aren't you pleased with us? We've just saved the man's job.'

A police helicopter appeared over the hilltop, searchlight sweeping the ground.

'Oh look, more polly-men!' Cobweb observed merrily.

Rick had had enough. Thanks to the twins, he couldn't even wait for Roxy. He would have to return for her when the coast was clear. 'That's our signal to go. Make a door.'

'I didn't come all this way just to leave. I'm going to look around first. We have goblin sacks of time—the polly-men are busy with the train and not interested in us. I glimpsed a lovely little ruined castle just back there over the hill.' Cobweb cast a little hag's haze to hide herself from the helicopter and started walking—hopping over a stream meandering across the moor. 'Archer, are you coming?'

Archer rubbed his hands. 'Yes, I think we have time for a little adventure. No point rushing back.'

As if the train hijack wasn't adventure enough!

Peony nuzzled Rick gently.

'Your breath smells of cheese and onion crisps.'

Peony snorted.

'OK, I'll get on. We'd better follow those two nutcases before they do anything else insane.' He mounted the horse, exhausted by the aftermath of his rage. 'Can you trail them while I contact Roxy?'

Peony trotted off in the wake of the twins. Behind them the clatter of the helicopter landing on the far side of the train drowned out the noise of angry passengers.

Having told Roxy where to meet them on his shell, Rick did not expect her to arrive much before midday, so was surprised when she reached their camp soon after dawn.

'Hey, anyone home?' she called, as she scrambled up the slope of the old moat.

Rick was having a wash in a stone trough by what had once been the stables. Aethel bathed in a patch of sun beside him. He shook the water from his eyes and smiled with delight as Roxy hurried towards him.

'I'm all wet,' he warned her.

That didn't stop her giving him a crushing hug, which he returned.

'How did you get here so fast?' he asked.

'I caught an overnight coach to Glasgow because some idiot had hijacked a train.' He had already confessed this in their shell conversation.

'Imagine that,' he said dryly.

Roxy grinned, a pixie clip of green feathers in her hair fluttering. 'The coach took me nearly all the way here and I was able to get some rest. I got out when I saw the helicopters and police vehicles, then followed my nose.' She rubbed her palms together. 'So, where are your companions in crime?'

Rick held up his hands. 'I'm innocent, really I am.'

She nudged him. 'Of course you are. The Rick I know wouldn't go round purposely creating havoc.'

'It seems to follow me anyway.'

'Result of a Fey upbringing, I guess. How're your magic levels?' She flexed her hands, releasing a little shower of gold and silver sparks.

One of the side effects on the changelings of coming to Earth, the source of green power, was that they were super-charged, the capacity for wielding magic developed in Avalon filled to overflowing. Rick rolled his shoulders. 'I'm OK. I ran myself dry with a hover charm on my horse.'

'*Your* horse?' teased Roxy. 'You sound like a pixie.'

Rick gave her a sheepish smile. 'You should have seen him dodging the elfshots and lightning bolts the ogres threw at us—amazing. Peony and I have formed a partnership. I can't really think of him as Queen Mab's any more.'

'Escaping death by the skin of your teeth does that to you. What about your new friends? Is their magic under control?'

'Yes. They've not noticed any change. It was the same with the other Fey bloods we met here, remember: only humans seem to get the added boost. I wonder why?'

'Because we've come home.'

'That must be it.' He put his arm around her and they stood for a moment looking over the misty glen. 'Amazing, isn't it? So beautiful and, well, normal. Just ordinary life but it's a miracle.'

'Yes, it is. We can't let Oberon spoil it, Rick. I know humans have already messed up big time taking too much, but handing it over to Oberon is no answer. He's going to be here very soon—I just feel it.'

Rick wished the peaceful moment could have lasted but Roxy was right; they needed to prepare for the crisis that was fast approaching. 'You're more right than you know. I heard him announce that he's getting rid of humans and taking over the Earth power source.'

'What!'

'It's not just us changelings now on his hit list.'

Roxy muttered a string of inventive pixie curses.

'Do you think it's the best plan, going to fetch Arthur?' he asked.

'I'm sure. My pixie friend, Trix-E, even suggested he might look after us. She thinks of Arthur as a kind of surrogate dad. Pixies are really big on family.'

A surrogate dad? Rick had longed to know his own parents but the tide of history had carried them out of his reach. He didn't even know where they were buried, his old Anglo-Saxon home covered over by a supermarket car park. Naturally, he had heard the stories about King Arthur, but no one had ever mentioned his capacity to be a good father as far as he could remember.

Roxy must have sensed the direction of his thoughts. 'We need someone to train us—someone with experience; someone used to Round Table magic—if we are going up against Oberon. Arthur seems the best choice as he's like us and will understand our enemy.'

She was only repeating the arguments he had already made to himself, but somehow with her saying it out loud he felt more confident. 'Yes, we need him. I know I'm the eldest, but I just can't look after everyone when I'm not even sure of how to protect myself.'

'Oh Rick, you twit,' Roxy batted him in the stomach, 'we don't expect you to look after us. Haven't you notice how rubbish we are at listening to you? So you can give up that idea already. No, we need King Arthur. Only thing is, I'm a bit worried that Arthur's been in solitary confinement for some years now, about sixteen if I've counted right. He might not react well when we break in on his isolation.'

Rick put his jacket back on, hot where the sun had warmed the leather. 'Or he might be so grateful someone has come to get him that he welcomes us with open arms. I wish we had a way of checking on him.'

'Ah, funny you should say that.' She produced the scrying glass from her bag with a flourish learned from the pixies. 'I am now the proud owner of the mirror, formerly Morgan's, and, before that, the centrepiece of the Round Table.'

Rick shook his head in amazement. 'You've got Morgan's mirror?'

'More accurate to say it's *Merlin's* mirror.'

'How on earth did you manage it?'

Roxy decided it was time to come clean. 'I didn't.

When I tried, I got put in the stocks. Miz-Begotten and Trix-E took it for me. If you really want something stolen, ask a pixie.'

'Go on then—see if you can locate Arthur with it.'

Roxy sat cross-legged on the ground. 'The thing is, Rick, I've not mastered the magic yet. I got a glimpse of you, but when I looked for Tiago and Linette I saw nothing.'

'Give it another go—we've got a moment or two before I have to wake the twins.' He sat down beside her and watched with interest as she breathed on the surface.

'What are you doing?'

'I'm trying to hold Arthur in my mind as I mist the glass with my breath.'

'Is it working?'

'Um, no.'

'Try again.'

'Duh!' Annoyed by him stating the obvious, she puffed at the mirror. This time their reflections vanished. The surface of the mirror cleared and tiny knights rode across a bleak moor. At their head, on a black stallion, rode a tall man with long brown hair and a piercing gaze, looking very cross about something. He wore lightweight armour worked from leather and decorated with embossed dragons. A circular shield was slung over his shoulder and at his side hung a jewelled scabbard with Excalibur written in gold wire down the length.

'Got him!' Rick bent closer. 'Amazing—do you see how he holds himself in the saddle?'

'Yes, but this must be from the past, right?'

Rick's finger hovered over the surface as if he wished to touch the man in the glass. 'Probably. Is that how this works?'

'I was told it shows the past and present. The future is beyond even Merlin's magic.'

'So can you find Arthur now?'

Roxy closed her eyes and tried to imagine what he would be like today, but it was impossible to dislodge the hero in the mirror from her head. She tried making him sixteen years older, but the picture didn't feel authentic, and when she opened her eyes the mirror returned to showing their two faces in its surface.

'Sorry. That was a bit of a failure.'

'Don't say that. You did well. I bet it takes years of practice to master. When you get a chance, perhaps you can see if there's any glimpse of Merlin as well.'

Roxy wrapped up the mirror again and lodged it safely in her bag. 'I think we'd better get going. As soon as we cross back into Avalon we'll be losing time rapidly here.'

'OK. Ready to meet Archer and Cobweb? I told them you were coming.'

She shuddered. 'I think I'd prefer to meet Peony. I'm not sure I'll warm to anyone who is so closely related to Oberon. Oh, before I forget.' She retrieved Rick's sword from her bag and handed it over.

His face lit up when he saw what she had brought him. 'Thank you—I thought I'd lost it for ever.'

'I have a feeling you might need it.'

The twins were still asleep, lying in a bed of heather, back to back, Archer with his hand on his bow, Cobweb grasping her sword. Peony stood to one side, grazing on a patch of grass peeping between the stones. Rick cleared his throat. The Fey sprang to their feet, ready for battle, Cobweb holding her sword low, Archer with his arrow fitted to the bowstring aiming over her head.

Rick waved cautiously to show them it was friends approaching. 'Good morning. Roxy's arrived so we're ready to go when you are.'

Cobweb sheathed her weapon. 'You could've been killed. Don't startle us from sleep again, human.'

'And how exactly am I supposed to wake you up then?'

Roxy muttered something that sounded like 'bucket of cold water should do it'. He tried not to laugh.

'You don't wake us up.' Cobweb cast a little spell

on her hair which obediently began winding itself in a braid for her. 'Our servants know they can only come in when we give them permission.'

'Actually, he's not your servant,' said Roxy.

Cobweb raised one perfect arch of a brow. 'This is your little friend, I suppose? The one who ruptured the timeline?'

Roxy folded her arms and tapped her foot. 'I was escaping your father's murderous guards at the time. They left me with no other option.'

Archer tugged his sleep-rumpled tunic straight. 'She's a fiery little human, isn't she? Perhaps we should leave her behind. I don't think Mother would like her. We can't risk bringing badly behaved creatures into her retreat.'

'Badly behaved!' snorted Roxy. 'I'm not the one who hijacked a train for a lark!'

'She'll be fine. I'll vouch for her,' said Rick quickly. 'Are you ready to go yet?'

Cobweb stretched languorously. 'I suppose so. I could do with a proper bed tonight. I don't much like sleeping on the ground. But I do like this castle. Do you think we could come back and repair it?'

She snapped her fingers, casting a brief restoration illusion over the place, letting them all enjoy the image of the castle in its heyday—soaring grey stone walls, scarlet banners and blue flags flying.

'No time,' said Archer.

She let it shimmer back to its actual state. 'We'd better go then. I do want to see Mother again. She'll be on our side about Mab, I'm sure of it.'

'And she'll give us breakfast,' added Archer, beginning to weave the door.

'Do we need to do something to keep the balance?' asked Rick, mindful of the near miss they had had the day before.

'I'll send a few forest creatures through. I think that should hold the balance for now.'

'Nothing too magical.' Rick had a sudden vision of white Fey stags wandering the Scottish glens. They would blend until they started producing sparks from their antlers in the rutting season.

'You will cease to speak to me as if I am stupid!' Archer's spell rose from his palm, a coil of magic. It bent, split and hovered over them like a rainbow on a waterfall. He poked his head through the tunnel-sized gap then retreated. 'Good, exactly where I wanted us to be—on the doorstep of Deepdene Sylvan Palace. It's a hunting lodge, but quite comfortable. And here they come.' He stood back as five enormous silver bears ambled through the doorway between the worlds.

'Bears. You've swapped us for wild bears?' Roxy exchanged a look of misery with Rick.

'This country has bears. I checked before selecting them.'

'*Had* bears. They were hunted into extinction. And none of them were ever silver.'

'Well, now Scotland has them again.' Archer smiled at the family group sniffing the stone ruins. 'One of them is expecting cubs, so that's a bit of luck, isn't it?'

'Do they act like this all the time?' Roxy asked Rick in a low voice.

Rick nodded. 'I've learned just to go with it. It saves wasting energy on futile protests.'

'Come on then, if you are sticking to your idea of finding this Arthur person you mentioned.' Cobweb called over her shoulder as she strode through the door.

'You told them about Arthur?' whispered Roxy furiously.

'Not the full plan—just that I wanted to find out if he were dead or alive. I had to say something to explain why we wanted to go through, and why we're not staying with them.'

'Do you trust them?'

'Well . . . um . . . maybe.'

'I see.' Taking a calming breath, Roxy put her hand on Peony's mane and walked through with him. Rick and Archer brought up the rear.

'Welcome back to Avalon,' Cobweb said, circling back to face Rick, her eyes glittering with mischief. 'I think we'd better put you in chains.'

Chapter 13

'WHAT! Why?' Roxy flew at Cobweb to push her away from Rick. Rick hauled Roxy back before spells started to be exchanged.

'Calm down, human.' Cobweb's hand went to the hilt of her sword but she didn't draw it. 'A little touchy, aren't we?'

Roxy's reply sounded more like a growl.

Archer stepped in to separate the girls. 'Human, my sister is right. Even in exile, our mother's court is full of our father's spies. If we march in with you running loose, he'll have the excuse he's waiting for to make her exile even harsher.'

'And you didn't think to mention this before?' asked Rick. Like Roxy, he was quick to be suspicious of any Fey politics. Humans never came out well.

'We didn't know you were going to come all the way with us.' Cobweb took a set of silver chains from her belt and dangled them before Roxy's nose.

Roxy took a step back. 'Can't we just leave and, you know . . .' she nodded towards the west where the ocean lay, 'go check on Arthur.'

Archer shook his head. 'You can't travel through this forest without our mother's permission. The guards will shoot you on sight.'

'Do you believe them, Rick?'

Did he? 'I think it'll be OK.' He held out his wrists. Going through Titania's palace looked as though it was the quickest and surest way of proceeding with their quest. 'I'm going to put my faith in your word, Archer. I hope I won't be disappointed.'

Archer moved behind him and took Rick's sword from his scabbard. 'I'll look after this. We can't bring you in chained up and still armed.'

'You'd better look after it.' Rick hated being without his weapon having only just regained the sword. He still had magical defences, and plenty of them, but nothing felt quite so secure as being able to wield his favourite blade. Aethel curled a little tighter round his arm. No one would be removing her without a fight.

Roxy only reluctantly offered her wrists for the chains. Her eyes were blazing with fury. 'If you let us down, Archer, I'll seek you out and extract the most painful revenge I can think of!'

Archer laughed and chucked her under the chin. She snapped at his finger but he had removed it in time. 'You should have more faith in our word, little human.'

'Why should I? I've met your father.'

His smile dimmed.

Now they were secured to the twins' satisfaction, Rick had a chance to look around. They had arrived in a paddock that stretched behind a beautiful rambling mansion built of golden stone. The moss-covered roof was decorated with many towering chimneys, so that the whole place looked like something that had grown out of the surrounding forest rather than been imposed, a grove of stone saplings seeking the sun. A gentle hum filled the air—bees wandering from flower to flower, the rustle of leaves, the murmur of a nearby stream somewhere in the forest. Even the tree canopies were honey-gold and caramel, decked out in festive autumn colours.

Archer took the harness off the horse and placed it on the top bar of the fence. 'Stay here and rest,' he told Peony. 'I'll send a groom to tend to your needs.'

Kicking up his hooves, tail fluttering like a flag, the Barbary galloped to the other end of the field, wheeled round and passed them, enjoying his holiday. At least someone was happy.

Forging a path through the long yellowing grass, the Fey twins and their prisoners approached the house. There were no formal gardens. The forest clearing extended to the main entrance. The lack of flowerbeds was made up for by the abundance of butterflies and moths that flitted from stalk to stalk. A heavy, almost sleepy atmosphere permeated the air. Rick could sense magic seeping through the soles of his feet; the link to the green power of Earth must be strong.

'Where does this forest draw its energy from?' he asked.

'The sunken ring of volcanoes that stretch between Ireland and Scotland—Giant's Causeway one side, Fingal's Cave on the other. It is dormant now, but still provides a steady trickle of power,' answered Archer. 'It was magnificent in its day they say—the Fey used to cross over to watch the explosions. That was before you humans arrived.'

Rick blinked. Archer seemed more majestic in this place—more than he had in his father's cold palace of stone courtyards. His blue eyes glowed as if lit softly from within. Cobweb too seemed more . . . well, just more.

The heavy front doors of the palace were carved of golden oak. The figures were taken from the forest: stag, boar, squirrel, wood sprite. In the centre was the likeness of Cerunnos, forest prince, with his magical horns—the most mysterious of the Dark Folk, older even than the Fey. Legend said he resembled a stag, yet could walk on two legs as well as four.

'Does Cerunnos rule here?' asked Rick.

Archer shook his head. 'I don't think so. But neither is he ruled by our father. He keeps himself to himself in the wild places. He wouldn't be found under a roof like this. I believe his magic and his mind are far older than ours, and my father would no more claim to order his business than he would the waves of the sea. There would be no point.'

'But your mother has him on her doors.'

Cobweb grinned. 'No doubt to anger Father.'

'I've changed my mind: I think I'm going to like your mother,' muttered Roxy.

Archer knocked on the door with the hilt of a dagger he kept on his belt. There was a sound of scuffling and locks being turned, then the doors swung open. A short, fat pixie with a mop of black spiky hair took one look at the visitors before bowing low with evident dismay.

'Your highnesses! If only you had sent word! To greet you like this—O, bless my toes—please, come in, come in.'

'It is no matter, Joll-E. Can you tell our mother we have arrived?' Cobweb handed him her sword, which he placed reverently on a side table.

'Of course, your highness.' The little butler almost fell over as he backed away, still bowing.

'No wonder they have such big heads,' Roxy whispered to Rick, 'if their servants treat them like this.'

Rick nodded, but his thoughts were still on this palace of marvels. The entrance hall stretched two storeys above them. A stained glass window over the door bathed the area in multi-coloured light, birds and trees spilling on to the rush carpet. It had to be spelled glass because the reflections were moving like the animals and plants they depicted.

'I like this place.' Rick rubbed his hands in the golden light, feeling as though he were taking a bath in sunbeams.

'Yes. It feels somehow warm and real.' Roxy stood so that a humming bird light could flit across the bare skin of her forearms.

The sound of footsteps approaching rapidly drew them out of their private conversation. A Fey robed in pale green was running towards them, hands outstretched. Behind her came her courtiers, all eager to greet Titania's children.

'My clever darlings! You came to see me!' As tall as her son and daughter, Titania caught them in a hug, her primrose-coloured hair mingling with their dark and fair heads. Her complexion was as pale as Cobweb's, making her appear delicate, though, in view of what Rick knew about the Fey, that was probably a false impression. Most of them were as hard as nails. 'Does your father know you're here?'

'We had to flee,' admitted Archer. 'Mab has been trying to force us out ever since she married him.'

Titania flinched at the name of her rival. 'Then you are doubly welcome here. But what are these creatures you bring with you?'

'Humans. They've escaped their prison but have been useful to us on our journey here. We promise to keep them under control.'

Titania embraced her children again. 'Humans—how peculiar! But, of course you will control them. Come—tell me of your adventures. Shall I have one of my attendants see to these humans of yours?'

'That won't be necessary. We are responsible for them so we'll keep them with us.' Archer gave Roxy a quelling look, aware she was about to explode at his high-handed tone.

A severe Fey with hair tugged back in a complicated knot at the nape of her neck gave a cough.

Was that a resigned sigh from Titania? 'Yes, Lunila?'

'Perhaps your ladyship is not aware that the king has ordered all changelings be captured and turned over to his guard. Would you like me to summon his troops on your behalf to fetch these strays?'

Titania tapped her cheek with one perfect mother-of-pearl fingernail. 'When did he give this order?'

'Earlier today, your ladyship.'

'And how do you know this?'

Lunila looked a little uncomfortable. 'I . . . er . . . keep abreast of the news from court in hopes of finding a way to restore you to favour, my lady. This is one such opportunity.'

Cobweb exchanged a covert glance with Archer. Rick could almost hear their thoughts—that at least one spy had just revealed herself. They had warned him that the court was riddled with Oberon's agents.

'Did your news make any mention of my children?' Titania's question appeared carefree, but there was no mistaking the hint of steel behind it.

'Only that the king is desperate to know their whereabouts.' The Fey touched her chest gracefully. 'His heart was pierced by their defection, but he wishes to forgive them. Their safety is his main concern.'

'How kind of him. I am sure no one here will doubt that they are safe with their mother.'

There were murmurs of agreement from other members of the court.

'Perhaps you would be so kind as to tell him that I will keep them with me for the present. He will be relieved to know that they are in good hands. Their wayward behaviour is doubtless explained by being kept from me for so long.' She brushed Cobweb's hair behind her ear affectionately.

'I . . . I will see if I can pass such a message on. But the humans?'

'They are not important.' Titania gave a dismissive wave of a petal-like hand. 'Leave them for the moment. I am more interested in my children's future. I trust you will make my case persuasively.'

Lunila bobbed a curtsey and withdrew.

Titania watched to make sure she had truly gone. 'Come, my children: we have much to discuss. Joll-E, prepare my private sitting room in the arbour for my guests. Cobweb, collect your weapon.' She lowered her voice so that only those close to her could hear. 'We are not safe even here.'

Roxy slipped her hand into Rick's. He shared her feeling of unease. They were so worthless to the Fey, even those who had acted as their allies; it would be no surprise to find them being turned out, or turned over to Oberon, if that suited the former queen.

'I wish we'd stayed on Earth,' Roxy murmured, as they followed on the heels of the three Fey.

They left the house through a set of crystal-glazed doors and proceeded across a field of poppies. A little party of pixie servants trotted ahead of them, laden with silk cushions and a tray of refreshments; they were making for an arbour made of the entwined trunks of a ring of silver birches, Titania's private retreat.

'What do you think they'll do about us?' Roxy asked.

Rick squeezed her hand. 'I see no reason why they won't let us go after Arthur. They don't seem anxious to please their father so the suggestion of sending us back as some kind of peace offering will be ignored. Probably.'

'And if it isn't?'

'Well, I've not revealed how strong my magic is to them. How are you feeling?'

Roxy rubbed her ribs. 'Pretty full. But you know I'm really rubbish at strength spells; my magic is more of the pixie sort—charms and cunning.'

'We'll probably need both if things go wrong. And there's Aethel. Archer knows about her, but he doesn't understand exactly what she can do.'

Dismissing her servants, Titania sank down prettily on a long, low sofa, arranging the watered green silk of her gown in a graceful swirl over her legs. Her children sat on cushions at her side. There were no seats for Rick and Roxy so they were left standing to one side. Titania poured three cups of lemon-scented tea.

'We cannot talk freely with your pets listening. You will have to put them somewhere else,' she announced, nibbling a feather-shaped biscuit.

Archer got up and stretched. 'If you insist. Really, Mother, they have been loyal to us. I do not suspect them of treachery.'

'Have you learned nothing from court, Archer? They may not want to betray you, but if they hear and are then captured it will not take your father long to wring the information from them. It is safer for all of us if they do not know anything.'

Rick cleared his throat and bowed. 'Your ladyship, we would prefer to leave. We came here on a mission.'

Titania raised one sculpted brow.

'They want to go to the Isle of the Dragon,' Archer explained.

'And do what?'

'Speak to that human Morgan trapped there—Arthur.'

Titania began to laugh—it wasn't a nice sound. 'You must be mad! He is vicious.'

'You've met him, your ladyship?' Roxy dared to ask.

'Once, shortly after he was caught, when I was still married to the king. It was thought to be amusing to visit the patient in his asylum. He ranted away at us, promising he would return and finish us off, shouting about swords and wizards and round tables—quite entertaining, I suppose, if you like that kind of thing. I found him rather pitiable. Then again, he was suffering from his wounds, had some kind of fever I believe. Perhaps he is quieter now. Or dead.' She shrugged. 'But no, I cannot let you go there, not with my former husband's spies watching my every move. He will immediately charge me with conspiracy. You must be confined somewhere where you can do no damage. See to it, Archer.'

'What!' Roxy's face flushed with anger. She turned on Cobweb. 'You gave your word!'

Cobweb shook her head. 'I've not broken any promise to you. You won't be harmed. Just obey my mother and nothing bad will happen to you.'

Archer sighed and got up. 'Come on, you two. I've somewhere in mind where you can wait comfortably.'

Rick felt the magic tug on his wrists. Archer was dragging them after him even if they refused to go. Roxy had dug in her heels but that only succeeded in her creating furrows in the grass as she was towed along. He decided to go with more dignity so walked quickly after the prince.

'At least open a door and send us back!' he pleaded, addressing Archer's back.

'Can't do that either. You've been seen.' He took them down a flight of mossy stone steps to a pool, empty of water but half filled with dead leaves. At one end was a cage made of a strange lattice of knobbly sticks. 'The old firebird pen. This should keep you safe.'

'Keep. Us. Safe!' Roxy was spitting with rage. 'Archer, you are a pile of troll dung. I'm not going in there. Get these chains off me before I bite you!'

'You can try.' He gave another shrug as if to say she didn't stand a chance. 'Go in, or do I call the guards to push you inside?'

The magical drag on the chains stopped at the door to the cage. Rick took a step away. The pull started again. 'What . . . ?'

Archer shoved Rick in the back so he stumbled inside. He then poked Roxy in with Rick's sword. 'Go on. You'd be happier together, wouldn't you?'

Roxy flounced in, her eyes bright with something that looked suspiciously like tears of anger. 'I hate you. I hate all Fey. I hope you rot in a bog with mushrooms growing out of your ears.'

Archer seemed amused. 'Good threat. I'm warming to you, human. But it isn't as bad as you think. If you used that brain of yours, you'd work that out for yourself.' He closed the door and chucked in a key. 'For the chains. You won't need them in there. I'll come back for you later.'

Rick snatched up the key before Archer changed his mind.

'You trusted them,' Roxy said bitterly, sitting down on the leaf-strewn floor of the cage.

Rick felt a pang of self-loathing. 'Yeah. My character judgement isn't great. I liked Professor Marmaduke at the start, didn't I?'

'And he turned out to be a mad Mage rebel in disguise.' She held out her wrists so Rick could undo her chains, then did the same for him. 'Do you think they planned this?'

Rick sat next to her. 'No. They just aren't that interested in helping us either. They regard us as somewhere only a little above a faithful hound, so you can understand why we've ended up in this ridiculous position—a hobspitting cage!'

Roxy turned to meet his gaze. 'You're angry too?'

'Of course, I'm furious—at myself mostly, as I should've guessed. But I thought, if we got this far and they left us, I could blast our way out. It doesn't solve the problem of getting back to Earth but it would at least get us on our way to see Arthur.'

'Who is insane and rants?'

'Yeah, that's the one. Though as his character reference came from a Fey queen, perhaps we should ignore it and go anyway?'

'OK. Go for it. What spell are you going to use?'

Rick ran his fingers over the structure. He hadn't met anything quite like it before. 'If it was a cage for firebirds, I guess it was made flameproof. I think I'll use elfshot. Take cover in case of splinters.' They hunkered down in the leaves. 'Ready?'

'Yes.' Roxy's reply was muffled as she had covered her face with her arms.

Rick drew a thread of magic from his supply and spun it into a hard bullet of elfshot, priming it to explode on impact. 'One, two, three!' He threw it like a cricket ball, aiming for the bars as if they were an undefended wicket. The shot cannoned towards them—then vanished.

'Have you done it yet?' Roxy asked.

'Hang on a moment.' Rick threw another shot but the same thing happened. 'Roxy, there's something wrong with my magic. Look.'

She raised her head in time to see a third bullet of power puff out of existence. 'Let me try.' Her own shot, less powerful but still good enough for the job, flew from her fingers and disappeared before hitting the bars. 'It's not your magic—it's all magic.'

Rick examined the bars more closely then knocked his forehead against one. 'I understand now.'

'What?'

'These aren't branches. These are bones—dragon bones.'

Roxy's expression darkened. 'And you can't perform magic on dragons. The perfect Fey prison.'

Chapter 14

ROXY paced the cell while Rick tried kicking out the bars. It was no good: the dragon bones were welded together and his boot made no impact on the hard grey surface. The only result was an aching foot. He limped to a pile of leaves and sat down heavily, letting his arms drop wearily by his sides.

'Hey!' cried Roxy. 'What about Aethel? Can't she get out?' Roxy tapped Rick's arm bracelet that had slid from beneath his cuff.

'And what good would that do us?'

'I don't know, but maybe she could go and find the key to the door.'

It was worth the attempt. Rick shook the snake off his wrist. 'See if you can get past the barrier, Aethel.'

The snake slid to the bars—there was plenty of space for her to wriggle through. She had got to within an inch of them when she suddenly stopped, her head turned back to metal, her body writhing impatiently behind, still in flesh form. She was stuck. Rick pulled her out of range and the head snapped back to life, angry and hissing, ready to strike.

'What happened there?' asked Roxy, wisely keeping well back until the snake cooled down from the indignity of being half and half for a moment.

'Aethel is a torc turned to magical snake, not a snake turned to magical jewellery,' Rick explained, stroking Aethel to calm her. 'When she got near the bars the dragon anti-magic must have made her go back into her original form. She's not happy about it.'

'Don't blame her.' Roxy shuddered. 'It looked horrible.'

'Sorry, Legless, but we had to try.' Rick wound her round his neck and let her settle back to her favourite form, resting on his collar bone where she had a good view of the world.

'So that's not going to work. What's left?' Roxy paced the cage again.

'I'm going to sleep.' Rick made a nest in the leaves and curled up.

'What! How can you sleep at a time like this?'

'I can't see any other use for this cage, can you? I guess Archer is going to come and let us go eventually. I could either fret, like you are doing, or I could catch up on the sleep I've missed since yesterday.'

Roxy slumped down beside him. 'Why do you have to be so sensible?'

'Because I've run out of mental energy to be anything else. But you go ahead; I know you like stomping.'

She pulled a face. 'I won't give those terrible twins the satisfaction of seeing me all het up thanks to them.'

Head resting on one arm, Rick smiled at her comical expression. 'Quite right. Make it look as if you are enjoying a holiday.'

Roxy threw a handful of leaves at him for being so infuriating.

Rick had another idea that might placate her. 'You know, you could use the time to look in the scrying glass again.'

'I might as well, I suppose.' She sat down beside him and took it out of her bag. 'But I'm so tired I'm not sure this will work.' The mirror rested in her lap like a giant's frozen teardrop. She bent over it and breathed. Unlike her previous attempts, the glass instantly cleared to show an image of Tiago asleep. His dark hair was spread on a white pillow. 'I did it! I was thinking of Tiago and how tired I was and there he is!'

Rick rubbed his eyes, trying to work it out. 'So the mirror responds when you get both the mood and the memory in tandem. It showed you Tiago when you were tired; Arthur in the old days when he was frustrated by something—that matched your mood. How did it first begin?'

'I saw you on the train when I laughed.'

'Yeah, that was pretty funny in a totally dementing Fey kind of way.'

Roxy gazed a little longer at the peaceful image of their friend. 'I wish we could wake him up and talk to him.'

'It's not a window, Roxy. That image might be from way back in the past.'

'Still, it's nice to see him.'

'Yeah, it is.'

They watched the sleeper for a few more moments then Roxy let the image fade. 'And if you're right, I just have to get in the right mood for the vision.'

'Tricky.'

'But that's Merlin's magic, isn't it? Twisty and complicated—and very, very powerful. Thinking about it, I don't envy Tiago and Linette having to find him.'

'Let's put it away for now. You can try again when you've slept.'

'OK. Budge up.'

Rick made space for her on the leaf bed and they managed to fall into an exhausted doze. Rick had only snatched a few hours' rest before he heard people approaching. He opened his eyes to find that the sun was setting, casting long shadows across the cage. The dampness under the leaves had begun to soak through; Rick's neck felt stiff when he sat up.

'Over here, mistress. Prince Archer locked them up so they wouldn't cause trouble.' It was the voice of the little butler, Joll-E. Rick's spirits lifted, hoping for refreshments at the very least.

The butler stopped on the edge of the dry pond above them, his form silhouetted against the sunset. A willowy Fey stood beside him, her long robes flapping in the breeze against her legs.

'So they are in some kind of cage, are they? I'll kill them first before we remove them from their pen,' Lunila announced. 'Oberon does not care if they are returned dead or alive.'

'Very good, my lady,' replied Joll-E, with a high-pitched giggle. 'I'll have some footmen help you carry the foul beasts away before Lady Titania notices.'

'Blood-thirsty little pixie!' Roxy growled, tumbling out of sleep straight into the crisis, her hands raised to form a magical shield.

Rick gently pushed her hands down. 'No need, remember?'

Lunila's blast of brute energy hurtled towards them—then vanished. She muttered a curse, then tried again. It was futile: no spell would reach them, even though they were sitting ducks.

'So that's what Archer meant about the cage being not so bad.' Roxy gave the Fey a taunting wave.

'Yeah, he made sure we were protected while stuck in here.'

'I feel a tiny bit better about him now. Just the smallest, microscopic bit, mind, but it might stop me poking him with your sword when he lets us out.'

Rick scrambled to his feet. 'Look out—she's coming in.'

Lunila had given up on the spells from a distance. She took the cage key from the butler, who had a huge ring which looked like it held the master copy of every key for the household, and swept down the steps towards them.

'Stay back!' she ordered, pointing a long quivering finger at them. 'So it is made of dragon bones—how unusual. I'll have to do this myself, I see.' She unfastened the door and stood back. 'Out, out—let me kill you out here.'

Roxy looked at Rick with incredulity. 'Does she really think we are that stupid?'

'Apparently so. The Fey have no idea about what it means to be a human.'

Lunila was shooting white sparks from her fingertips. 'Why don't you do as I say?'

'Maybe because you're a murderous old crone? Yeah, that might have something to do with it,' jeered Roxy.

'I'm afraid, my lady, you'll have to come in here and get us.' Rick was all politeness, which was somehow even more galling than Roxy's more apparent defiance. 'Aethel, guard.' The snake slid down his body and took up position in the open gate.

Lunila jumped back, lifting her skirts above her ankles. 'Joll-E, Joll-E, they've a snake! Dispose of the creature at once!'

The pixie darted forward, hesitated on seeing the hissing, spitting serpent, but then made a game attempt to strike Aethel back with a broom left behind by the gardeners. Aethel was too quick. She wriggled under the flailing besom and captured his leg.

'Get it off me!' squawked the pixie, trying to pull the snake from his plump calf.

Aethel sank in her metal teeth.

'Aargh! It bit me—it bit me!' he yelped. 'I'm going to die!'

'Control yourself, pixie!' barked Lunila. 'You're not dead yet, are you? Come away from the door and I'll destroy it.'

'Quick, Rick! Aethel is still in snake form even though they are in the doorway,' Roxy whispered urgently.

That meant the dampening field must not be strong enough to spread across the gap. Acting in unison, Rick and Roxy fired elfshots through the chink in the cage's defences. Skimming over the pixie's head as he hopped in agony, they struck Lunila squarely in the chest, propelling her back against the marble wall of the empty pond. She slumped to the ground unconscious. Rick and Roxy pushed Joll-E out of the way and burst free of the cage.

The pixie immediately cowered on the ground, hands over his head. 'Don't hurt me, don't hurt me!' he whimpered.

Aethel slid away from him in disgust.

'What do we do with them?' Roxy asked, kneeling down by Lunila to check that the Fey was still breathing.

'Obvious, isn't it?' Rick prodded Joll-E into the cage. 'Does Lady Titania know you serve another, pixie?'

'Please no—I'll be a good friend to you, I will. Just let me go. I won't tell anyone you escaped— I'll help you leave.' The pixie curled his little hands around the bars.

'No dignity—that's what I really don't like about you,' said Rick, as he helped Roxy drag the Fey into the cage. 'As if we'd trust anything you say after seeing you betray your employer.'

'I know pixies who would be ashamed to admit you were one of them.' Roxy glared at the pitiful butler.

'Please, kind, pretty human girl, please don't leave me here with her.' The pixie cast a petrified look at Lunila, who was beginning to stir. Rick turned the key on the cage.

'Hmm, I thought we were foul beasts? Release you—I don't think so.' Roxy skipped up the steps and did a little jig at the top to celebrate their victory. 'Yay, free at last!'

A hand landed on her shoulder. Rick rushed to help her, but too late—Archer had her in his grip. 'What is going on here?' The prince looked down on the new inhabitants of the cage. 'Why are they in there?'

'Let Roxy go!' Rick gathered a bolt of magic to force Archer to comply if necessary. He let it spin in his fist and gather strength.

Archer shook his head. 'No need for that, Rick. I only came to get you out.' He patted Roxy's shoulder. 'See, she can go if she likes.'

Rick reabsorbed the magic. It soaked back into his skin, leaving a little shimmer behind. 'Sorry. I'm just a bit touchy at the moment, what with those two trying to slaughter us.'

'Did they really?' Archer frowned at Joll-E.

'I'm disappointed in you, pixie. I thought you served my mother, not my father. You are the last member at court whom I would've suspected.' He bowed to Roxy and Rick. 'I thank you for revealing another traitor—an unexpected but useful outcome of your short imprisonment.'

'What are you going to do with us now?' Roxy rubbed her shoulder where his hand had been resting.

Archer caught up a curl of her hair and examined its coppery colour. 'Wonderful. Hmm, what was that?'

Rick wasn't sure he approved of Archer's newfound interest in Roxy. She seemed a little uncomfortable under his scrutiny. 'She asked what you were going to do now.'

Archer shrugged. 'The spies can stay in the cage until Mother has time to deal with them. You two can come with me.'

He led the way to the stables. Night had fallen. The fireflies were out in their battalions—little torches lighting the shadows under the branches of Deepdene Forest—matched above by the much more powerful glitter of the stars. Even the dark sparkled here.

Cobweb was waiting for them in the yard, Peony already saddled, along with a grey with a silver mane and tail.

'I imagine you must be hungry by now,' the princess announced, wasting no time on greetings. 'We've packed supplies in your saddle bags.'

'You're letting us go?' asked Rick.

'Of course, Elfric Halfdane. When you've found out if that man is alive or dead, return here and we will make a door to send you back home.' Cobweb led the grey to Roxy. 'Her name is Dewdrop. Treat her well.'

'Your mother agrees to this?' Rick checked Peony's harness and noticed that Archer had remembered to strap his sword to the saddle. They really did mean to let them go, then. 'Or is this another Fey lady we'll need to avoid in future?'

'She does.' Archer held out cupped hands to assist Roxy onto her horse. 'She would be here to wish you farewell but we decided it would be better for her to occupy her court so no one sees you depart. We may have caught two spies—'

'Two?' interrupted Cobweb. 'Who is the second?'

'Joll-E, can you believe it?'

'The toad! That will break Mother's heart. He knew the plans to build up the alliance.'

'Hush, no more about that, Cob. We don't want to burden our friends here with the knowledge. Indeed, I'm grateful they have been the instrument for revealing Joll-E's treachery to us. Despite my earlier doubts, it was right to bring them here. I'm sure Mother will agree.'

Rick's heart leapt at the hint of an alliance being formed—against Oberon surely? 'If we can help you with the thing you're not going to tell us about, please let us know. We might be able to help. You won't beat your father's armies alone.'

Archer laughed. 'You're very quick, human—too quick maybe. Thank you for the offer. I, for one, have learned today not to dismiss the help of changelings.'

'Oh, we're not that great, not compared to the Fey.'

'Hmm, let me think.' Archer started counting on his fingers. 'Hover charms on horses, a wide variety of glamours, elfshot to put out a powerful Fey and a very interesting choice of neck jewellery—no, I won't misjudge your usefulness in future.'

'And he's sweet.' Cobweb winked at Rick.

'I told you not to say that.' Archer closed his eyes in disgust.

'But it's true. Humans make very entertaining pets.'

'We're not pets!' Rick and Roxy said together.

Cobweb chuckled. 'I knew that would annoy you! You're such fun to tease.'

The twins were hopeless. There was a danger if he spent any longer in their company that Rick might begin to like them.

'Do you know the way to Arthur's island from here?' Roxy asked, prompting a welcome change of subject.

'The Isle of the Dragon. Peony and Dewdrop will show you. Just follow them.' Cobweb scratched the grey's nose in farewell.

'When you get back, don't come directly into the palace. You never know who might be watching there.' Archer adjusted the stirrup on Roxy's saddle. 'Send us a message and we will come and make the door for you.'

'How will we do that?'

Digging in his pocket, he passed over a shell. 'It is spelled to communicate with mine, just like the ones you and Rick have.' He met her eyes, letting her see a mischievous twinkle in their depths. 'Call me. Any time.'

Chapter 15

ROXY had not ridden since she was small. Living with the pixies, she had ridden bareback on the cart horses, but their ambling pace was nothing to what this fleet-footed mare could do.

Deciding she had to admit what the horse could no doubt sense, she leaned forward. 'Go easy on me now, please.'

The mare snickered, but not unkindly.

Actually, it turned out to be easier than she feared. The mare trotted along behind Peony on the narrow forest trail, resisting the urge to try any tricks to unseat her nervous rider. Roxy was helped by the high front and back of the saddle that made her almost as comfortable as sitting in a chair. She would have to do something very stupid to get thrown from Dewdrop.

Rick's glow-ball spell hovered in the air in front of them, lighting the path.

'I like this forest,' Rick said, after some time had passed. 'I spent the other night in the one by Dark Lore and that was horrid—a thick tangle, vicious. This one seems almost gentle.'

Roxy knew what he meant. The spaces under the trees were not choked with bushes and brambles but either grassy or thick with leaves. It reminded her of a huge deer park. 'I wonder how it came to be like this? It looks, well, sort of managed, if you know what I mean.'

'Maybe it is something to do with Cerunnos, the forest prince. I sense that his is a kind of magic far older and more natural than Oberon's. Archer said as much.'

'Where does he fit into the politics of this place? I thought Avalon drew all its green energy from Earth?'

'That's right. We've evolved to rely on each other. I wonder what world Cerunnos really belongs too? Perhaps, as a nature sprite, he came from Earth first?'

'Maybe. The stories about him are ancient.'

'Or he could belong to both somehow. I'd like to meet him.'

'Sadly, we'll have to postpone a visit—we've got a king to drag out of retirement.'

After a few hours' riding, the stately trees of Deepdene Forest gave way to a ridge of chalk hills. As the sun came up over the pastureland, Roxy noticed a herd of white deer grazing under an isolated Fey oak tree, bronze leaves blazing in the horizontal shafts of light. The air smelled different—no longer heavy with wood and earth, she could taste the salt of a nearby sea. She glanced up, scanning the skies. A few birds flew up high, tiny scratches on the pale blue.

'Do you think it's safe to continue in the open?'

'We've not much choice.' Rick raided the saddle bag and passed her an apple and sweet bread roll before choosing the same for his own breakfast. 'I'm hoping that Oberon has no idea what we're planning. I think he dismissed Arthur from his thoughts long ago. Still, we could travel under a glamour.'

'White deer?'

'Yes, that'll be good.'

'I've not had much practice casting glamours over more than myself.' Roxy bit into her apple.

'Thanks to the twins, I've been on a crash course. Just think of your personal space ballooning out to include Dewdrop. If she's anything like Peony, she'll not mind.'

Rick was right: it was easier than she antici-pated. Practising while she finished her meal, she was quite pleased when he complimented her on her illusion.

'You should stop doing yourself down, Roxy,' Rick said. 'You keep saying you only do small magic, but I'd say you have way more skill than you think.'

'Really?'

'Yes, really.'

Perhaps he was right. She had, after all, managed to blast those three muggers away from Simon back at the Notting Hill carnival.

Rick's thoughts, however, had been travelling forward to where they were going, not back to Earth. 'What do you think Arthur will make of us?' Rick asked.

'Honestly?'

He nodded.

'I don't know. He's been cut off from everything for so long. He won't know about us or about what's been happening on Earth. We at least had our train-ing, a library, and access to TV to see the pictures.'

'Modern life will be even more of a shock to him than it was to us. But I meant what will he think of us personally?'

'Well, you he'd think a dork and me charming, of course.'

'Thanks for that.' Rick hadn't taken it as the tease she intended.

'You know I don't mean that. Your dorkishness has plummeted recently; you are almost normal.'

'Wow, carry on piling on the compliments, why don't you.'

'Really, Rick, I don't know what he'll think.' Roxy knew he was desperate to impress a man he was already looking on as a father-figure, or mentor at least. 'Don't get your hopes up too high. He could be batty like Titania said.'

'She was OK in the end, wasn't she?'

'Surprisingly, I have to agree.'

'Wonders will never cease. I felt a bit jealous seeing the twins with her.'

'So did I. But I don't think I'd like her for my mother.'

'No?'

Roxy brushed her hair from her face. She had made it into a loose braid and tucked it inside her T-shirt at the back but bits kept flying free, bobbing behind her with the feathers from her hair clips. 'I suppose I already have parents in a way—the pixies.'

'I thought you said they were a nightmare?'

'To control in the human world, yes, but otherwise they are wonderful. They treat me like a daughter.'

'I didn't know that. I think I'm feeling envious of you now.'

'I know I'm luckier than most changelings. But don't build up your hopes about Arthur being like that for you, please. I don't want you to get hurt.'

Rick didn't answer.

Roxy sighed. 'Come on: let's pick up the pace. I think the horses want to gallop.'

They had no more conversation until they reached the coast. The Downs came to a sharp end with a sheer white cliff plunging down to a narrow rocky beach. About half a mile from the shore floated the misty blue shape of the Isle of the Dragon, its shape resembling the creature it was named after—sharp spine and two promontories recalling spread wings.

'How are we going to get there?' Roxy asked.

'Hover charm. Do you know how to do one?'

'In theory.'

'Best practise then, before you try it on Dewdrop.' Rick swung out of his saddle and put one of their bags on the ground. 'Go on, give it a go. Make this fly.'

Her first attempt was not encouraging: the bag almost plummeted over the edge of the cliff. Dewdrop gave an alarmed whinny.

'I totally suck at this,' Roxy declared, dispiritedly.

'Yup, you do.'

'What!' That remark annoyed her immensely. It was OK for her to criticise her own performance, but not Rick. She narrowed her eyes at the bag and made it hover in the air, then do a loop-the-loop. 'See!'

Rick applauded. 'I thought it wasn't like you to give up at the first failure. I knew you'd do it just to prove to me that you could.'

'Were you manipulating me?' Roxy directed the bag to bash him over the head.

He ducked down, laughing. 'Totally. Aren't you grateful?'

'Go kiss a bog frog.'

'You want me to kiss you?' He staggered towards her, fending off the bag. 'Certainly.'

She batted him away. 'Stop it.'

'Only if you control that missile of yours.'

Roxy ended the play-hostilities by allowing the bag to sink to the ground. 'I did it.'

'Yes, you did. Ready now?'

'I am. Let's go find ourselves a king.'

'Do you think he'll be guarded?' Roxy shouted over to Rick as they approached the island. Her voice had to compete with the wind whipping the tops of the ocean waves in a stinging spray but at least Peony and Dewdrop were enjoying the chance to gallop in the air just above the rolling sea. They had decided a low approach would be less noticeable than circling in from on high. The horses revelled in beating the waves, diving dangerously close to the surface; from their whinnies it seemed that even the slap of the spray on their faces was considered fun.

'Hard to say,' Rick called back. 'He's been in Avalon for longer than any of us so he'll have more magical power.' He steered Peony closer so he wouldn't have to shout. Doubt felt like a hard pellet lying undigested in Rick stomach. 'What are we letting ourselves in for, Roxy? For Arthur, England, or Albion, is only just coming out of Roman occupation. To him the top technology is a sword and his people would only have a vague memory of anything approaching civilization. How is he going to adjust?'

'Well, it's a good thing then that I sent the changelings to make camp at Stonehenge—at least that'll be familiar.'

He appreciated that she was able to make light of the situation. 'Probably make him feel superior: the ancient Britons didn't even get round to putting a roof on it.'

Roxy gave a nervous laugh. 'It isn't his awareness of modern times we are after—it's his skill at binding together a bunch of misfits: that's a definition of the Round Table if ever I heard one.'

A picture flashed into Rick's mind of shining armour and floating pennants. Too perfect to be true. 'The legends probably whitewashed the reputations of his men. I don't suppose for one minute it was as romantic as the stories say.'

'It never is, but even if he is a bit more rough-edged that the noble king of legend, he'll be useful to us. Oberon isn't a nice Fey; we need a hard man to counter him.'

After a brief over-flight of the barren looking island, the horses landed on the narrow strip of beach facing the mainland. The first thing they noticed was a raft made of lashed driftwood, the second was a rickety ladder scaling the cliff.

'Looks like someone comes down here.' Rick gestured to the raft and the nets stretched out on stakes to dry. 'Arthur?'

'He's had, what, sixteen years here?'

'About that. He was the last British ruler to withstand the Saxon invaders. With the help of Merlin's magical genius, he was said to have bound the little fiefdoms together for a while to stand against the newcomers from the east.'

'He might've been able to hold on for longer if the Fey hadn't got involved and sent him into exile. That was a piece of bad luck for him.' Rick's own time had been some three hundred years later, long after the Angles and the Saxons had become the settled inhabitants of England harried by the next set of invaders, the Vikings. They were each like successive waves on a beach, taking the land from those that came before. He was looking forward to meeting someone who was even older than he was in the history of the British Isles. Sometimes with the other changelings he just felt so ancient in their eyes. 'I don't see any guards, do you?'

Roxy scanned the beach then the cliffs above. 'Nothing. Oberon must have decided he wasn't an escape risk. So, do you think we go up there?' She nodded to the ladder.

Rick waded into the water to get a better look at the cliff. 'I think it goes into a cave—I can just glimpse the entrance on some kind of ledge.'

'I'll go first.' Roxy strode up the beach, sliding back slightly as the sandy ridge gave way under her feet.

'No, I'll go first.' Rick hastened to catch her up, muttering a quick spell to dry his soaked boots.

'Shut up, Rick. I'm not going to be argued out of this. Anyway, I've a good reason. I look less threatening than you. If Arthur is vicious as Titania thinks, he might hesitate to take on a girl.'

Rick hated that she had a point. 'But he might be mad enough to chuck you over the edge anyway.'

'Yes, but now I have the hover charm: I'll just charm my shoes to hold me up.' She did a little surfing motion to demonstrate.

'It's harder to do that stuff in a panic,' Rick argued, remembering his own sickening slide down the castle wall. He'd not even thought of using a hover charm.

'I won't panic. I'm prepared for any kind of insanity. Our life to date has been nothing but one long series of crazy events so I'm used to it.' She began climbing.

Rick let her go. This wasn't worth the argument. He'd just keep close so he could help if necessary.

The first ladder linked to another, and then another, so they were able to scale the sheer cliff with relative ease. The rungs were worn, showing that they were in frequent use. One strut had been repaired with a splint of wood lashed to the break. The ladders looked handcrafted and made from material available on the island: driftwood, and twine made from fibrous plants twisted together into a primitive form of rope.

Finally they reached the opening to the cave. Another ladder lay against the rock wall on its side. It looked just long enough to reach the top of the cliff above, but Arthur had cut off the approach from that way. The entrance to the cavern itself was barred by hundreds of pointed stakes facing outwards. It was like looking at the back of a porcupine.

'Not exactly encouraging of visitors is he?' murmured Roxy, peering into the darkness. 'Do you think he's in there?

'I didn't see any other signs of buildings when we flew in; I'm guessing this is his bolthole.' The island had appeared flat on top, covered with tough maritime grass, pitted with burrows for Fey puffins, which were large multicoloured cousins of the ones found on Earth. 'Bleak, isn't it?'

Roxy examined the heap of oyster shells lying near a stone seat. It was all too easy to picture the lonely king sitting here to watch the sunset, eating his supper of seafood. 'Imagine living here alone for over a decade. Whatever has he been living on?'

'Oysters, obviously. Then fish, eggs, seabirds, maybe seaweed, perhaps some berries: I hope he's kept his strength on that diet.'

'Maybe Oberon sends him supplies?'

'And maybe I'm a blue baboon.'

'Yeah, well, just a thought.' She pushed at one of the spikes. 'How do we get past this?'

'We could blast it, but I've got a feeling that will really annoy our host. I think we should try knocking. Excuse me, Aethel.' He tapped the snake in metal form against the rock. She obligingly made a ringing sound. 'Your majesty? Arthur? Are you home?'

Nothing. Rick gestured to Roxy to have a go.

'Mr Pendragon . . . ?'

'Roxy, he's a king.'

'I know—but I'm a republican.'

'Can we have this debate another time? Just don't annoy him before we've even said "hello".'

Roxy gave him a fulminating look but modified her approach. 'Sir, we are from Earth. We'd like to speak to you. We need your help.'

A creaking sound alerted them to the fact that the spiked doorway was rolling back. The porcupine quills flattened against the walls of the tunnel.

'I think that means we can go in.' Roxy took a cautious step forward, hoping it wasn't some cruel joke which would end up with them both pinned on the spikes like butterflies in a display case. She lit a ball of magic and let it hover in her hand to light the way. 'OK, let's see if he feels up to visitors.'

Rick drew his sword from its scabbard.

Roxy raised an eyebrow.

'No harm in being prepared for anything. We don't even know that it is Arthur letting us in.'

'True.' She walked ahead of him, shoulders slightly hunched against attack. A drip of water fell on Rick's neck, making him jump with its sudden icy touch. The tunnel was dank; sad to think that the great king was reduced to living in this hole.

They continued for about a hundred metres until their way was barred by another gate, this one solid. Roxy knocked.

'May we come in, sir?'

It would be a good defence to trap visitors between the spikes and the door, thought Rick. He hoped Arthur was feeling above such tricks today. He glanced behind—just in time to see a broad-shouldered warrior step out of a hidden passage behind them. He had a sword levelled at Rick's chest before he'd even had a chance to raise his. Roxy gasped, her magic light faltering for a second before blazing with renewed power.

'Who are you?' growled the man, as if speaking was strange for him.

Rick held his hands wide apart, sword loose at his side. 'Sir, we come in peace.'

'I asked *who* you are, not *what* you want!' The man's face was in shadow but Rick could make out keen eyes set either side of a hawkish nose. His hair was a long tangle, his beard ragged, but there was nothing slovenly about the way he handled his weapon.

'I'm Roxy Topley. Human.' Roxy stepped to one side of Rick so the man could see them. 'I'm originally from Ireland but, like Rick here, I've been a changeling in Avalon for most of my life.'

The warrior nodded and seemed to ease back

a little. 'And you, young soldier, who are you?'

'I'm Elfric Halfdane. I come from Mercia—'

'What! Half *Dane*? One of the invaders dares step on my land!' Not waiting for an explanation, Arthur swung his blade up to strike Rick's head from his shoulders. Rick only just managed to raise his sword to intercept the blow. Roxy screamed but had the sense to keep back. Arthur rained strike after strike at Rick, each one he parried until his arms ached with the strain. He felt like a tree that Arthur was trying to fell with wild blows.

'Stop it, stop it!' yelled Roxy.

Rick gathered a pulse of magic for an elfshot in his left palm and threw it at Arthur's chest. The king repelled it with the flat of his sword, hitting it like a baseball so it crashed into the tunnel wall just above Rick's head. Disappointed not to have hit Rick in the face, Arthur bared his teeth in a snarl.

'Know such tricks, do you, Dane? Try this then.' Arthur directed a bolt of energy through his sword. Rick dived out of its path and the wooden gate burst into flame.

An elfshot flew from Roxy's fingers, distracting Arthur from the killing blow he was about to land on Rick's exposed side.

Arthur swung round like a bee-stung bear. 'Keep out of this, wench! I have no quarrel with you.'

'I'm not a Dane!' panted Rick, scrambling to his feet. 'Not in the sense you mean—not an invader!' Added to his own danger was the fear that one of them would hurt Roxy in this wild battle in a confined space. She'd backed as far away as she could, but dread of hitting her was hampering the swing of his sword. He was left with cramped, defensive moves. 'I'm an Anglo-Saxon—a later people.' He dashed the sweat from his brow with his sleeve. 'Only my grandfather was Danish.'

That was no better to the invader-hating Arthur—Saxon, Angle, Jute, or Dane: all were the enemy. 'Then you will die for your mongrel blood, Halfdane.'

Smoke from the burning door filled the air making it hard to breathe or see further than the end of his sword.

'Roxy!' Rick coughed, his eyes blurred with tears.

Understanding his plea, Roxy blew the smoke away with a charm that summoned the breeze. The smoke cleared to reveal a larger space beyond, somewhere for them to retreat from this murderous passage. She jumped over the remains of the door and into a vast cavern. Her light reflected from the quartz lined walls and the still lake that stretched across half the floor. The roof arched above like a cathedral, dripping with candle-shaped stalactites.

'Rick, in here!' she shouted.

Rick was still engaged in a punishing exchange of blows in the narrow tunnel. He was attempting to keep Arthur busy so he couldn't brew another of his sword bolts. Unfortunately, he couldn't retreat without leaving himself exposed.

'Rick, get in here. I've a plan,' called Roxy. She had spotted a pile of nets on a flat coffin-shaped stone.

'Quiet, wench! I'll deal with you next!' bellowed Arthur. Sparks flew as his sword hit the edge of Rick's blade.

'Roxy, I'm just a bit busy . . . fighting right now!' gasped Rick.

'Trust me! Close your eyes *now*!'

Rick shut them. His arms jolted as Arthur's latest blow met his, but then Roxy let her light flash at intense brightness, blinding Arthur before he could strike again. He staggered back. Rick opened his eyes to see that she used the hover charm to cast the net over the king. It dropped sweetly on his head, catching his sword in its strings.

'Quick!' Roxy seized a length of rope. She threw an end to Rick and they wrapped up their angry host so that he could no longer attack. 'There. Maybe now he'll listen!'

But she had underestimated the king. Calling on his magical reserves, Arthur radiated a ferocious wave of power that reduced the net and rope to fiery embers and travelled on to knock Roxy and Rick off their feet. Rick sailed through the air and fell half in the lake, head briefly submerged in the freezing water. Arthur shook himself free of the sparks and ran towards Rick, sword raised to strike.

'No!' screamed Roxy, throwing herself across Rick's chest and dousing him in water again as his elbows collapsed under her weight. Seeing her chance, Aethel quivered to life and slithered up and across Roxy's collar, putting her body at risk to defend both humans.

The sword stopped a thumb's breadth from Aethel's neck. 'Out of the way! Take the enchanted snake with you, wench, or I will cut it in two!'

Aethel hissed.

'No, you've got to listen to us. Please!' Roxy eased off Rick, allowing him to shuffle out of the water. Neither of them attempted to rise as it seemed less likely Arthur would cut them down in cold blood. Rick quickly gathered Aethel to his chest: Arthur would have to kill him first before he struck Aethel.

'Why should I listen to you?' Arthur's gaze was fixed on Rick and Aethel; he barely noticed Roxy as his predator's instincts honed in on his prey.

'Because England needs you,' Rick said quickly. 'You have promised to come to the aid of your kingdom—you've waited for the call for years—and here we are: we are your summons.'

Arthur spat in the water at Rick's side. 'They sent a Saxon to get me—I doubt that. No, you are one of Morgan's tricks and I won't fall into her trap again.'

'Do we look like one of Morgan's people?' scoffed Roxy, holding her hands out wide. 'Come on—I hate her more than you can possibly imagine. She's kept us in prison since we were infants—stolen us from our parents. At least you got to live most of your adult life on Earth. You even got to be a world famous king! All we got were lessons in how to spy on our own kind.'

'We're on the run from her, and from Oberon,' Rick added. 'That's why we need you.'

Arthur let his sword fall to his side and gave a creaky laugh. 'I have waited all these years to help two little sprigs of humanity, have I? I enjoy your sense of humour—for that alone I will consider sparing your life, Halfdane.'

'You don't understand, sir.' Rick placed his sword on the ground in front of him in a sign of good faith. He coaxed Aethel to wind round his arm in a less threatening position. 'It's not just us—it's all the changelings—and England too.'

'The whole world really,' added Roxy, 'if you don't mind expanding your mission a little.'

Arthur roared with laughter now, holding his sides. 'I have not been more entertained since Gawain kissed the loathly lady! How long is it since I heard such a good joke? Sixteen years?' He swung round to look at the calendar he had scratched on the wall. 'Yes, sixteen years next solstice. If you have indeed come to fetch me home and my castle at Camelot is still standing after Mordred's attack, I'll offer you the position of jesters.'

'Um, about that,' Roxy slowly got to her feet, testing out his changed mood, 'I'm afraid things aren't quite how you remember them.'

Arthur grabbed her arm, dirt encrusted nails black against her pale skin. 'You mean the Saxons overran us after the battle? I won it only to lose the war, did I? I feared as much when Morgan lured me away to her "healing" island. Pah, healing island, my foot: it's been my prison ever since!'

Roxy glanced at Rick, her expression asking how to break the bad news.

'Shall we, er, sit round a fire and have a drink together?' Rick shook the water from his hair. 'We can tell you what happened after you left.'

'No, stay where you are—all three of you. I will take counsel.' Arthur strode away from them, pacing the shore of the lake. He was talking loudly to himself, punctuating his discussion with wild gestures and barks of anger. The roof echoed his words until it sounded like he kept company with a pack of wolves.

'He's cracked, hasn't he?' Roxy whispered, not daring to move.

'Yeah, looks like it.' Rick's spirits sank to see the great king reduced to this bizarre behaviour. 'Though I suppose he's only had himself to talk to for over a decade; it's not surprising really.'

As suddenly as he had left them, Arthur advanced on them. To Rick's relief, he sheathed his sword. 'I am starved for news here. I will trust you thus far, Halfdane. Come, I will offer you my meagre hospitality in exchange for your tidings.' He knelt by the fire laid in a ring of rocks and began to chip away at a flint to produce a spark.

'Here, let me.' Rick knelt beside him and lit the kindling with a flash of magic.

Arthur sat back on his haunches. 'How do you do that?'

'Magic, like yours.'

'I've magic?'

'Yes. That power you used on the door—and to blast the net.'

'Nonsense: that's my special fighting strength granted me by God. Merlin's the one who does magic for me.' Arthur warmed his hands in the glow. His cavern, though splendid, remained at a chilly temperature. The fire did little to warm it beyond the small radius of heat it gave out.

Roxy sat gingerly on Arthur's other side, approaching him a bit like a lion that she wanted to befriend but feared would bite her head off first. 'Actually, sir, it's from this land. The longer you live in Avalon, the more powerful you are. I guess no one told you that?'

Arthur turned to study her expression. He had forgotten how to behave with people: his examination was too intense to be polite. 'No. The only ones I have seen in the last few years have come to taunt me, not teach me. I could have been lighting my fires like this all this time?'

'Yes, sir.'

That seemed terribly sad to Rick. Arthur had been sitting on a well of power and not known how to use it for anything but fighting, like a thirsty man ignorant of the spring running a few inches beneath his feet.

'Ah, I see they have made a fool of me.' Arthur reached for a clay jug. 'Only one cup, I'm sorry to admit. I don't get visitors. You may have herb tea or water. I have no grain for beer or grapes for wine.'

Roxy slipped the bag she had been carrying from her back and dug out the empty lemonade bottles Rick had kept in his pack from the train. 'We can use these for water.'

Arthur took the clear plastic container in his fingers and rolled it around gently. 'What is this? A kind of glass?'

'A bit like that. It doesn't break so easily and is lighter. We call it plastic. It's made from oil.'

'Indeed?' Treating the cheap bottles as if they were made of diamond, Arthur filled them with water. 'I can offer you only dried fish to eat. I've not been hunting yet today.'

Rick dug a chocolate bar out of his jacket pocket—another souvenir of the train journey. 'Here, try this.'

Arthur studied the wrapping as closely as he did the biscuit inside. He took a bite, letting shortbread crumbs and a strand of toffee fall on his beard. 'Sweet. Like honey. It is very good.' The smooth chocolate flavour hit his taste buds. 'Very good indeed. You perhaps should become a baker in my kingdom, Halfdane, rather than a jester. You will make your fortune. And this wrapping is ingenious. Is it magic too? See: there are tiny words far smaller than a scribe can write upon it. I can't read, but no doubt it is a spell of great power.'

'It's the list of what is in it. And I didn't make it.' Rick felt they were getting further from where they wanted to be with these distractions, like a swimmer swept away from shore by a strong current.

'Ah, the mage who made this lets all know his spell, does he? That is unwise of him. Merlin would counsel against such practices.'

'Yeah, I'll tell Mr Twix that when I see him next,' murmured Roxy.

Arthur held up his cup. 'To news-bearers!'

Rick and Roxy copied his gesture and took a swig from their bottles.

The moment had come. Rick nudged Roxy. 'OK, you tell him.'

'No, you.'

Arthur leaned back against a stone and crossed his feet in front of him. His clothes were well worn: rusty brown tunic and grey cloak, linen leggings gartered to his legs with twine. He wasn't wearing armour but Rick could see chainmail and leather armour laid out on an altar-like structure at the water's edge; a shield rested against the plinth. Arthur had clearly not considered him threat enough to risk damage to his most prized arms and had come at him with just his sword. 'Now, children, stop arguing among yourselves or shall I go back to trying to kill you again?'

His flash of humour was unexpected, giving Rick hope that there was a sane man under the rather unpredictable exterior. 'I'd prefer it if you didn't. My arms are aching,' Rick admitted.

Arthur's pale green eyes warmed a little as he

looked at his adversary. 'You did well, squire; you held your own against a full grown man. There are gaps in your defence, though, and you make some basic errors. I would have beaten you if we had continued.'

'I don't doubt it, sir.' Rick warmed to the praise, the first he had ever received from an adult man.

'Then in payment for my lesson at sword play you will tell me the news. How fares my kingdom?'

Rick cleared his throat. 'Um, the first thing you need to understand, sir, is that time here in Avalon and time on Earth travel at different speeds. Roughly one year here lasts about a hundred on Earth.' Feeling awkward, he threw a pebble in the still surface of dark lake, watching the rings spread until they lapped at the shore.

'Ah.' Arthur's expression was bleak. He moistened his lips. 'I see.'

'You are a great hero still though,' Roxy added. 'Every child knows of King Arthur and his knights.'

'My queen—my knights: what of them?'

'I'm not sure exactly.' Rick rubbed his knees meditatively. 'I think some survived that last battle with Mordred; they must have done because we have the stories. I remember reading that your wife lived until her death near Glastonbury and was buried there, but to be honest the facts are hard to come by. So much time has passed that people have made up a lot of stuff and attached it to your name. We're not sure what was you and what came from the imagination of bards through the ages.'

Arthur threw his own stone. It skipped six times before sinking near the middle of the lake. 'When is it now?'

'We've reached the twenty-first century.'

'I cannot imagine that. And England?'

'She's at peace, thankfully.' Rick wondered what was important for him to know, to understand, today. 'You wouldn't recognize much about modern life but the people enjoy a good life, live up to about eighty years on average.'

'You jest, surely? No one lives that long unless extraordinarily blessed by God.'

'No, I'm telling the truth. We might get a lot wrong but most of us live in a kind of comfort your time—and my time come to that—couldn't even dream of. Doctors cure rather than kill their patients. People are warm and well fed. They can travel around the world with very little trouble in flying machines called aeroplanes. Nearly everyone can read and write.'

'The men have all become scribes?'

'And women too,' chipped in Roxy.

'Where are the warriors?'

'Countries still have armies but they fight with different weapons, terrible ones, more like your bolt of energy than your sword. Only a few men and women join these forces; most of us are classed as civilians,' said Rick.

Arthur sat silently, finishing the last of the chocolate bar as he pondered this basinful of news. His expression was sad but not disbelieving. He had evidently decided their tales were too outrageous to be made up.

'My world has gone then,' he said at length, brushing the crumbs from his tunic.

'I'm afraid so, sir.'

'And all these years I have been sustained by the hope that my time was yet to come.'

'Maybe it has.'

'Hmm.' He did not believe them. 'So why do you need me? What use am I in this modern world of old people living to miraculous ages, universal scribes and clever doctors?'

Rick didn't rush to answer. He picked at a hole that had appeared in the hard-wearing trousers of his dragon keeper uniform that he still had on. The morning visit to the Stormridge seemed years ago but it had only been a few days. 'Well, you see, sir, you are like us. We are children out of our time. I belong to the eighth century, Roxy here to the tenth. Oberon stole about a hundred of us over the years and imprisoned us with the intention of sending us back to act against our own people. We were taught that we had been sold by our parents—abandoned. It was all lies. I think he suspects that we know the truth, but in any case, he has changed his mind about our usefulness and wants to kill us all.'

Arthur's eyes sparked with interest. 'You want me to defend you from him?'

'That's part of it, but the problem is bigger than that. He's planning to invade Earth and take it over, destroying human civilization.'

'Why? What possible business does he have meddling in Earth's affairs?'

'It's the exchange. Do you know about that?' Roxy asked.

Arthur nodded. 'Aye, Merlin told me about it. It was what powered our Round Table.'

'It is under threat, partly because humans have been stupid and ruined the world's environment. The green power is declining, which means magic is fading. It might have to be rationed soon if it gets any worse.'

'And Oberon thinks the cure is to invade? That sounds like him.'

'I'm not claiming humans haven't made mistakes, but I think a Fey invasion is no way to solve the problems,' argued Rick. 'The thing is, people won't understand how to defend themselves and repel a Fey attack. Only we changelings do.'

'And what has that to do with this old man?'

'Old, sir? I thought you were in your prime.' Arthur chuckled at that. 'But we're young, unprepared. I'm the oldest surviving changeling and, as you said, not exactly a match for a full grown warrior. We all have magic though—and are the only hope humanity has if we are to stop Oberon's plan to take over. But that's not enough on its own. We need a leader to organize us.'

Arthur shook his head slowly, looking terribly lost and uncertain of himself.

'We need you,' Roxy said softly, daring to slip her hand in to Arthur's. Rick understood the impulse: when he wasn't trying to kill them, there was something so sorrowful about the king.

Arthur looked down at his scarred palm enclosed in her slim fingers. 'I've not touched another human for sixteen years.'

She squeezed his hand. 'We know.'

'This is a lightning bolt from clear skies to me. I will take some time to think before I give you my answer.'

'Of course, but we don't have long. We've got to go back as soon as we can.' Roxy released his hand.

Arthur got up and walked slowly away, this time heading for the tunnel leading back to the cliff.

Chapter 16

'THAT was brave of you—to take his hand.'
Rick put his arm around Roxy's shoulder.
'Well done.'

'I felt I should. He's been so alone. I'd want to
feel another human's touch if I were him.'

'You've got good instincts, Roxy. Shall we clear
up a bit? We've made a mess of his home.'

'Yes, let's.' Together they swept to one side the
ashes of the door and the burnt net, using the little
breeze charm which Roxy taught Rick. They disturbed more than they expected: scores of shiny
feathers swirled in the wind before resettling on
a nest of hay in one rocky niche. Too small to be
Arthur's bed, they had no answer as to what it was.

Still Arthur did not return.

They then passed the time competing to skip stones on the lake, their voices echoing in the roof space. Even with all this activity, Rick felt as if nothing could take the chill from this place: it felt like a magnificent tomb.

He made a stone skip five times, rings rippling out to cut across each other. 'Don't you think sometimes, Roxy, that we are a bit like these stones?'

'No!' She laughed. 'I hope you're not saying we're flat and round—I'd take that as an insult.'

'I was thinking of something a bit more complicated than that; you know how our lives cross with Earth—we bounce in and the ripples spread but we are from another dimension, moving at a different speed.'

'I never knew you were a philosopher, Rick?'

'Neither did I.'

She threw a rock so that dropped into the lake with a plop and no bounce. 'I want to be more than a skipping stone.'

'Yeah, it's a mad life. Sucks to be us sometimes.'

'Do you think we should go after him?' Roxy asked after an hour had passed.

Rick scratched the back of his neck, aware suddenly of how tired he felt. He must have been running or searching almost continually for a couple of days now. 'I think we have to give him as much time as he needs.'

'But every hour here is four days on Earth. I'm worried about the others. They've been alone now for, what, for well over three months?'

'Yes, I know. But we can't rush him. It's not fair. We are asking him to trust us and he has very little reason to do so.'

'But I have decided to nonetheless.' Arthur had walked up on them in total silence. The big warrior moved like a leopard, powerful footsteps made without a sound. 'I will come with you to this new England. Experience tells me that I should answer the call when it comes, not argue with my fate.'

'You'll help us changelings?' asked Rick.

Arthur gave a ripple of a shrug; the big muscles of his shoulders bunching. 'I will try. I will not promise to follow your tactics until I have had a chance to survey the field. Perhaps there are other ways to stop Oberon. A commander does not accept the word of a green boy.'

'Thanks,' said Rick, cut by the dismissal.

'It is not an insult but the truth. You yourself told me you needed a leader. Don't be surprised if you get what you ask for.'

'We realize you aren't going to be a pushover, sir,' Roxy said quickly, before another argument could brew between Briton and Saxon. 'Do you need long to pack?'

'Hah! You see all I have around me, wench.'

'Roxy,' she corrected him. 'That whole wench thing went out long ago and might earn you a slap on the face for rudeness.'

'Very well, *Roxy*. I have no wish to offend the maidens.' He winked at her, a slightly laboured gesture as if he was only just remembering the use of his facial muscles. 'All I need do to be ready is to collect my weapons and my armour. I trust we do not need supplies if we are going to the place of the wonderful food you gave me?'

'We're covered in that direction, sir,' Rick answered, understanding that he was not to be granted the same teasing relationship that was forming between Roxy and the king. 'The main problem is how to get back to the mainland. We have a couple of friendly Fey who will create the doorway to our world—as you might know, only Fey bloods can do it.'

Arthur nodded. 'So I was told by Morgan, with great glee, I might add. I hoped for a long time that Merlin might come for me but, when he did not, I decided he, too, had to be dead.'

Rick shook his head. 'It's possible he's still alive on Earth. There are rumours.'

'Then why did he not come for me?'

Good question. 'I don't know, sir. We are working on finding him, and then you can ask him. We brought just two horses with us. I suppose two of us will have to ride double.'

'Yes, that would be best. I can carry you over to the mainland on my raft. I've been once or twice over the years but found there was no welcome for me there.'

'No need. We can fly, sir.'

Arthur looked at Rick with new respect. 'Fly? Now this I have to learn.' He threw his shield over his shoulder. For the first time, seeing it in the light of the fire, Rick noticed the lovingly-crafted dragon swirling on the surface, catching its own tail in its mouth. Gold metal wire had been beaten into the surface to outline the creature; it shimmered and rippled as if almost alive.

'Sir, does your shield do anything . . . well, anything odd?' he asked, reaching to stroke Aethel who had worked her way under his shirt to rest her head on his collar.

Arthur tightened the straps across his chest. 'Not that I have noticed. Why do you ask?'

'It's just that after a time Avalon has a strange effect on things brought from Earth. My sword transforms very easily under any spell, and my torc . . . perhaps I'd best show you. Aethel, greet King Arthur.'

Aethel coiled round Rick's head to arch above it like Cleopatra's headdress.

'Your fighting snake. I assumed it was an illusion made to fool me in battle.' Arthur reached out but Aethel wasn't as forgiving as Rick and hissed at the warrior who had had a serious go at killing her owner. 'A vicious little thing—I like it.' Arthur gave her a nod of approval.

'No illusion. She's alive. Aethel, mind your manners.'

Aethel tickled Rick's ear with her tongue.

'How did this wondrous creature come into being?' Arthur watched enviously as Aethel slid down Rick's chest to coil on his arm.

'They brought her with me as a neck torc when I was taken. I'm not sure how it happened, but over time she became like this. I was just wondering if your shield had showed any signs of, well, life?'

Arthur turned round to display the dragon to Roxy and Rick. 'What would you say? It has kept its shine over the years even though I have not the ingredients for polish or a smithy to burnish it anew. Merlin said he had dipped it in dragon tears to make it withstand enchantments.'

Roxy cautiously reached out and ran her finger along one gold wire. She shivered. 'It doesn't feel quite as I expected—not inanimate, but not alive.'

'Hmm. Then maybe I should experiment with my power, now that I know I can do more than fight with it.' Arthur frowned, reminded again of the trap of ignorance he had been in for so many years. 'I only have one more thing to do before I go. Let us proceed to the cliff.'

Stamping out the fire, Arthur led the way to the end of the tunnel. They had been in the dark for so long that Rick was surprised to see that the afternoon was still fairly young, the sun high in a blue-washed sky. Less time has passed than he had feared.

'Wait here.' Arthur put the ladder against the wall and climbed up to the top of the cliff. He returned with a puffin tucked inside a cloth sling made from his cloak. Rick sincerely hoped he did not intend to make it lunch. Its eyes were far too intelligent to consider eating it.

'This is Peter,' Arthur said gruffly. 'He will be coming with us.' He looked a little embarrassed by the announcement, pulling at a scarf knotted around his throat as if it had become too tight. 'He has been my guard dog for many years, alerting me to any Fey visitors flying in. I wonder why he missed you?

'We landed on the beach, sir, not above where the puffins live,' said Rick.

'Ah, that would explain it.' Arthur patted Peter's head in a practised gesture.

Roxy flashed a quick grin at Rick. At least Arthur had not been entirely alone, then, if he had befriended one of the island's inhabitants. 'May I stroke him?'

Arthur nodded.

Roxy ran the tip of her index finger over the black stripe on the puffin's head, which separated the two white patches around his alert eyes. Peter made a purring sound, not unlike a cat. 'What a beak.' Triangular, it was coloured like a rainbow, even fancier than its Earth counterpart, and his feet bright orange. Nicknamed the clown of the sea, puffins didn't have to do anything but be themselves to be funny. Both Rick and Roxy were smiling—it was impossible not to. 'He's so much bigger than the ones in our world, isn't he?'

'Indeed. And cleverer, when he can be bothered to think.' Arthur cleared his throat. 'I am ready now. Where have you left your horses?'

'They wait below.' Turning away to hide his grin, Rick headed for the ladder and began to descend.

Peony and Dewdrop greeted them joyfully. Arthur picked up his pace, kicking the sand with his boots, delighted to see horses again after so long in his island exile.

'What wonderful creatures—I had almost forgotten.' Arthur ran his hands over their neck and flanks. 'Good, strong mounts, both of them. They will have no trouble carrying a man in armour and two youngsters between them. Which will do which?' Dewdrop butted him in the chest. 'Ah, you volunteer, do you?' He smiled and scratched her nose. 'You are a very fine mare. I am honoured to be your rider.'

Roxy shrugged. 'I suppose I am no competition to a legendary king.'

Rick was relieved he had not been asked to give up Peony; he and the horse had bonded over the last day, and he would have struggled to see another on his back. 'Shall I help you up, Roxy?'

'Hadn't you better teach Arthur the hover charm first?'

'I have a better idea,' said the king dismissively. Clearly he had never learned how to make his suggestions without sounding arrogant. 'I do not know how to wield magic in the ways you both use, so why not let the maiden ride with me while Halfdane carries my armour and shield? You can instruct me in such things when we have more time. I would not like to discover that I have no aptitude for such magic while sailing this noble creature above the ocean.' He slung his shield off his back as if the matter was settled and passed it to Rick.

'OK, we'll do that then,' Rick said, hoping only Roxy picked up his amusement at the king's high-handed ways. Arthur was used to command so it was not really a surprise to see him assume his word would be obeyed. Rick packed Arthur's goods around him. Of the armour, the mail shirt proved to be the heaviest piece. Arthur lashed it to Peony's saddle with leather ties, double checking that it was secure.

'Don't get it wet or you will be up all night cleaning it, squire.'

Since when had he become a squire? Rick wondered. But then, if he had stayed in his own time he would have expected to serve an apprenticeship with a knight. Perhaps it wasn't too late for him after all? 'Aye, sir.'

Arthur's eyes met Rick's. He huffed, then patted Rick's leg—the first non-combative touch he had offered him. 'I forgot myself for a moment. Having a boy around reminds me of my past and I thought that I . . . Well, look after it, Halfdane.'

'I am honoured to be entrusted with your arms,' Rick said, giving him a formal bow from the saddle, a little kick of delight in his heart.

'Then you will take my mascot too?' Arthur passed him the sling containing Peter.

'With pleasure.'

Peter made no fuss about the exchange, nestling against Rick's chest as happily as he had Arthur's.

The king smiled. 'He's a useless bird: an indifferent guard and very lazy, but affectionate.'

Rick thought that Peter was really far from useless in Arthur's estimation; the puffin had probably been key to helping Arthur cling on to his humanity during the long years of exile.

The transfer of extra weight made, Arthur swung up in the saddle and held out a hand to Roxy. 'Maiden, if you would?'

She stepped on his boot and wedged herself in the saddle behind him. 'This is cosy,' she laughed to cover her embarrassment. She gripped his tunic at the sides to steady herself.

'Let's fly!' Arthur spurred Dewdrop along the beach and Peony followed. When the horses had gained sufficient momentum, Roxy and Rick released the hover charm and they began to stride over waves rather than sand.

Arthur let out a battle cry. Peter surprised Rick by echoing it in a shrill call.

'Careful, or I'll drop you!' Rick cautioned, trying to settle the puffin in the sling against his chest.

But that was exactly what the puffin had in mind. He escaped from his papoose and plunged into the waves, diving through Peony's hooves to do so.

'Arthur!' called Rick. 'Peter's jumped!'

Arthur roared with laughter. 'Excellent! Don't worry, squire; he is just stretching his wings.'

True enough. The puffin emerged from the waves, swimming at a pace to match the horses.

Skipping like a flying fish, he then dived again, silver bubbles in his wake. When he came up, he had a sand eel in his beak. Rick relaxed. The puffin was in his element.

The horses landed at the base of the cliff to allow the puffin to rejoin them. Rick tucked the wet bird against his chest, wrinkling his nose at the strong fishy smell that now came from the damp feathers.

'How's your magic, Rick? Roxy asked.

'I've still got an hour or so of flying left in me.'

'I'm pretty empty. Let's gallop the next bit. I wouldn't want to arrive back at Deepdene with no power. Just in case.'

'Do you mind, sir?' Rick asked Arthur.

'Not at all. I would relish a gallop over good solid earth.'

Once back on the Downs where the white deer grazed, they swapped over. Peter and the armour went on Dewdrop, Roxy came with Rick.

'There's a bit more space with you in the saddle,' she said, putting her arms around his waist. 'And I have to admit, Arthur smells a bit musty after all this time with no soap.'

Rick chuckled. 'We did suspect the reality was not going to be as romantic as the stories.'

'I know it isn't a priority, but I'm itching to hand him a comb and a razor.' Arthur's hair straggled down his back in dreadlocks.

'I'll leave the grooming tips to you.' Glancing back at her, Rick realized he had seen that mischievous look in Roxy's eyes before, when she had plotted his makeover from Anglo-Saxon prince to twenty-first century teenager. He guessed Arthur was next on her list. 'I think he wouldn't take it well coming from me.'

'No, squire. He'd probably give you a cuff round the ears and order you to polish his armour with a toothbrush.'

'No, he wouldn't.'

'You sound very confident about that.'

'Because he doesn't know what a toothbrush is yet.'

They took a break from riding when they were far in to Deepdene Forest. Night had fallen and all were in need of rest. Arthur surprised Roxy and Rick by dismounting, casting aside his cloak and sword belt, then throwing himself on the ground in the bracken.

'What's he doing?' whispered Roxy.

Rick shrugged. 'Best leave him to it, whatever *it* is.'

Roxy was about to warn Arthur that he could pick up Fey ticks that way, but bit her tongue. He was revelling in being in a forest once more; it would be a shame to spoil his moment. He thrashed his arms and legs—if there had been snow on the ground she would have said he was making an angel.

'Ah, can you smell it?' the ancient king groaned. 'Leaves, wood, and water.' He got to his knees and murmured a prayer of thanks for his deliverance.

Roxy and Rick waited a little awkwardly for him to finish his devotions. Arthur jumped to his feet, reinvigorated by freedom. He seemed to be bristling with energy, like a dog shaking droplets off his coat after a dip in a stream.

'Now, tell me who else will be at this place you are taking me to—Titania's court-in-exile—and why should they help us?' He rubbed his leather gloved hands together and checked his weapons, this time putting on his chainmail shirt before strapping on his sword belt. As his head emerged from the slit at the top of the mail and the rings fell into place, Roxy had the impression that the true Arthur of the stories was also coming back.

He drew his sword, displaying the name graven on the blade: Excalibur. For the first time, Arthur Pendragon stood before them as a fully-dressed knight of ancient Britain, in possession of his mind and strength. Roxy began to hope that their plan to fetch him might actually have been a good one.

Rick quickly explained their odd relationship with Oberon's twin children. 'We have no illusions about them, sir, but they're not hostile towards us, not like their father or Morgan, our old commander at Dark Lore.'

The expression in Arthur's eyes heated on the mention of his adversary. 'Morgan La Faye—she still holds a position of trust here, does she?'

Roxy nodded. 'Yes, she's Oberon's favourite lieutenant. I've seen them in battle together. Do you mind me asking why she took you in the first place? Was it on Oberon's command?'

Arthur gave a bark of mirthless laughter. 'Nay, it was her plan from the start. Do you know that she is only half Fey?'

'No! She kept that quiet.' Roxy thought back over the years she had known the commander. 'I suppose it explains why she seems to hate us more than most of the Dark Folk.'

Rick smiled sourly. 'I bet she despises what she would see as her mongrel blood.'

Arthur twirled his sword to flex his wrist and continued. 'Morgan's mother was a Welsh wise woman of a princely house; her father a Fey who visited her at Imbolc, the late winter festival when the Earth is most hungry. Morgan was the result.' He sheathed his sword, found fault with its positioning and fastened his belt another notch. 'The baby never lost the hunger, though for her it was for power not food. She was part of my household for many years until she learned the secrets of her Fey inheritance; then she transferred her allegiance to Avalon.'

'I wonder how that happened?' mused Roxy.

'Merlin may know; I do not. She went, but not before taking her revenge on those who had committed the crime of offering her shelter and raising her as a lady of worth. She did not want us to be happy—or spread the tales of her parentage.'

'Does Oberon know the truth?'

'He probably suspects, but her life is devoted to repudiating her human heritage, hence her decision to trap me here and destroy the kingdom she had lived in and any chance for peace.'

'I wonder what she thought when Oberon put her in charge of us humans?' Rick responded to Peter's begging by feeding him a scrap of bread roll from the supply in their saddle bags. 'I bet she hated it.'

'Aye, she would, though doubtless she did it to the best of her ability to prove to Oberon she could be trusted.'

'I wish Oberon had given us to the pixies: we could've had a wonderful time,' said Roxy. 'They helped raise me for my first two years here.'

Arthur picked Peter up. 'Pixies? I do not think I've met any of them.'

'No, they love being free to roam. They helped us break out of Dark Lore.'

Arthur furrowed his brow, considering. 'So we do have allies among the Fey. I must revise my thoughts as to the best strategy against them. It is always better to fight a divided kingdom.

'I am eager to meet these allies of yours, but first we must snatch what rest we can. We should rise before dawn if we are to make as fast a journey as our brave horses can manage.'

Chapter 17

FTER a short rest, each taking an hour of the watch, they proceeded more cautiously as they approached the palace. No one spoke, but they could all see and smell that they were heading towards trouble. A column of smoke rose in the air above the place where they expected to see Deepdene, top flattening to hover over the trees like a dark mantle. Arthur reined in his horse.

'Your friends are in that direction?'

'Yes, they're the only ones we know round here who will do the magic to make a door back to Earth.' Roxy felt in her pocket and pulled out the shell. 'Archer gave me this to contact him. If it is OK with you, I'll see if he is answering.'

'What is that?' Arthur touched it gingerly with a fingertip.

'A kind of whisper carrier,' Rick explained.

'How could anyone have thought of such a strange device? How useful that would be in a battle!'

Roxy refrained from adding just then that almost everyone on Earth used something very similar. Arthur had enough adjustments to make as it was.

'Proceed carefully: I do not trust these allies of yours.'

'Archer? Are you OK?' Roxy asked, hearing the prince's voice at the other end.

'Roxy, you've made good time.' His voice sounded clearly in her ear, confident if a little harried. 'Unfortunately, my father's troops have also travelled quickly. We're trapped in the palace.'

'We can see the smoke.'

'He sent Morgan with dragons. Lunila and Joll-E must have got a message out before we caged them. Morgan is laying siege to this palace until we give you up.'

'But you don't have us.'

'She doesn't believe us. She thinks we've hidden you somewhere and won't stop until we give in.'

'Where are the troops?'

'In a ring around the house. They are burning the gardens with dragon fire, threatening to destroy the palace with all of us inside next.' His tone was admirably cool but Roxy could tell the situation for those inside was dire.

Arthur tapped Roxy's arm. 'Ask him how many there are.'

'Is it a big army, Archer?

'No, just a crack squad under Morgan's command, but it doesn't need to be. With the dragons, there is little we can do against them, and this house is not built as a fortress. I'm in counsel with my mother as I speak. She advises you to run while you can. Our hope is that we can persuade Morgan we are not harbouring you in the house.'

'Can one of you get out and make a door for us?'

'I can't see how I can—we're surrounded. Have you no other allies who will make your door?'

'Frankly, no.'

'Ah.'

'And even if we go and hide, she might not believe you don't have us until it is too late.'

'Worried about me, little red-head?'

'Yes, of course. You are our passage home, remember?'

He laughed at that. 'Only because of that? You have a Fey heart, Roxy.'

'I was taught by the best, wasn't I?'

Arthur held up his hand. 'Cease this chatter, wench.'

'Roxy!' she hissed.

'Maid Roxy. Tell your prince to stand by for my orders.'

Rick cast his eyes to the heavens. Roxy heaved a sigh: like that was going to work!

'Um, Archer, Arthur Pendragon is going to come up with a plan. Do you mind holding on for a moment while we discuss it?'

'So the old human king is alive! I'll listen to what he has to say, but tell him not to forget whose kingdom this is!'

'Right, like that's a really helpful argument to be having at this time. Just a minute.' Roxy put the shell down and gave them a brilliant smile. 'He's delighted to wait for our suggestions. What's the plan?'

'I doubt Morgan really wants to burn down the palace.' Arthur shifted the shield off his back. 'She may speak boldly of killing Oberon's children, but she can't be sure the tyrant will not regret his permission and blame her afterwards. It is a ruse to flush you out.' Arthur gestured to Rick. 'Can you draw me a map of the house and grounds?'

'We don't know it well but I'll try.' Rick sketched out on a patch of earth the main building, stables, arbour and gardens.

Roxy knelt beside him. 'If they are burning the gardens, they are very close to the house. The meadow goes right up to the front doors.'

'So far all the advantage has been Morgan's. She

248

knows who is in the house, she has knowledge of you and your abilities; there is only one element in this situation she has not anticipated. Me. If I take her on, I should prove sufficient distraction for your allies in the house to break out and join the fight.' He twirled his sword in his fist to warm up his muscles. 'But how to neutralize the dragons?'

'I've got an idea about that,' said Rick. 'They aren't willing participants but slave labour. If we get them free of their harnesses, they are likely to flee or turn on their Fey tormentors—either outcome is good for us.'

'Yeah, but what if they turn on us too?' asked Roxy.

'There is that danger—and I didn't say it was perfect, did I? Just an idea.'

'There is no need to apologize, squire, it is a sound idea.' Arthur paced, quickly assembling his plan. 'No venture in a battle is without risk, especially of being turned against you. That is an acceptable one for the advantage it would bring us. So, there are two points to our strategy: I will take on Morgan and you, squire, will free the dragons if you can.'

'And me?' Roxy frowned at Arthur. She wasn't going to sit on the sidelines while they went into danger.

'Roxy, you've the scrying glass—you could try

turning that to see our enemies, as it used to work in the Round Table,' suggested Rick.

'By the dragon, how did you get Merlin's mirror?' Arthur rubbed his hands. 'No, don't tell me now—there's no time. But it gives us a tactical advantage I did not know we had.'

'Yes, but I don't know how to work it properly,' Roxy admitted. 'Do you, sir?'

Arthur looked surprised to be asked. 'Me? No. It was always Merlin's device.'

'I'll do my best, but I'm not promising much.'

'Find our foes in the glass and defend our retreat or all will be lost.'

'No pressure then,' muttered Roxy.

Deep in battle mode, Arthur missed her dry tone. 'Now, tell your friends in the house what we plan.'

'Archer wishes us good luck.' Roxy reported as she slipped the shell back in her pocket.

Arthur had been reviewing his arrangements. 'Maid Roxy, there is one thing I should have asked before making you chief of our defensive line: do you have battle skills? I know Halfdane's ability with the sword but what can you do?'

Roxy flexed her fingers. Pickpocket wasn't exactly a fighting asset. 'I'm not on Rick's level.'

Rick wasn't having that. 'She's brilliant in a tight spot, sir.'

'Good, I would not like to leave you in charge of Peter and Peony without defence. As for you, squire, free the dragons and get back here in one piece.'

Roxy wished she could stop Rick taking such a huge risk but couldn't see any alternative.

'And you, sir?' asked Rick.

'I intend to take the fight to Morgan. She and I have a score to settle. Come here.' He beckoned them closer. Turning first to Roxy, he put his hands on her shoulders. 'Maid Roxy, if I do not return and you survive this battle, I ask you to see Peter to safety. Will you do that?'

'Yes, of course. I'll make sure he's looked after.'

He studied her face, liked what he saw there, nodded and kissed her brow. 'Good. You are one of the warrior queens, I see.' He addressed Rick next. 'Dragons are perilous; however, I have every confidence in your abilities.'

'Thank you, sir. I'll try not to fail you.'

Arthur clasped Rick's forearm, the warrior's version of a handshake, then patted his back. 'I look forward to taking a hand in your training. The raw material you give me is so promising. Keep safe.'

'And you, sir.'

Brandishing his sword in a salute, Arthur swung on to Dewdrop's back and spurred her into a gallop.

'You know something,' Roxy said, her gaze on the king as he disappeared into the trees, 'I don't think he is mad after all.'

Rick laughed. 'You've just watched a man rush away to face a battle with one of Avalon's most powerful Fey and you think he's sane?'

Roxy choked. 'Yep, you're right Rick. I'm the crazy one. My standards of what is sensible and what's not have got kind of mixed up lately.' She gave him a hug. 'You'd better hurry.'

Rick rested his chin on the top of her head. 'Yes, I know. Waiting for that burst of courage. Would almost be easier to do what Arthur did—have a horse to carry me off with a flourish.'

'How are you going to make your approach? You've got to get near the dragons without being seen.'

'I've got an idea that should take me right up to the no-magic field around them.' He stepped away from her and drew on his power. With a shimmer he cast a glamour over himself, arms unfurling into wings, neck stretching, face morphing into the reptilian head of a small black dragon.

Roxy shrieked. 'Hobspit, Rick, that's really weird!'

The dragon's jaws cracked in a serpent's toothy grin. 'I set the twins' dragons free so thought I'd just borrow their shape. The dragon keepers might think I've just come back to them because I'm hungry or too well trained to escape. It might buy me a few minutes.'

'I've got an idea.' Roxy spread out a blanket from Arthur's bedding roll. 'Enchant that and you'll even be able to fly.'

Rick stepped onto the cloth. His magical energy was lower than he would like but it only had to last until he reached the dragons. After that it would be of no use in any case. 'See you soon.' The blanket began to ripple under the waves of magic he sent down through his feet. Rick spread his arms to keep his balance as he began to rise. It was like trying to surf but with wool rather than water under him.

'Good luck, Rick,' called Roxy.

Finding a stance that worked, Rick was able to risk a look down. The top of Roxy's head got smaller and smaller until the leaf canopy hid her entirely. Once the blanket had spiralled above the level of the trees, Rick had a clearer view of what was going on around the palace. Morgan's squad had surrounded the building by staking seven dragons at strategic intervals. Their keepers prodded their blinkered charges to produce bursts of angry flame, penning any resistance inside the house. Roars of dragon distress echoed off the walls. Ogres headed the two-legged troops, waiting for the order to move in once the fire had done its job. A dozen sycacopter soldiers hovered over the roof, repelled for now thanks to arrows shot by the defenders who were positioned at attic windows. Morgan had placed her dragon opposite the front door but had removed herself from his back so she could use her magic. When a puff of wind cleared the smoke a little, Rick saw that her mount was Oberon's own Stormridge, the creature who had promised to eat him rather than leave him to the king's execution.

Would that help or hinder his plans to free them? Rick had no idea.

A horse charged out from the forest, a rider crouched low on its back. Dewdrop's hooves stirred the scorched earth and soon her sides were streaked with soot. Embers flared briefly in the wind created in her wake. Arthur's cloak flapped like wings, his shield shining in the sunlight. Shouts of alarm from Morgan's soldiers warned her just in time of the peril approaching from behind. She spun, her cruel serrated sword held high, her face a picture of astonishment. Rick could see her mouth the single word 'Arthur!' even though he was too far away to hear her. The king did not stop. He made straight for her, throwing himself from the saddle to bring her crashing to the ground under his weight. Dewdrop galloped on, under orders to get clear of the danger zone.

Rick only had time to see that Morgan had not been crushed in this first shock attack. Both fighters were on their feet, exchanging blows. Then an arrow whistled through what would have been Rick's wing if his dragon shape was more than an illusion. He blasted the next missile from the air with a fire spell, hoping they took it for dragon-flame, though the alignment of simulated mouth and his hand was probably way off. Circling down, he let the blanket land not far from the Stormridge. Dragon keepers ran to encircle the 'free' dragon, keeping back as they well knew the peril an unfettered beast posed to them. Out of the corner of his eye, Rick recognized Gorth, his old tormentor and trainer, and Jacques, the one who had taunted him in the kitchen. He flexed his pretend tail in the head keeper's direction, wielding it like a whip to drive him back.

What do you do here, little human? The Stormridge had sensed the false dragon as soon as Rick had landed. Rick could see him sniffing the air. Blinded, it was scent that had given him away to the old dragon.

'I've come to free you, sir.'

'Sir' is it? You give your captives such respect? I should blast you for that alone!

'Not my captives. I did not chain you here. Morgan is using you against those who resist King

Oberon. She is using your fire to drive them out of their sanctuary.'

The Stormridge swung his head towards Rick and spat a tongue of flame in his direction. It had the perhaps unintended consequence of setting one venturesome dragon keeper alight before he could get a harpoon chain into Rick-the-dragon.

'Thanks,' gasped Rick, quickly thrashing his tail in a circle to keep others back.

For what?

'I think you just saved my life.'

How unfortunate. I was hoping to burn you.

This wasn't going well. The appeal to the principle that the enemy of my enemy is my friend wasn't going to work on this creature. He was too cynical to distinguish between good and bad, changeling and Fey.

'What will it take to persuade you to let me release you without you killing me?' Rick asked. The dragon keepers were creeping closer again; one was levelling another harpoon at him. He threw flames in that direction, but they weren't as powerful as the Stormridge's own and fell short. The dragon keeper fired the harpoon. The missile hit where the illusory dragon's neck would be, a hand's span above Rick's head. The trailing chain knocked him from his feet. The glamour vanished, leaving Rick lying exposed on the ground in a ring of dragon keepers.

Only their confusion saved him. Rick scrambled to his feet and dived to take shelter, if it could be called that, under the Stormridge's wings.

'Please don't eat me. I'll free you, I promise.' Rick crouched against the rough scales of the dragon's foreleg. They both knew the Stormridge could reach down with his jaws and put a sudden end to Rick's life.

The dragon chose to be amused. *Interesting: you choose me over your fellow dragon keepers.*

'I was never really a dragon keeper. I was always bait. You know that Oberon wanted you to break me.'

The Stormridge reared up, neck stretched. He strained on his harness. Rick feared he was about to be squashed under the dragon's clawed feet, but then the Stormridge swung his head in a semicircle releasing a wall of flame at the approaching keepers. Three were caught in the blast, their screams of pain music to the dragon's ears. *I am no toy to do Oberon's pleasure. This must end!*

'And I can end it. Just, please, grant my friends and me our lives. We have no quarrel with you, or you with us, I hope.'

Avalon belongs to the dragons, not to humans, not to the Fey.

'I don't want Avalon. I want to save my friends. Can we agree on that much?'

Why? Why should I help you?

'Because you can. And maybe . . . just maybe, because I released two of your kind already for no reward.'

You did? That claim can soon be tested. A clawed foot clamped Rick to the ground as the dragon let out a shrill cry. It rose higher and higher, going beyond the capacity of the human ear to hear. *If you lie and the two young dragons who did not return to the stable have been harmed, then I rend you apart before I eat you.*

'I did not hurt them.' Rick struggled to breathe against the talons pinning his chest to the earth.

We shall see.

Roxy covered the piles of earth from the trap she had excavated with leaves and twigs, thanking fate for giving her magic to do the heavy lifting. Looking into the scrying glass in a vigilant mood, she had quickly seen the hidden threats that Morgan had seeded through the forest: reinforcements of hob-goblins waiting to round up anyone who tried to flee. Standing at the edge of the trench, Roxy drew on her power to spread a sticking charm over the floor of her trap, a silvery spider's web of magic that would cling to any who fell in. It was far less cruel than sharpened stakes, but hopefully as effective. She had made some preparations against attack but now all she could do was wait. Peony rested, one hoof lifted from the ground. The puffin, however, had burrowed into the earth, only his beak visible as he gazed in the direction Arthur had gone.

Branches snapped as something large moved towards them at speed from the direction of the palace. Roxy held herself ready to defend her position until she saw Dewdrop cantering back to them.

Had Arthur fallen already? Reaching for the shell, she called Archer in the hope he had a better view of the events on the field before the house.

'What's happening?'

Archer's voice sounded tight with excitement. 'Your king is exchanging blows with Morgan on our doorstep. No one can get close as they keep blasting each other with magic bolts, the shock waves are enough to drive us all back.'

Roxy heard a boom at Archer's end of the conversation. He coughed then came back to his shell. 'That was the roof and window over the entrance. I'm showered in glass. We are about to sally out and assist, as Morgan's troops are circling. Problem is that Rick hasn't freed the dragons so things are liable to get a bit too hot for our liking.'

'Can you see Rick?'

'I'm sorry, Roxy. It doesn't look good for him. He got really close to the largest of the dragons but then disappeared under the creature. If things change, Cobweb and I will try to retrieve him from the battlefield before the dragon gets him. I've got to go. I'll do what I can for your friend.'

Roxy stuffed the shell back in her pocket. She couldn't wait here, no matter what Arthur had ordered. She had to help Rick. But she had no weapons, not even a staff to use against the dragons, and magic would be useless.

'What shall I do, Peony? Dewdrop? Peter?'

The horses pricked their ears forward and Peter let out a shrill squawk, going into what she recognized as his guard dog mode.

'What?' Roxy put her back to Peony. 'What's wrong?'

She could hear them now, and smell them. The hobgoblins had caught their scent and were coming to investigate. Roxy grabbed the puffin from his shallow burrow and swung up on Peony's back.

'We're going to lead them away. Dewdrop, follow us! Jump when we jump.'

The baying of the hobgoblins grew louder.

'Go!'

Peony surged forward, following a forest path that led away from the palace. Even if they could not defeat a pack of hobs, they could at the very least reduce the numbers Arthur, Rick and the twins had to fight.

That's if Roxy's trap worked. If it didn't, they'd be the next course on the hob menu.

Chapter 18

RICK'S head rang from the dragon's cry. The Stormridge had not moved for some time, ignoring the harpoons fired at his gnarled hide. He appeared to be waiting for a sign.

Rick did not hear the reply when it came; he only knew that something had changed when the clawed foot on his rib cage lifted.

You tell the truth, human. The Stormridge's tone was filled with wonder. *You released Girax and Jontil. They are coming.*

'Will you allow me to free you then, without turning on me?'

I could have turned on you already.

'I know, but you're hoping that I will free you without any promises on your part. I'm not stupid.'

Girax says you freed him without any vow of safety.

'Not an experience I'd want to repeat.' Rick glanced under the Stormridge's wing and saw that Arthur's sword arm was trailing by his side; he was now fighting left-handed. Morgan was limping, unable to press her advantage. They were too closely matched for a swift outcome.

Release me. The dragon dipped his head, a snide smile curving his jaw. The Stormridge knew full well that Rick had no bargaining power. *Quickly now, the keepers are approaching with their nets. I find it hard to struggle against those razor wires. You had better free me now.*

The Stormridge was right: Gorth was ordering a band of keepers to surround the tethered dragon with a large net. His choices had just evaporated. Rick reached up and started to unbuckle the complicated fastening of the harness. First he removed the blinkers. That act was immediately rewarded with a pinpoint accurate flare from the Stormridge that caught a troll leading a pack of hobgoblins towards Arthur's unguarded back. Encouraged, Rick clambered up on to the dragon's spine ridge and tackled the place where the tethers were fastened to the harness. He worked to loosen the screw pin that secured the chains at the centre. It was much more elaborate than the harness that the twins had used; battle gear was meant to ensure the dragons could not turn in the heat of the fight against their masters, so it was made to be more difficult to undo than the ordinary flying saddle. Fortunately, he had had a lesson in how to achieve a fast unshackling as part of his dragon-keeper training.

The pin came free and the tethers whipped to the ground as the dragon heaved himself clear. Next to slide was the saddle with Rick still clinging on to it. He found himself clutching an empty harness with the tip of the Stormridge's tail flicking through and cutting his cheek with its sharp scales. The dragon turned on the keepers, who had the sense to panic when they saw the most vicious of their charges was free. Running did not help Gorth; he disappeared in the first blast of fire with a ghastly shriek.

Release the others. I will drive back the guards, ordered the Stormridge.

Still deeply unsure of just what he was unleashing, Rick did as he was told, running from dragon to dragon. None offered any resistance; the only injury that threatened was getting caught by their thrashing as they wriggled free of their chains. After the cut from the Stormridge's tail, however, Rick knew to jump clear. When the seventh and last was untethered, Rick took stock of what this meant for the battle. He counted nine dragons on the field. Nine? Two small ones had joined the others. Having tracked Oberon's forces from the air with hopes of releasing their fellow dragons, Girax and Jontil had just flown in to share the freedom celebration. Rick was relieved to see that so far the dragons had kept their attention on Morgan's forces, ignoring the Fey resistance fighters who had come out of the house to battle alongside Arthur. Morgan and Arthur were still to be seen striking at each other in the midst. Cobweb was battling a troll twice her size; Archer stood on the top step, picking off reinforcements as they arrived on sycacopter wings, sending the odd dart into the troll to help his sister in any pause in the aerial threat. Even Titania was fighting, sending formidable shockwaves at the troops who tried to approach the doorway.

Drawing his sword from its scabbard, Rick raced towards Arthur.

After a short dash down a forest path and hurdling over a fallen tree, Peony leapt the deep trench Roxy had excavated earlier. Dewdrop followed the tricky double jump without hesitation. Roxy turned in the saddle in time to see the hobs filling the forest path, and yet still more followed. She could not believe how many there were: at least two dozen were on her trail. Urged on by their troll handlers, the hobs bounded over the trunk—and fell into the pit. The trolls were too dim-witted to imagine even so simple a ruse from a human and stumbled in after. In trying to heave their hobs out, the trolls got caught in the sticking charm and dragged into the mess. Their cries and curses were deafening and promised her a painful death when they finally caught up.

'Come on!' Roxy urged Peony. 'We've done all we can here. Let's go find the others.' She was desperately worried for Rick.

Roxy reached the edge of what once had been the beautiful meadow but was now a trampled battlefield. It was impossible to know who was winning. There appeared to be at least seven different skirmishes happening in as many directions. At the centre of six of them were vengeful dragons, causing havoc among the diminishing numbers of troops fighting in Oberon's colours of grey and silver. The thickest knot of fighters was gathered at the doorway to the house, so Roxy urged Peony in that direction. As they approached, Peter flapped free and dived into the fray, a flash of black, white and rainbow beak darting between pounding feet and swirling swords.

'Peter!' Too late, he had gone. 'Arthur's going to kill me for losing him.'

Roxy now spotted Rick fighting back to back

with Cobweb near to Arthur. The king was standing in front of Titania, the queen doing an excellent job of picking off the opposition as they tried to storm their position. Morgan had rallied her personal guard of ogres and was pushing forward; it looked as if, despite the chaos reigning elsewhere on the field, this was one position she was about to win. Her foot had reached the bottom of the steps. Gathering the last of her magic, Roxy spurred Peony forward. She let the elfshot spin in her hand, gathering force as she had seen Rick do. She released it like a bowling ball, sending it in low at the legs of the guards. Bam! They went down like ninepins, losing the momentum of their surge forward.

The resistance took immediate action, reversing the push. Morgan was forced back on to the scorched earth. Roxy didn't have time to appreciate her contribution because the soldiers at the rear of Morgan's battalion were looking for the source of the blast and quickly saw her. Two huge ogres broke off their attack and began running towards her and the horses.

'Oh.' Roxy's mouth went dry with terror. She was out of magic and out of ideas.

A shadow rippled over the ground in front of her and the faces of the ogres turned from aggression to terror. A huge lava-grey dragon ripped through her attackers, chucking them aside with careless strength. Peony, so fearless up to this point, began to sweat and quake, dancing in a circle. Dragons in all directions, it was only a matter of time before they were the next target.

Rick brought down his ogre, but received a shallow wound to his upper arm in payment. He tied a quick bandage around the cut. Cobweb was still battling a very persistent troll, but appeared to be prevailing, her lightning speed making up for her slighter stature. She had already defeated two and was tiring. Morgan's reinforcements just kept on coming. Arthur was still defending the steps, though his left-handed strokes had become more about brute strength than skill. Only determination to fight until his last breath kept the king going; they were all drained of magic now. Thank goodness for that unexpected explosion of elfshot knocking out the bodyguard. Rick had no idea where it had come from but he hoped he lived to thank the person who had sent it at just the right moment.

Then, to Rick's horror, he saw Arthur stumble, weariness catching him. Morgan had been waiting for such a chance and swung her sword in an arc above him, lining up a shot to cleave his head from his shoulders. The stroke went wild. Her face was covered by a squawking flutter of black feathers and scratching orange feet. Batting Peter aside, Morgan tried to regain her position, but Arthur was already on his feet and on guard once more.

'Look behind you, Morgan!' shouted Arthur. 'The dragons are destroying your troops; you will have to sue for shelter from us if you do not retreat while you can.'

With a piercing shriek of rage, blood dripping from Peter's scratches on her brow, Morgan shot a red fire bolt into the sky. It exploded with a sound like a booming bell. 'Retreat! Retreat!' she cried. But there was nowhere safe for her soldiers to go. Some realized this more swiftly than others and broke discipline, running haphazardly for the cover of the trees between the skirmishes that dotted the field. Morgan was now in grave danger of being left without support.

Yet she was too powerful a Fey to be caught without an emergency spell to aid her. She swirled her hand, spinning a magical wind from the air. A little twister wound its way to her, knocking friend and foe out of its path. Rick held on to the balustrade to stop himself being blown over. Titania stood flattened against the wall, her primrose hair and pale apricot robes spread against the stone. Archer held Cobweb to the ground with one hand while he grasped a window ledge with the other. Morgan dived into the heart of the mini tornado and was whisked up and out of sight, disappearing into the smoke clouds above.

'Take prisoner all who surrender!' Arthur shouted above the noise of the storm, barely pausing to acknowledge that he had beaten his old foe. He stood braced against the wind, cloak flapping wildly behind him. 'It is not over until the palace is secure!'

Then Rick saw something that made his heart plummet. 'Sir, Arthur! Roxy!'

Roxy was stuck in the middle of the field, stalked on two sides by dragons. She had dismounted and stood between Peony and Dewdrop, her copper hair gleaming against the swirls of smoke rising from the smouldering earth behind her. Girax and Jontil had decided to play with this unusual quarry of two horses and a human. They were coming in pincer formation, like bat-winged cats, shoulders moving up and down like the slow turn of a piston, heads low. They ignored easier quarry running past their noses, eyes fixed on her.

'With me, squire!' Arthur sprinted towards Roxy, shield bobbing on his back. Rick raced after him, leaping the fallen, tripping over weapons and armour discarded on the field of combat. He had no idea what they were going to do when they reached her. Die defending her most likely.

Roxy appeared to be trying to send the horses to safety but they were refusing to go. Instead they flanked her, neighing quite hopeless challenges at the dragons. Arthur reached her side and held out his sword in his left hand; his right dangled useless. He shrugged the shield from his back so it hung over his weak side. Rick reached them, taking his position on Arthur's right hand.

'To the forest—go!' Arthur ordered the horses.

Peony stamped his refusal.

'Go, I tell you. There is nothing you can do here. You are good faithful steeds, but this is no battle for you.'

'Please, Peony, save Dewdrop. She won't leave without you,' Rick urged.

With great reluctance, the stallion led the mare away. The dragons barely flinched as they galloped by, their ebony eyes still fixed on the bright gleam of Roxy's hair.

'Go back—we are not your enemies!' Rick yelled at the dragons.

You look edible enough for our tastes, one replied.

'I did you a favour once: is this how you repay me?'

We owe no debts to two-legged creatures, Fey or human.

Rick wished he had forced the Stormridge to make a bargain for his freedom; he had nothing left with which he could persuade the dragons.

'It's no good, sir, they aren't going to spare us just because I did them a good turn.'

Arthur nodded, showing no surprise. 'Then we fight. Ever battled a dragon, squire?'

'No, sir.'

'Their weak points are their eyes and their throat. Forget all other targets: the hide is too tough.'

'What about their fire?'

'I suggest you try to avoid it,' Arthur said with grim humour.

Roxy was shivering. 'We could split up—run in different directions. Some of us will get clear.' She knew that the dragons had become mesmerized by her and would chase.

'No, we stay together now, Maid Roxy. The time for running is past.'

Rick heard the deep breath that gave warning of a flame about to be thrown. 'Incoming, sir!'

'Behind the shield!'

Arthur held out the barrier, Rick and Roxy pressed to his side. They all expected the shield to melt away on the first touch of dragon fire; but it held. As the flames licked the gold wire pattern on the surface, the shield grew heavier and heavier. Braced against each other, Rick and Arthur struggled to support it.

Then a flash of light burst from the shield, stunning all who stood nearby. A serpentine shape unwound itself, weaving out into the air, shaking its wings free. Made up of only a network of golden threads, it took the unmistakable form of a dragon. It rollicked in the flames, swimming in them as happily as an otter in a stream, gathering strength and substance as it took in the blast.

Girax and Jontil broke off their attack, crouching in disbelief and awe before the creature they themselves had awoken. The Stormridge landed behind them and cuffed them away with a swipe of a paw.

Bow to the Pen Draig, he ordered.

The two youngsters made little bobs of their head to the swirling golden marvel, then retreated as fast as their short legs could carry them until they gained momentum to fly. This was incredible. Only the Stormridge seemed to have any idea what was happening.

'A Pen Draig?' Rick asked. 'What is that, sir?'

The Stormridge hesitated, but Rick suspected he wanted to share the marvel with someone, even a boy. *A Pen Draig, or Pendragon, is a chief dragon. I am one. Your king has the honour of bearing another. She is one of the spirit dragons that live in a realm separate from the one I rule.* The Stormridge watched the dance of the Pen Draig with deep appreciation. *They are rare and mysterious visitors to our worlds. She is the most beautiful I have ever seen in all my millennia of life.*

He was right. The golden Pen Draig moved like silk, winding in and out of her own coils. She did not need her wings to fly; they moved with her like rudders, steering her though the air currents. Her eyes were molten, glowing with power, shining with knowledge of a world beyond their experience.

Such dragons live in the world of spirits. They exist there ageless, but can choose to inhabit magical objects in our worlds if they so wish, taking a brief leave from eternity to experience life in corporal form. Your king is much blessed. No dragon dare attack the keeper of the spirit Pen Draig, nor his companions. You have your pledge of safety at last, little human.

With that, the Stormridge bowed to the Pen Draig and leapt into the air, gaining height with powerful downbeats of his wings. Then a most wonderful thing happened: his skin shivered and became iridescent like the scales of a rainbow trout, a blush of pink down his flanks. With a cry to the other dragons, he gathered them in a circle revolving over the battlefield, each one shaking off the dull colours of captivity and returning to their natural skin tones—heraldic red, moss green, sky blue, tawny brown. At last, thought Rick, this was how the dragons were meant to be; he gazed with delight at their splendour. Only the two little black dragons remained in their old livery, though they added a silver glint to their wingtips. Each paid homage to the Pen Draig before following the Stormridge and flying north in a 'V' formation, recalling a flock of huge geese on migration to new lands.

Their retreat left the field in the possession of Titania's forces, Arthur, Rick and Roxy stranded in the centre with the swirling dragon.

'Stars!' whispered Roxy. 'She's really something, but what do we do with her?'

'I don't think we do anything—it'll be up to her.' Rick could feel Aethel humming around his neck, her body quivering with excitement. 'Hey, Roxy, I think Aethel's up to something.'

Torc turned to snake. She coiled onto Rick's head and began to weave in the air, following each gyration of the Pen Draig. The snout of the airborne dragon whisked over Rick's head and snatched Aethel into her jaws.

'Please! Don't hurt her!' Rick called, hands spread to catch her in case she fell.

The spirit dragon flipped Aethel into the air playfully a few times, then slowed to coil around the three humans. Her head rested on her fore-paws, eyes locked on Rick.

Bad child. Slipped away from my realm for adventure in yours. The dragon's voice was a whisper in Rick's mind, so much gentler than the strident tones of the Stormridge.

'Child? Do you mean Aethel?'

You called my child 'Noble' in your tongue? Thank you, princeling. You have been a good friend to her, but I fear she has learned many bad habits here.

'Your child? But she can't be a dragon: she doesn't have wings.'

She does in our form, not while in a material golden body here. This foolish little one does not know this. She was not ready to come here and has made many mistakes. I came to return her to her rightful home. I am grateful to you, for you have brought our paths together again and I can take her back and teach her all she needs to know.

'You're taking her?' Rick wanted to howl.

You would grieve?

'Deeply.' He couldn't imagine life without Aethel; it would be like losing his right hand.

The Pen Draig let her tongue flicker over Aethel's golden head. *Your lives are so brief. Perhaps it would do no harm for us to stay to see them through to the end. I will still have plenty of time to curb her wilful ways.* The Pen Draig's gaze fell on Arthur. *I am also bound by gratitude to the one who bore the shield that allowed me access to this realm. Yes, we will stay.*

'May I ask, my lady, why are you able take your living form in the presence of the dragons and Aethel can't?'

She can if she releases herself from her material form.

But to stay in that body and be untouched by dragon anti-magic she would need to be dipped in dragon tears as I have been. Until then, she is vulnerable. We must take good care of her. She licked the dent Rick had made in Aethel's neck with his slide down the castle walls. The notch disappeared.

'May I take her back—just for now?' Rick wasn't ready to hand Aethel over any time soon, even to an awe-inspiring Pen Draig.

The Pen Draig nudged Aethel in Rick's direction. *You may keep her for a little while. I will return to my home in this realm.* Spinning like water draining away, the Pen Draig diminished until she once more sat on the face of Arthur's shield, seeming nothing more than gold wire and gilt paint. Aethel slid back to Rick and settled around his arm with a contented hiss.

Chapter 19

'EXCUSE me, but what just happened?' asked Roxy. She had not heard the dragon-side of the conversations Rick had been conducting.

'I don't know exactly—but it was awesome.' Rick cradled Aethel to his chest. 'The shield is a Pen Draig and in some way she is Aethel's mother or guardian, I'm not sure which.'

'Pen Draig?' asked Arthur, sheathing his sword. 'That was the title given me as the chief of my men on Earth—Arthur Pendragon. It means leader, does it not?'

'It seems likely that the humans borrowed the titles from the real dragons, sir. Maybe a higher power had a hand in making it part of your legend because the dragon said that bearing the Pen Draig on your shield keeps you safe from all dragon attacks.'

'An excellent advantage.' Arthur smoothed the edge of his shield. 'She was a beauty, wasn't she?'

'Incredible—and I don't think we've seen the last of her.' Rick's brow creased in a frown as another thought struck. 'Though, as she lives in eternity, her idea of what a moment is might differ from ours. She seemed to think my request to keep Aethel for my lifetime was the equivalent of staying five minutes longer at a party.'

With a whoop and a whistle, Archer and Cobweb came running over to them.

'Elfric, you're alive! Thank the stars!' exclaimed the princess, kissing him exuberantly on both cheeks. 'I thought you were a dragon's dinner. But what was that wondrous creature we saw in the air, and where did it come from?'

Archer lifted Roxy off the ground in a fierce hug, then brushed a scratch on her forehead with a fingertip. 'You are hurt?'

'I'm fine. I got a little roughed up by the brambles, but the enemy didn't lay a finger on me.' She took a step away from him as soon as he released her. The twin's attitude to their two human allies was a little overwhelming. Rick wasn't sure if it was flirting, or more like an owner feeling responsible for a clever pet. He suspected from Roxy's expression that she felt equally confused.

Titania arrived at a statelier pace, her fine robes stained by battle. Rick preferred the twin's mother when she looked like this: she appeared less formidable and more, well, human, if that wasn't an insult to a Fey. 'Elfric is injured, Archer, as you should have noticed immediately,' she said, with her usual crisp delivery. 'So is King Arthur. We must take them into the house and see to their injuries.'

'My lady.' Arthur bowed. 'Are your people in command of the palace grounds?'

'Ever the commander, aren't you, my lord?' Titania examined the bloodied warrior before her. 'I am pleased to see you recovered from your fever and restored to your full abilities. I hope no ill will lies between us for your captivity after we have fought together today?'

'My argument lies with Morgan La Faye and King Oberon. Those who oppose them are my allies. What news from the field, my lady?'

She smiled wryly at his persistence. 'The field is mine. I have posted sentries; we should be safe for a brief time. I must make preparations to leave the palace by tomorrow at the latest and find a place that we can defend now it has come to open war with Oberon.'

'Aye, my lady, that would be the wisest course.'

'Come, I will not have an ally go untended while I have feysicians who can treat your injuries, and my servants will find fresh clothes for you all.' She began the procession back to the house.

'Has anyone seen Peter?' Arthur asked, scanning the battlefield anxiously.

'Peter?' asked Titania. Two Fey passed carrying a fallen comrade on a stretcher.

'A puffin, my lady.'

'Ah, the creature that flew at Morgan's face? I did wonder what manner of beast it was. No, I've not seen the valiant bird but I will make sure every corner of the field is searched. Here are two more that deserve our praise.' Titania pointed. Peony and Dewdrop were trotting towards them. Roxy and Rick hugged them and rubbed their velvety noses, congratulating them on their cleverness and bravery.

'I must seek Peter before I can myself find rest.' Arthur hurried towards the site of his confrontation with Morgan, turning over shields and searching among the fallen. Rick and Roxy helped but there was no sign of the bird. Dread filled Rick as he imagined what might have happened. It would have been so easy for the puffin to have been trodden on by friend or foe in the heat of combat, or injured by a swipe of a sword. Then, as they approached the steps to the palace, Peter fluttered out from under a fallen block of masonry, looking a bit dusty but none the worse for his first battle. He flew to Arthur's shoulder and perched there like an odd species of pirate's parrot.

'Not so useless after all,' said Arthur gruffly. 'You saved my life and I thank you.'

Peter purred and preened, quite content to be named the hero of the battle.

Once inside the palace, a narrow-faced feysician saw to Rick's wound. The spike on the ogre's mace had sunk in deep but the healer closed the puncture with magic, leaving only a faint silvery scar on his bicep. Arthur's arm proved to be trickier to cure as it had been broken in several places. Knowing how important it was for a warrior to maintain the strength in his fighting arm, two feysicians sent Arthur into an enchanted sleep while they conducted the painful realignment and knitting of the bones. Peter refused to leave the king's side while the treatment went ahead, squawking whenever he judged the healers to have been too rough, purring when they achieved their goal of a complete mend.

While Arthur was receiving the best care available in Avalon, Rick and Roxy were able to bathe and change into clean clothes in the wing of the palace that had escaped fire damage.

'It's a shame that this beautiful old house has had such a battering,' said Roxy, brushing and braiding her hair by an open casement. 'Particularly the magic window above the entrance. I loved those dancing creatures but they've all been destroyed.'

'I know, but I can't help thinking how many lost their lives in defence of Deepdene—friends to Titania and the twins.' Rick came to stand beside her, arms folded. The beautiful gardens were now nothing but blackened earth.

'What do you think of your first battle?' she asked Rick.

'Glad to be alive. I think I made a hash of the fighting—everything I learned seemed to go out the window.'

'Yes, it was ugly—and confused.'

'I imagine all battles are like that; it is the stories that follow that tidy them up and make them heroic.'

The evening meal took place in the banquet hall, which had survived with only a little damage to one corner. Stone pillars, shaped like the trunks of silver birch trees, held up the vaulted roof. Tapestries of woodland scenes decorated the walls. Arthur insisted on attending and had been placed in a chair next to Titania, an extraordinary sign of favour from the Fey, who usually ranked any human far below the least of their own people. Rick and Roxy were also invited to the high table and stationed between the twins. The food was good but plain: yesterday's bread, only slightly stale, creamy cheese with fragrant herbs, pale honeydew to drink, and the fruits of the forest for dessert.

At the meal's conclusion, Titania rose, her cup held before her. 'To the ones that no longer sit among us! May they be at peace.'

All got to their feet and echoed her words.

She turned to her companions at the table. 'I also drink to our new allies: the changelings. Without them, the outcome of today's skirmish would have been very different. To Arthur Pendragon, Elfric Halfdane and Roxy Topley.' The Fey court joined in the toast, Cobweb enthusiastically, Archer with a wry smile at the abrupt change in his mother's treatment of humans.

When the company had taken their seats, Titania addressed those at the table with her. 'We must make plans swiftly. Oberon will not accept this defeat, even of so small a force as he sent against us. He sent but a fraction of his troops to bend us to his will, little thinking he would be opposed. Next time we face his full might, and this house is not suited as a stronghold. We must now move our court.'

'Where will we go, Mother?' Cobweb asked.

'The Prince of the Wood, Cerunnos, has offered us shelter. His own magic protects his fastness in the heart of this forest. We will be safe there. He rarely takes sides so we cannot count on him to fight for us, but he will grant us space to send out messages to like-minded Fey and muster our forces.'

'And what of the dragons?' enquired Archer. 'Will they help us?'

Rick held up his hand, asking permission to speak.

Titania inclined her head.

'My lady, I think you'd be wasting your time trying to include the dragons in your strategy. In my dealings with them they have made it clear their plan is to get Avalon back for their own kind. A plot to change the Fey leadership would not interest them. The best you can hope is to per- suade them to stay out of it.'

'I believe you are right, Elfric,' said Titania gravely.

'Yes,' agreed Cobweb. 'We should not waste our limited time chasing an ally who is more inclined to eat than help us.'

Titania shook her head at her daughter's plain speaking. 'And what of you changelings? What plans do you have?'

'We must go back. Tonight if we may,' said

Roxy. 'Our mission there is urgent and we've been here a couple of days now—and that means months and months in human time. I left the others with some pixies, but we know that Earth is also on Oberon's list of targets. If he comes after us before we are ready to defend ourselves, we will be wiped out.'

'And I go with them, my lady,' announced Arthur. 'I will train these youngsters to defend their world. We, however, stand ready to aid you in your struggle because all of us who are pitted against Oberon are really part of the same battle.'

Rick was relieved he made no mention of setting up the Round Table. Ally though Titania was today, he felt it best that they kept that as a surprise to all Fey, not just the hostile kind.

'We must maintain our communications. Archer, Cobweb, you must go with them and see their stronghold so we can find them again at need.' Titania rose, preparing to begin sketching the doorway between the worlds right there at the high table. 'Don't be long away as I will give the order to move out from this place at dawn.'

'Yes, Mother. We'll only take a week or so. Human time is so useful for snatching holidays,' whispered Cobweb to Rick. 'And we get out of the tedious business of packing!'

'I heard that!' said Titania, not sounding too cross. She kissed her daughter in farewell. 'Don't do anything rash, and listen to the humans.'

Roxy and Rick's eyes met. As if.

'What about the horses?' Rick asked. 'I'm sure Peony would like to come.'

'And Dewdrop,' added Roxy.

'Then by all means take them if they wish to go. All creatures should be free to realize their own destiny. That is where Oberon errs, wanting to trap and contain.' Titania raised her voice, addressing those Fey listening in on the conversation rather than the humans. 'I do not claim his kind of power; I seek to lead only by consent. If you follow me, I will try to bring a change for the better to all our lives.'

Rick guessed they had just been present at the first public speech of the new rebel leader of Avalon. It sounded very promising—if only Titania could survive to see it through rather than be snuffed out by her ex-husband's superior strength. Her chances of success were slight. But then again, so were theirs.

Titania's doorway from Deepdene could not take them all the way to Stonehenge as that was too far south. The closest she could manage was a copse in the Peak District, an area of rolling hills near

Manchester, but two hundred miles north of their destination.

Roxy and Rick had left in late August and came back to find the following summer had arrived. The trees were carrying their full canopy of leaves, the flowers in a riot of many colours and the fields lush with grass.

Arthur looked about him, running his hands over a tree trunk, plucking and crushing a leaf to smell the scent. 'Why, so little has changed! I was afraid my world would have completely disappeared with the passage of time.'

Just then an aeroplane flew overhead on its path to the airport, the noise shattering the peace. A tractor came into view as it churned its way up the muddy track leading to the woodland, huge tyres splattering mud in all directions. Arthur dropped the leaf and drew his sword.

Rick placed a restraining hand on the king's forearm. 'I think, sir, you had better put that away. Much *has* changed since your day.'

'What are those things? Some new kind of dragon? Then I need not fear them.' Arthur held his shield towards the approaching tractor, expecting it to bow before the Pen Draig.

'No, they are machines, driven by a kind of human magic called the combustion engine. The one overhead is a plane—it carries people long distances at great speeds. That is a tractor: farmers use them to plough instead of oxen.'

'You have brought me to a time of miracles!' Arthur shook his head in amazement.

The driver slowed when he saw the party of strangely garbed folk by the side of the track. Caught up in calming the nerves of the king, Rick had not had time to agree a glamour with his companions, and now it was too late to try one.

'You lost?' the farmer called. 'Bridle path's that way.' He pointed down the hill towards the village at the bottom of the valley. He didn't seem surprised by their appearance, which struck Rick as decidedly odd.

'Thank you. Yes, we must have missed our way,' agreed Roxy, beaming up at the farmer as if she hoped a friendly expression would be enough to deter awkward curiosity.

'Dressed like that, I expect you're headed for the jousting tournament at Chatsworth.'

Ah, that explained the man's attitude.

'We are? I mean, yes, we are,' agreed Roxy.

Arthur looked positively eager to hear a contest was to be held. 'Tell me, my man, which king has summoned the knights to fight?'

The farmer chuckled. 'Very good at this, aren't you?'

'Aye, Good Ploughman, I am deemed most accomplished in the noble art.'

The farmer gave them a friendly wave in parting. 'You're a caution, you are. I hope you win. I'll look out for the pictures in the local newspaper.'

The tractor trundled its way up the track and over the brow of the hill.

Arthur rubbed his hands. 'So where's the tournament? I told you things hadn't changed so much.'

Rick groaned. He could just imagine the mincemeat Arthur would make of a bunch of actors who did recreations of medieval jousts for the tourists. He would probably wipe the floor with them—literally.

'It's not how you think,' Roxy said quickly. 'It's just pretend—a game.'

'Of course it is a game—but an important one as it trains a knight for the battlefield.' Arthur began walking in the direction of the village.

Roxy ran to catch him up. 'Not now it doesn't. It's just a bit of fun—padded lances, actors dressed up as lords.'

'Sounds tedious,' commented Cobweb. 'What's the point without real danger?'

'They make a mockery of a serious sport? I must set them right on the matter.' Arthur picked up his pace. 'At once.'

Rick decided this was the wrong way to argue

the question. 'Look, sir, we can't waste time going to a tournament that will likely take all day. We've got to find a way to reach Stonehenge.'

'What about taking a train again?' suggested Archer.

'No!' said Rick and Roxy quickly.

'What about one of those planes you mentioned?' said Cobweb, gazing eagerly at the sky.

'Absolutely not,' said Rick.

Roxy stopped at the gate barring their way. 'Actually, with two horses to transport, I think we should perhaps go to the tournament after all, Rick.'

Rick swung round to cover her mouth with his hand. 'Don't you dare suggest he takes part! He'll kill someone.'

Roxy pulled his palm away. 'If you'd let me speak, Rick, I'd tell you what I had in mind. I was just thinking that where there're horses there are horse *boxes* and drivers.' Rick looked blank. 'The people today transport horses in a kind of trailer called a box because it's, well, like a box with wheels. A little bit of persuasion and I'm sure we can *charm* someone in to giving King Arthur a lift south.'

Roxy wasn't foolish; she was brilliant. 'That's not bad, Roxy, not bad at all. Well, it is bad, of course, some poor guy is going to be spending his weekend driving us about, but it is a very neat solution.' He glanced over at their companions. In their long flowing robes and armour, the twins and Arthur would fit right in at a medieval pageant. 'Bit of a high-risk strategy though. How are we going to restrain them?'

'Their mother told the twins to listen to us.'

'So?'

'Yeah, you're right. When has that ever made a difference? OK, but it might be entertaining— as long as we persuade Arthur not to take on all comers.'

'Hmm, I'll do my best. It's a plan; let's go and see what happens.'

To say that the actors employed for the Chatsworth tournament were surprised to find 'King Arthur' and his retinue turn up to compete would be an understatement. The display team had set up on the lawns in front of the stately home; they had done a good job at setting the mood, pitching marquees with fluttering pennants bearing heraldic symbols, and roping off an arena like the lists of yesteryear, a wooden barrier down the centre and various other knightly games around the edge. The leader of the little troupe was speechless when the king announced his attention to show his prowess on the field of combat.

'Look, mate, I don't know who you think you are—' the man spluttered.

'I've already declared my titles before the herald,' said Arthur severely, nodding to the lady at the microphone who had obeyed his demand to be introduced to the curious crowd.

'Well, *King Arthur*, you can't just ride up and ruin our carefully choreographed display. It's dangerous for one thing. Health and Safety would have kittens if they heard. You're blowing huge holes in our risk assessment.'

Arthur leaned forward in his saddle, Dewdrop pawing the ground before him fretfully. 'I think you, sirrah, do not understand the rules. We do not fix battles—they must be fair and free. No cheating is allowed in my realm. Squire!' He snapped his fingers for Rick's attention. 'I think we should show these paltry fellows how it is done. Maid Roxy, guard Peter for me, if you would be so kind.'

'Sir, Arthur,' Rick hissed, 'we don't need to do this. All we need is a vehicle to take us south and Roxy has already found someone who will drive.' Roxy had located the owner of a roomy horse transporter who had happily agreed to do the deed, thanks to his susceptibility to her persuasion spell.

'I do not steal the war gear of another knight. His horse, transportation and armour are only forfeit when I win them in a fair battle on the field of honour.' Arthur spurred Dewdrop into a gallop and cantered round the arena. 'Who dare face King Arthur? Come forward all challengers!'

The crowd gave a rousing cheer. Cameras flashed from every part of the arena.

Arthur let forth a battle cry. The little gathering of actors on horseback scattered as he charged towards them wielding his sword.

'He's a nutter! I'm calling the police!' said the leader, running for the stewards' tent.

Rick urged Peony in pursuit of the king. 'Sir, my lord, we have to leave!'

Arthur pulled on the reins. Dewdrop reared impressively. 'So I have won the day without a blow being struck. These poor people are disappointed.' The crowd booed the actors who were now hiding behind a marquee. 'You, squire, you and I will show them how true knights fight.' Arthur sheathed his sword and took a lance from the rack standing at the edge of the field. 'Choose your weapon!'

'But sir, I haven't jousted before!'

'Then it's time you learned!' The crowd cheered, thinking this all excellent entertainment.

Rick felt a dull sense of inevitability about how this would end. 'If I do this, will you then leave quietly?'

'But of course. Honour will have been satisfied, the people pleased, and the day ours.'

Rick took a lance from the rack. It was heavier than it looked—he had been hoping these were play-props like the actors' armour. He patted Peony's neck. 'I'll try not to hit you.'

Roxy passed him a helmet from the actors' gear, then a wooden shield. 'It will be quicker this way, you know.'

'Want to take my place then?'

'No fear. But I'll stand by with a cushioning charm when I see you fly from the saddle.'

Rick faced Arthur at the far end of the lists. The announcer had got into the spirit of the occasion and was playing a rousing rock song to encourage the crowd to clap along. Arthur was revelling in the attention, conducting the applause as he waited for Rick to be ready. Roxy stood in the centre of the field and dropped a white scarf, signalling the start.

Rick and Peony headed for Arthur and Dewdrop. Even though he knew Arthur was his ally and had no intention of inflicting serious harm, Rick couldn't help feeling terrified at the sight of the ancient king bearing down on him, his face hidden by the visor of his helmet. He just hoped Arthur hadn't suddenly recollected that Rick was one of the hated Saxons. Arthur's lance struck his shield dead centre; Rick's aim was wide. With a feeling of momentary weightlessness, Rick was born back and out of the saddle, landing with a soft bounce on the ground. Roxy's charm had saved his behind if not his pride.

The spectators went wild, shouting and hooting. Arthur did a victory lap, modestly receiving their praise, though undoubtedly he would not consider unseating a clueless squire among his greatest achievements.

Roxy helped Rick to his feet. He took his helmet off and discovered that in the short time that had elapsed since he parted company with the saddle, Archer and Cobweb had decided to join in the fun and were entertaining the people with a virtuoso display of fighting with staffs while balancing on the fence down the centre of the lists. Arthur, meanwhile, was running at the quintain, hitting the target in the centre every time and elegantly ducking the swinging sack that span round to catch the unwary knight.

'Oh, what's the use in trying to hurry them along!' said Roxy, throwing her hands up in the air. 'They're enjoying themselves too much—it would be a shame to spoil it.'

It was all rather exciting; Rick couldn't resist seeing what Arthur would do next. 'We'll leave when we hear the sirens, agreed?'

Roxy nodded.

Arthur galloped by and pulled Roxy on to the saddle behind him. She gave a squeak of surprise but did not resist. Peter flew alongside, a streamer fluttering from his beak. As Rick watched, he saw Arthur pass Roxy his sword and encourage her to have a go at knocking the helmets off a row of poles set at head height. It appeared Roxy's knight training had also just begun.

Rick grinned as he swung back up into the saddle to join in. 'Welcome home to England, King Arthur.'

Chapter 20

THE obliging owner of the horsebox dropped them off on the main road near Stonehenge, slightly bemused to find himself in the south of England but happy enough with the little gold button Cobweb gave him for petrol money, at Rick's insistence. Her robes had many of them decorating the sleeves so she could well afford to part with it. The man drove off, leaving them on the verge as the dawn broke over Salisbury Plain.

'So, Maid Roxy, where do you think your friends will have made camp?' Arthur asked, stroking the puffin who was asleep in his arms. He scanned the horizon with an intent gaze, barely flinching as cars roared by on their way west. It had taken him a while to get used to traffic, but after many hours on a motorway Rick thought Arthur might finally be getting the hang of modern transport. They had to keep an eye on him, though, as he still had a tendency to wander into the path of oncoming vehicles, underestimating the speed of their approach.

'Well, I told them Stonehenge and there it is.' Roxy pointed to the small huddle of stones that, from this distance, looked fairly unimpressive. 'Let's get a bit closer and see if we can spot signs of their camp.'

She led the way; Arthur and Rick followed leading the horses; Archer and Cobweb came up behind, taking great interest in the oddest things. They had a little delay while the twins examined the workings of a litter bin, then a footpath sign. The silhouette of a man walking on the notice had them in fits of laughter.

'Humans have to be reminded to walk?' giggled Cobweb.

'Perhaps after sitting so long in those cars they forget.' Archer grinned at his sister.

'That's not how it works,' said Roxy grumpily.

'I don't think I'd try explaining if I were you,' murmured Rick.

They reached the fence that surrounded Stonehenge as the sun bobbed up over the horizon. The air had a cold nip as the sky was clear, but it looked as if they were heading for a hot summer's day.

'How long do you think we've been gone, as far as the others are concerned?' Rick asked. Aethel unwound from his wrist and slithered up to his neck for a better look.

Roxy rubbed her eyes. 'Let me think. We crossed over and spent nearly three days—half a day with Archer and Cobweb when they put us in that cage, one with King Arthur travelling to and fro from his island, and then the day of the siege of Deepdene. I guess it is nine months, more or less, since I left them in Hyde Park to meet up with the others at Paddington.'

'That's given them plenty of time to establish a camp and disguise it. It's a shame we haven't got a signal to let them know we're here.' Rick looked around the empty plain that circled Stonehenge. Apart from the road, the place was desolate.

A shaft of rosy sunlight fell on the face of the grey stones. They reminded Rick of ancient giant acrobats caught halfway through building a human pyramid and not quite managing the manoeuvre. A strange shimmer caught his eye. It danced behind the gap created by two uprights and one lintel stone.

'Roxy, when you said camp at Stonehenge, was there any reason for them not to take you literally?'

Roxy shrugged. 'No, I s'pose not. I was just thinking it looked a bit bleak and they might have moved somewhere warmer for the winter. Besides, what would they do all day out here?'

Rick pictured the busloads of tourists and a family of pixies. He then noticed the suspiciously large number of signs reminding visitors that English Heritage was not responsible for loss or theft of their belongings. 'My guess is that they have made a fortune. Come on: let's go and see if there's anyone at home.'

Letting the horses jump the fence, Roxy, Rick, Arthur and the twins took a more sedate path and climbed over.

'Can you see it?' Rick asked, confident now that he hadn't imagined the shimmer.

'There's a glamour cast over the whole site.' Archer waved his hand. 'A powerful one, as it is hard to spot.'

Roxy began running. 'Hey, guys, I'm back!'

Arthur caught the back of her jacket. 'Wait, maiden. We do not know if we are meeting friends or enemies behind that glamour.'

'Who else would it be?'

'You must expect the unexpected or you will never survive Oberon's tricks.'

Roxy stopped pulling away. 'You're right. Sorry. What do you suggest?'

'We enter the stone ring together. Squire, draw your sword. Archer, Cobweb, guard our backs. Peony, Dewdrop, stay here. We might need you for a fast escape, so be alert!'

The horses bobbed heads in agreement.

With Rick on his left and Roxy on his right, King Arthur strode into the centre of Stonehenge.

'Show yourselves!' the king demanded, glaring fiercely about him. 'Arthur Pendragon is here!'

The glamour rippled and dropped like a stage curtain coming down. Trix-E, Frost-E, Miz-Begotten, and the changelings surrounded them in a ring, an eclectic collection of weapons in their hands—axe, bow, spear and staff—but their expressions were far from warlike. Most of them looked rumpled and sleepy. Rick realized they had just woken them from their beds. The area in and around the stones was covered in little bell tents, bunting, and fabulous sculptures made of articles that had once belonged to visitors to the site. Most of the changelings were still in pyjamas.

'Roxy—Rick—you came back!' Tabitha dropped her bow and quiver and ran forward to give them a hug. 'We'd almost given up expecting you!'

'Is that why you set no guard?' asked Arthur.

Tabitha looked to Roxy for reassurance as Edgar hurried over to defend her.

'It's OK, Tabs. This is King Arthur. He's very hot on things like self-defence and taking precautions against Oberon,' Roxy whispered.

Tabitha dipped an awkward curtsey. 'Your majesty.'

The pixies cartwheeled over and folded Roxy in a group hug. Rick felt a touch of envy watching her exchange kisses from her adopted parents and sister.

'Who commands this camp?' Arthur asked severely, breaking in to the happy reunion.

Tabitha squeezed her hands together. 'I suppose I do, sir, with the pixies. But only while Roxy's been away.'

'A little maid?' Arthur's eyebrows shot up. 'You certainly do need my help then.'

'She's done a very good job, sir,' said Edgar belligerently.

'You have led them all this time and not lost a child?' Arthur asked Tabitha, surveying the changelings who were watching him with open curiosity.

'Yes, your majesty.'

'Then you have done very well—far more than many would have done in your place.'

Simon and Ahmed approached Roxy, waiting their turn to greet her.

'Roxy,' said Rick, 'can you find out if anyone's heard from Tiago and Linette?'

Roxy grabbed his arm and dragged him over to the group of changelings. 'You can ask them yourself, Rick.'

Tabitha gave him a shy smile. 'Hello, Rick. How did you survive dragon keeping?'

He gave a dry laugh. 'With difficulty.' The changelings grinned at him. 'Have you heard from Tiago and our human friend Linette while we've been away, Tabitha?'

Tabitha shook her head. 'No, but I've a good idea where they are. Give me a moment and I'll get it.'

She darted away to a nearby tent before he could ask what she was fetching. While she was gone, Roxy introduced Archer and Cobweb to the changelings and pixies. The changelings watched the twins like wary dogs meeting two newcomers for the first time, prepared for any sign of hostility. The twins were their usual superior selves, asking questions about the camp and dropping hints that an invitation to breakfast would be welcome. Frost-E took it upon himself to get the cooking fire going and began to juggle eggs in preparation for making a huge omelette. Peter perched on a stone to watch. Simon led the horses to an old bathtub of water so they could drink their fill. The pixies had clearly been scavenging since they had set up camp.

Tabitha came back with a newspaper. 'I go to the nearest town to get supplies a couple of times a week,' she explained. 'I picked this up yesterday.'

The headline read *San Francisco under siege from mystery wolf attack*.

'But San Francisco doesn't have wolves, does it?' Roxy passed the paper to Rick.

Arthur held up a hand. 'Explain what is going on.'

'This is a newspaper—it tells of events happening in other countries.' Rick showed him the photograph, remembering that Arthur couldn't read.

'Like a monastery chronicle?'

'Yes, exactly. And the story Tabitha pointed out talks of a night-time invasion of wolves running wild in the middle of a big American city. No one has been able to take a picture of them, despite modern technology, which has led to all sorts of strange theories as to what they are, including ghosts.' Rick passed the paper back to Tabitha. 'But you think it might be magic stopping them catching the wolves?'

She handed the article to Roxy. 'Yes.'

'And where there's magic there might be Tiago and Linette—or Merlin?'

'That's my guess. If wolves have been heard, though, I was wondering if hobs might be involved.'

Rick exchanged a worried look with Roxy. Tiago and Linette being pursued by a pack of hobgoblins in the human world: that sounded terrifyingly possible knowing Oberon. Morgan would have taken him news of Arthur's reappearance in the battle. If Oberon had realized that the humans were looking to defend themselves with the ancient king, he may also have worked out that Merlin was the next on their agenda, as Arthur never fought without the magician by his side.

'We've got to find them,' Rick said.

Arthur sat down on a fallen stone. 'Do not worry, squire, they may well be with Merlin already. He won't let any harm come to them. But of course we will go and find them. In what part of my kingdom are they?'

'Not your kingdom, sir. America.'

Arthur unbuckled his sword belt. 'Where? I've never heard of it.'

That was right—it hadn't been known in Arthur's day. 'A huge land to the west, many thousands of miles from here.'

'Ah. A place of legend. I heard stories of a land far over the seas. How do we get there?'

'Not by hover charm, that's for sure,' said Roxy. 'We'd run out of magic before we got west of Ireland. We'll have to fly.'

Archer took a seat next to Arthur. Cobweb returned from the campfire to join them, happy now that her breakfast was on the way. 'Did you say flying, Roxy? In one of those metal birds? I'm ready.'

Rick shook his head and groaned. He slumped onto the stone beside the king. Aethel slithered away to nose among the eggshells.

Arthur put his arm around Rick's shoulder, a fatherly gesture that rocked Rick's world to very core. 'Do not fear, squire, I'm in charge here. She is not your problem.'

Cobweb scowled. 'I am not a problem. I am a princess.'

Arthur gave her a cutting look. 'And I am a king. You are in my kingdom now, as your brother will be the first to acknowledge.'

Archer gave a reluctant nod.

'Then you will obey my commands.' Arthur stepped up onto one of the fallen stones. 'Now that is settled, it is time we began the summons.'

'Summons?' asked Rick. His spine tingled with anticipation. He could guess what was coming.

'Of course. Oberon is after us, the world is in peril: I must call all faithful knights to my Round Table for our mutual support and defence.'

'Shouldn't we wait for Merlin—and Tiago and Linette?' asked Roxy.

'Wait? Whatever for? It is for the king to summon the Table. My Table has always been much more than a magic spell performed by a wizard: it is a collection of willing hearts and brave souls like those I see around me. I have so much shaping and training to do that we must make a start now.' He winked at Roxy's worried expression and dropped his voice to a confidential tone. 'I'm sure Merlin will be along as soon as he can. He was never one to miss out on helping me stir up trouble.'

All right then. Rick and Roxy stood at Arthur's side as the king drew his sword and raised his shield to chest height. An excited ripple ran through the crowd clustered in the shadow of the menhirs of Stonehenge; they turned from their tasks and stood up to listen to his address.

'Friends and allies,' Arthur called out in a ringing tone. 'Your country, your world, needs you to defend it against the threat of the Fey king. I summon you to take up your places in the Round Table, sworn to defend humanity. Young knights, lay your swords and weapons at my service and I promise to care for you as I would my own family and lead you honestly, bravely, and steadfastly in the days to come.'

There was a pause as the changelings hesitated, unsure of the correct response; then Rick stepped forward and laid his sword at Arthur's feet. Roxy carried no weapon so placed the scrying mirror on the ground. Ahmed, Edgar, Tabitha, Simon—one by one the changelings came to lay sword, axe, bow and staff at the king's service. When each had done so, Arthur raised his shield in blessing. A golden mist swirled from the surface and touched each one on the crown of the head—a hint of smoke from the Pen Draig, adding her own stamp of approval on the young knights. Aethel slithered through the collection of weapons to Arthur's feet. He dipped his sword so she could entwine herself around his ancient blade. He held her aloft with a shout of victory.

'And so it begins!'

The changelings cheered and clapped. Arthur jumped down from the stone and went through the crowd, meeting his new recruits, handing back weapons as a way of discussing their talents with each one. After meeting all the knights, he turned to the campfire where the pixies and the Fey twins looked on with amusement. He sniffed the air appreciatively.

'Should we set off to fetch Merlin now, sir?' asked Rick.

'First things first, squire: breakfast. We'll set out for your friends and Merlin once we've eaten. No soldier can make good plans if he or she is hungry.

Let's celebrate the calling of the knights with a feast.' Miz-Begotten handed him a plate of eggs. 'This looks delicious. Anyone got one of those miraculous chocolate bars?'

Trix-E produced a box from her tent and passed it round.

Rick snapped open the wrapper and took a bite. Arthur was right. It was time to take brief holiday and enjoy the completion of the first stage in their plan: the summoning of the Table. He also took a moment to relish this chance to experience the simple things of human life, like friends, picnics and sunshine. Rick looked round the circle of changeling knights who were chatting with their neighbours as they helped themselves to breakfast, all so different yet pledged to stick together against their common enemy. The pixies, Archer, Cobweb, King Arthur, Peter, Aethel and the horses had all fitted comfortably into the little camp spread out across Stonehenge, Roxy moving between the various groups like a copper-haired humming bird, full of energy and encouragement for everyone.

Rick took another bite of chocolate. Yes, it was good to be home.

DESPERATE TO KNOW
WHAT HAPPENS NEXT?

DON'T DESPAIR!
READ ON FOR AN EXCLUSIVE EXTRACT OF
BOOK THREE IN THE YOUNG KNIGHTS TRILOGY

MERLIN

COMING SOON . . .

dagger. The point buried itself in the hob pup close by Morgan's feet. The creature gave a little yelp, a shudder, then keeled over. 'We must eliminate Merlin, crush the rebels, then take over the source of magic. Earth will be returned to its natural state—without humans. Its sole purpose is to feed Avalon, not rear these parasites.'

'I'll see to it at once, my lord,' said Morgan, backing away to carry out his orders.

'Oh no, commander. Not you.' At those few words, she flinched, her standing in the court instantly plummeting. 'I cannot afford another failure. I will see to this myself.' Oberon strode past her. 'Bring me my sword, troll!'

The mirror clouded as Roxy's grip on its magic slid away.

'Something wicked this way comes,' she muttered wrapping the mirror in its red satin cloth. 'Merlin's in big trouble.'

Rick stood up. 'Let's tell Arthur. We've got to hurry.'

They ran for the king's tent.

chamber by the stiff breeze. An armoured troll guard hurried to wrestle the window closed.

Oberon dropped his head on his hand, weary, almost sympathetic for a brief second, 'Get up, commander. I am not going to execute you—not today.'

The window blew open and banged against the wall. A pane shattered.

'See, Morgan, my hold over the weather in Avalon is already weakening. The supply of magical energy from Earth is failing—our enchantments are breaking. I have no time to punish those that remain loyal, no matter how much they deserve it.'

His brief weakness passing, Oberon leapt to his feet and strode to the maps strewn on his council table. He cracked his knuckles.

'The changelings have recruited Arthur, you say?'

Morgan rose warily. 'Yes, sir.'

Oberon picked up a dagger from the table and tapped his mouth with the hilt.

'I have made a mistake. I should have killed him when I had the chance.' He flipped the blade so that the jewelled handle rested in his palm. 'Still, he can do little without the magic of the Round Table behind him, and for that, he needs Merlin.' Quick as a cobra's strike, he threw the

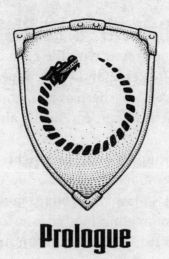

Prologue

STONEHENGE, Salisbury Plain, England.

IN the shadow of Stonehenge, Roxy and Rick crouched over Merlin's scrying glass. Remembering her few successful attempts to work the spell, Roxy breathed on the surface. A lock of copper hair flopped forward to brush the mirror. Rick reached out and tucked it behind her ear.

'Can you see them?' asked Rick.

'Wait: it's not that simple.' Roxy shut her eyes, hiding their familiar green sparkle, freckled nose wrinkled in concentration. She held the mood she wanted to match with their enemies. Vigilance. Intense dislike. She had to bring her own internal magic to sync with the enchanted mirror.

The glass flickered and cleared, pearly surface becoming as crystal sharp as a dragon's tear. Rick and Roxy bent closer, foreheads almost touching.

'Report.' King Oberon sat on his ice throne, carved white pinnacles echoing the points of his silver crown. Massive in build, powerful like a mountain dominating foothills, he ruled Avalon with an iron fist. Behind him, through the window, the sky blazed in a blood-red sunset; dark bars of clouds gathered.

'Your majesty, the rebels have fled.' Morgan La Faye knelt at his feet, long black hair curtaining her pale, battle-stained face. A sword cut on her arm dripped on the stone floor. A wolfish hobgoblin pup lapped up the blood.

'How could you let this happen?' Oberon's voice crackled with fury, his blue eyes burned with cold fire.

'Sire, I have failed you.' Morgan swallowed, bowing her head even lower as she waited for him to strike.

Lightning flashed, throwing the master and his most loyal servant into stark relief. Thunder boomed. Rain fell with the suddenness of a monsoon shower, droplets driven inside the audience